The Chronicles of

Judyann McCole

Adela Arthur and the Creator's Clock

Judyann McCole

ISBN: 1490322345
ISBN-13: 978-1490322346

ADELA ARTHUR IS DEDICATED
TO YOU

THE LOVERS OF
ADVENTURE,
STORYTELLING,
AND
ALL THINGS ***LIGHT***…

CONTENTS

PREFACE

She ran because she had no other choice. She feared what would happen if she dared to stop. There was no time to think. There was barely any time for her to breathe. On her broken ankle, she ran. With her bruised arms, she ran. With her bleeding sides, she ran because she knew today was the day she was meant to die.

Her bare feet, covered with everything from wet dirt to dried, dead leaves to cold ice, took her farther into the forest. She jumped over the fallen log, not caring that the bottom of her pants snagged on the tip of it. She went on, running deeper, running faster, trying not to think. Thinking would stop her. Thinking would make her want to survive. Thinking would cause her to fight, and today she could not fight. She heard the screeches; she had seen their dark eyes. They were confirming what she already knew in her heart to be true. Today was the day she was meant to die.

Snow fell gently on her like small glimpses of hope. She loved the snow. But even today it, too, was against her. It knew. It blanketed the ground and froze her to her core. She slowed, but she didn't stop running. Slowing was a mistake, though. Now she could feel the fatigue as it crept up inside her. She could feel the pain as it came into her ankle like burning knives slicing away at her. As the screeches rang through the forest, they too chilled her. Whether she slowed or not, she was meant to die today.

However, she had one choice, one option. What was to be her final ground? She had the choice of where she could die, and it wasn't going to be here. It wasn't going to be in the depths of the dark forest. It would not be fatigue, or hunger, or even the evil creatures that dwelled inside that forest. She couldn't die here. It wasn't good enough.

She ran, but again her pace slowed. What a fatal flaw that was, for now she tripped over the root of a skillfully hidden tree. Her body hit the iced-over, snow-covered ground, adding even more injuries to her collection. She touched her lip; seeing her blood on her hands shocked her, stilling her. She was bleeding everywhere, but for some reason that blood was what stilled her.

That was her final fatal flaw, because now she stopped running. Running had calmed her and now that was gone. A dry sob broke through her lips before the tears came. They broke so quickly they burned, blinding her.

She could think now. She knew to what her actions would lead. She knew she could hurt them all. But it had to be done; it was the only thing left to do. They would hate her. They wouldn't understand. They would have told her there was another way, but there wasn't. There just wasn't. They wished for it to be innocent, clean, easy—but it couldn't be. She knew there wasn't another way. They knew there wasn't another way. But they hoped, they prayed, and most of all, they feared. That they too were like her, that they too were only prolonging their agony. It wasn't always like this. I promise you it wasn't always like this. There used to be laughter and harmony, absolute and unfathomable harmony. They wanted that back. They needed that back. So she had to die today.

She heard it. She heard his foot upon the snow. Lifting herself from the ground with great ease, for she no longer hurt, she turned to him, all the anger in the world directed at him. He—with handsome red eyes and blond hair—he was the reason she would die today.

"I am not sure if you are the most reckless girl I have ever met or the wisest." His soft, gentle voice rang out—his voice never much higher than a whisper. It was a deceiving voice. It was the voice of a friend, a brother, a father; it was a voice of someone who cared.

"This you won't win. Haven't you heard? Light always wins. You scare and you terrify, but in the end, light always wins. So you are the most reckless man I have ever met, for trying to do the same thing so many others have tried and failed to do," she told him through her own tears.

He simply circled her before speaking again. "Now who lied to you, my dear? There is no such thing as failure. I have simply discovered ways that did not work."

She looked forward, not speaking to the man behind her. There was no point wasting the few precious breaths she had left. Her tears flowed from her eyes, rolling down her cheeks like miniature waterfalls. He was the reason she would die today.

"How tragic it is that you will not be alive for me to impart such a lesson upon you." That was the last thing she heard before the darkness came. She hoped, she truly hoped she did not die today for nothing.

CHAPTER ONE

THE BEAUTY OF ADOLESCENT MADNESS

"Good morning, Ashland! It is officially fall—" Slamming her hand against her alarm, Adela tried not to think about what today meant.

Oh, today is going to suck, she thought as she lay in bed. Today was a dark day, and on dark days you weren't supposed to go out.

"Adela, if you don't get your butt up, I am coming in there," the broken, scratchy voice called from the other room. Adela tried so hard to ignore him, burying herself deeper into the mattress and pulling a pillow over her head. All she wanted to do was rest on her dark day.

"Happy birthday to you! Happy birthday, my little bumble

bee." He burst into her room, singing dreadfully.

"I'm going! I am going," Adela yelled, jumping out of bed as she tried to dance around the older man singing in front of her, until she ran into the bathroom, slamming the door.

However, he continued on in his awful voice. "Happy Birthday—"

"I am in the bathroom. The water is running. You can stop now Grandpapa!" she yelled again as she leaned against the wooden bathroom door.

She sighed when she heard his laughter fade and the gentle slam of the door as it closed on itself. The second to last thing she wanted to do today was go to school. The very last thing she wanted to do was celebrate her sixteenth birthday. But did her grandfather listen to her? No. He was going to plan a "surprise" birthday party— which they could not afford—because turning sixteen is important, he said.

Apparently she was in the first stage of birthdays, the stage in which she should be excited to become older. He had told her there were three stages of birthdays. The first, the one she was in now, was excitement, the second was dread, and the third was pride. Pride that once again you had cheated death for another year. Despite her grandfather's age, he claimed to be in transition from the second to the third. He could, too. He didn't seem to look as old as he was, but she knew better. Stepping into the shower, her mind continued to race on.

As you could see, she wasn't a fan of her birthday. To speak frankly, she hated her birthday. At sixteen she was not a legal adult for another two years and could not drink for another five. In all honesty, to Adela, all the birthdays between twelve and seventeen were pointless. Anyone who told kids differently said so only to make sure teens didn't shoot themselves in the face before they turned eighteen.

Adela sighed. She didn't mean to be so cynical; she knew that was not the real reason she loathed her birthday. She hated it because it was a dark day. It was the day her parents died. It was the day she became an orphan. She could not remember it, the massive explosion that took them away. Each time she tried to call forth that memory, all she could recall was a bright light and sobbing around her. From what she was told, she was six at that time and should have been able to remember something: their voices, their faces, how their hands felt. However, she could not. It was her dark day.

She often wondered what they looked like. Each time she questioned her grandfather about it, he would tell her to look in the mirror—for she was a perfect blend of the two. So she looked in the mirror every day. Adela knew that she had inherited her mother's long, wavy black hair and hazel eyes, along with her father's height in addition to his fair skin.

Had she known where her old house stood, she would have surely gone back there. She would have walked among the rubble, trying to find traces of anything that linked her to them. It was for this reason she knew that her grandfather had moved them to Oregon.

Wrapping a towel around herself, Adela took a deep breath before wiping the steam off the mirror. She stared deep in to her hazel eyes, then spoke, "Happy Birthday."

Dressed, she began searching for the bus pass but could not find it anywhere. Ripping through her closet, dresser, and bed, she was still unable to find the blue bus pass, which hung from a panda bus-pass chain.

"I just cleaned this room." Adela sighed, pinching the bridge of her nose. It had taken her forever to clean her room, putting everything neatly in its place, and it took her only five minutes to destroy it.

She would have given up her search for her wallet—there wasn't much in there, just five dollars and an old movie stub, if she remembered correctly—however, the school buses in Ashland now required every student to have a bus pass. Grabbing her backpack, she marched out, hoping that she had left her bus pass and her wallet in the kitchen. When she walked into the kitchen, whatever her grandfather was cooking made her stomach grumble.

"You look nice," her grandfather told her as she rushed into the kitchen to search for the bus pass.

"Grandpapa, you're blind," she replied, looking inside the fruit platter.

Despite the fact that she was dressed incredibly plainly, something she cared less about, seeing as how they were poor. She wasn't joking: Grandpapa Keane was blind, and to the best of Adela's knowledge, he had always been so. Luckily, he had impeccable hearing, which made his job as a musical instrument repairer quite easy, but not many people went to the local blind man to repair their guitar.

He chuckled under his breath.

"Yes, but I believe you look nice," he told her in his dry, low voice.

Grandpapa Keane was a somewhat tall man with silver-gray hair that stopped at a little past his shoulders. A large wrinkle creased his forehead. But what made him truly memorable was his dry, scratchy voice. It sounded like he had a smoke stuck in his lungs, which he most likely did, given the number of cigarettes he went through. Grandpapa Keane always made sure to smoke outside whenever he thought she wasn't paying attention.

"Thank you. Have you seen my bus pass?" She smiled, leaning into the counter beside him.

"Adela, that's cruel. You know I am blind." He pulled his pale lips in to a thin line before he was unable to control his laughter.

"Ha-ha very funny. But if I cannot find my pass or wallet, I won't be able to get to school on time. As much I would love that, I would miss my own surprise party." Her dark long hair swayed as she moved toward the living room to continue her search.

He tried to deny it.

"There is no party," he claimed.

"Ok, Grandpapa." She knew better than to believe him by now. There was a party, there was always a party. The guest list was short; not many people could fit in their run down home at the edge of town.

"It's in the car." He laughed at her as he ate a strip of bacon.

"We don't have a—Grandpapa you didn't!" she complained. He just ignored her, dragging himself out of the kitchen and through the front door.

There, sitting comfortably in the weed- and fungus-covered driveway of their home, was a very old black and blue Honda Civic. The colors suited it well; it looked as though it had taken many beatings in its day. The paint was chipping off on its hood; the tires looked depressed and tired. She ran her fingers over it as if to make sure it was really there. Bits of paint came off at her touch.

Adela smiled as she stared at the car before her. "It's beautiful…," she told him.

They could not afford this; she wasn't sure how he had managed to even get her anything but a bicycle. That was why it was beautiful.

"I had the boy make sure it was safe." The boy he spoke of was Adela's best friend, Hector Pelleas, the smartest teen in all of Ashland, if not all of Oregon. You would not think him to be the car fixing type, but he just knew things.

"Stop overthinking it and go to wherever it is you go during the day," he said, throwing her the keys before walking inside.

She did not move, just stood there, shocked. She pulled on the door a few times; it seemed the rust on its outer edges had cemented it closed. When she took a seat the engine roared to life with great force before coughing like it realized it was not the grand car it once was in its prime. The whole car itself shook slightly as if it were a tractor-trailer.

"Hello?" she answered her old cell phone with the half-broken flip screen.

"Glove compartment. Now go or I will be forced to drive you myself," her grandfather said before hanging up.

The compartment revealed not only her bus pass next to her wallet, but it also let out a foul odor. One Adela did not even want to know the sources of. With a frown, she pulled out her license. It was hopefully the last time that thing ever saw the light of day.

With all the technology in the world, you would think they would be able to make the pictures flattering, she thought.

Shaking her head at the run-down house in front of her, Adela backed out of the driveway. It may have been the first day of fall, but it did not seem that way. She had only made it a few blocks from her home when the skies opened, a full-on downpour ensuing. But that was Oregon. One-minute you're enjoying a perfectly sunny day and the next you're under a cold waterfall. This was just one of the ways that today was going to suck. She could feel it. She didn't know why but she had this odd feeling, like something bad was going to happen.

She parked in the student parking lot and watched as the students of Ashland High ran under their jackets and books to avoid the rain, like animals clearing a watering hole. High school was a jungle, and something bad always happened in the jungle. She double-checked her zipper on her backpack before putting it over her shoulder. As she zipped up her old tattered jacket, she took a deep breath and prepared herself for the mad dash she was about to take. The minute the door was open, she felt the cold water soak her jeans. Closing the door quickly, she ran as fast as she could into the brick building.

Only when she reached the safety of the school building did she slow. The halls were just as crowded as always; people tended to linger for some odd reason, forcing her to fight her way over to her locker, where she prayed it would open. It always seemed to have a mind of its own.

"Ahh!" she groaned, banging her hand against the red locker when it didn't open, but that did nothing, as usual.

This locker always brought out the worst in her. All she wanted was her physics book. That was it. Today, the one day in history Mr. Watkins was giving an open book test, and she couldn't get her book.

"You can use mine." Adela turned to face the owner of the meek voice.

There, standing beside her and opening his locker with great ease, was Hector. She had known Hector for years. He lived on the other side of Ashland, the one with the nice homes where the porches didn't break, and you didn't have to share your bathroom with the friendly neighborhood daddy long-leg. If it were not for the fact that his mother and her grandfather were friends, then they never would have been friends, either. He was a short guy in comparison to the other guys his age. It did not help that he lacked muscle tone, either. He was thin and wore clothes that only highlighted that fact. All of this, plus the ridiculous ties he wore around his neck all the time and his untamed sandy brown hair and glasses made him the very definition of a nerd.

"Are you sure?" she asked him as he handed her the large textbook.

"Photographic memory, remember." He laughed at her.

"Cheater." Adela frowned at him as they walked to class.

"Jealous," he responded.

She frowned even more because he was right. Taking her seat by the window, she noticed that there was no end in sight to the rain. Mr. Watkins strode in, business-like as usual. He was one of those teachers that didn't have fun or a life outside of school. Pushing his glasses farther up his hooked nose, he held in his hands a stack of crisp white sheets of paper.

I wonder how many trees had to die for this one test, she thought as she flipped through the hieroglyphic-covered pages.

Even with the book at her side, it would not have given her enough time to decode any of the symbols in front of her.

"If a cannonball has a mass of 150g and is shot from a muzzled cannon toward you with a velocity of 960m/s, what is its kinetic energy?" What did it matter if she were dead? Who in their right mind would stand there wanting to know how much kinetic energy was behind a cannon ball? Move. Problem solved; you're alive and it did not matter what the kinetic energy was.

When the bell rang she sighed in both frustration and defeat. This was the bad feeling she had: failure. There was no way she was passing physics this year.

"That bad?" Hector asked. She just nodded, walking into the girl's bathroom.

She hated to fail at anything. She hated letting people

down; she hated letting herself down. She tried her best in everything, but for some reason she did not understand physics at all. Washing her face, she hoped the water would calm her down. As she dried her face she stared into her reflection. There was a small crack in the glass.

All of a sudden, she no longer saw her own reflection. In her place she saw a woman with long, snow-white hair and black eyes. There was nothing else, just pure darkness. The paleness of her skin showed even more so with the green dress she wore. Adela moved and the woman followed. Suddenly, a wicked smile crossed her pale lips. Her hand reached out toward Adela, coming through the mirror. Adela backed away until she was up against the red stall doors. Pushing, she moved farther back, falling on the bathroom seat. She could not tear her eyes away as the hand reached forward.

It seemed like the woman's whole body was coming through the mirror. A deafening scream broke from her lips as she slammed the bathroom door closed. With all her might, Adela tried to hold the door closed. Her heart pounded so vigorously that she could feel the ringing in her ears. Her arms grew weak and the stall flew open. The woman was gone and in her place stood Principal Pelleas, Hector, Wilhelmina, and her followers.

"Miss. Arthur, are you all right?" the redhead she recognized to be Principal Pelleas questioned as she reached out for her. Adela was frozen, not just from her residual fear but also from confusion.

"No one is going to hurt you," the principal told her softly as if she was a child. She squatted before Adela, waiting for her to take her hand.

Adela blinked for a moment, trying to gather herself. Nodding, she took Principal Pelleas's hand. Rising, she gazed into the mirror, until she couldn't any longer. Nothing was amiss; however, she knew what she saw—or had she just imagined it? Principal Pelleas looked between the mirror and Adela, her red hair swaying softly.

"Let's go to my office, okay," she told her, a hand on Adela's back. "The rest of you head back to class," she ordered.

Wilhelmina and her girls just stared at Adela with smirks on their faces before leaving. Hector followed, but not before looking back one last time. Adela knew without a doubt as she stepped into the crowded hallway that the whole school would hear about her episode in a matter of seconds. What was worse was that she could not stop it. The only way to kill a rumor before it became a monster was to shoot it down early in the game.

Taking a seat in the leather chair in front of Principal Pelleas's desk, she tried to avoid her green eyes. *Principal Ellen Pelleas,* the plate on her desk read. She was Hector's mom and basically her surrogate mother. Getting in trouble with her always followed them home. She knew her grandfather would most likely be talking to her sometime today or the next. Adela was not really okay with him knowing of her episode.

You would think Principal Pelleas would have her accomplishments plastered all over the walls. Instead, she had pictures and small trophies of students from the school. There was even a picture of her on desk of the Grande Ronde River with a younger looking Hector, the only proof that that boy did more than read. There were quite a few plants in the room and everything seemed to be made of wood. It was very Zen and earthy. The antique-looking mirror on the wall threw her off.

"Adela?" Adela turned to the older woman in the large chair in front of her.

"I am fine, Principal Pelleas," she told her. The longer she stayed in this office, the worse the rest of the day was bound to become.

"Would you like to go home? I could call your grandfather," Principal Pelleas asked her as she picked up the phone, preparing to dial.

"I'm fine. Besides, it would make it harder to pull off that surprise party I know you both are planning." Adela couldn't help the small smirk that played on her lips. The look on Principal Pelleas's face said it all. She knew her grandfather was planning something; the car was just to throw her off.

"Fine, you may go," Principal Pelleas said, placing the

phone back down. The principal and her grandfather had known each other for years. How, Adela was not sure. He had said something about a pottery class they had taken.

"And Adela," she called, causing Adela to stop near the door. "Try to look somewhat surprised when you get home."

Adela sighed before nodding and closing the door as she walked out.

All day people stared. They whispered behind her, and teachers shot her worried glances. You would think it was the first time a high school girl ever cried in the girl's bathroom. She wasn't popular by any means, so she did not understand why people even cared to begin with. People stared at her as if she had two heads. This was not the type of attention a girl wanted on her birthday. Sighing, she put her head on the lunchroom table.

"On a scale of one to ten, how bad?" she grunted up at Hector.

His sandy head rose from its place within the large textbook. He tilted his head to the side before glancing around the poster- covered, overcrowded cafeteria.

He pushed his glasses back up his crooked nose while he thought for a moment. "Eight and a half."

"Urg, I hate high school," Adela said, putting her head down on the table.

"Some good has come out of it, though." He looked back down at her. She raised her head up, staring at him oddly.

"Mr. Watkins is reviewing his test on account of the rumor."

"What rumor?"

"That the physics test was so difficult it caused you to have a panic attack in the bathroom."

Great, she thought. That was probably one of the nicer things being said.

She bit into her apple, trying to ignore everything around her. She just had to make it one more day. It was Thursday. Someone was bound to do something stupid over the weekend, and by Monday no one would care about her anymore.

"Hey, loser!" someone called. It made her mad that Hector's head lifted back up as if his name had been called. She knew who it was, which was why she wasn't going to turn around.

"I was talking to you," the voice said. Sighing, Adela turned around and came face to face with Wilhelmina White.

She was *that* girl in high school. You know, the one who seemed to be just too pretty be real, the one who would wear something ridiculous and the next day every single person had it on. Her flawless chocolate skin, brown eyes, and gorgeous soft dark hair made her the queen of Ashland. She had even done some modeling. People like her were the reason girls like Adela hated school.

"What do you want?" Adela snapped, rising up to be on equal footing with her.

"Cool down, tiger. I just wanted to say thank you." She smiled raising her hands up in defense, the girl behind her smiling, too.

Adela didn't trust any of them. Wilhelmina did not say thank you, and she didn't even believe she had heard the words before.

"I'm serious. If you weren't such a freak, I would be making up Mr. Watkins's test right now." She and her hyenas laughed before walking off to hunt for their next victim.

"I hate her," she told Hector, but he wasn't paying attention. Instead, he just packed up his stuff before walking away.

She stared at him oddly as he retreated. She would have stayed where she was sitting had it not been for the laughter she heard. Whether it was for her or not, she wasn't staying. Walking over to her locker, she found Hector standing there beside it, staring into his as if he was searching for something.

"What's up with you?" she asked him, her arms folding across her chest as she leaned against her locker. She wasn't even going to try to open that thing again. It was a bad omen.

He said nothing to her before sighing. Reaching into his

locker, he pulled out a small white box with a perfect blue bow on it.

"I, uh, wanted to give it to you before but you were freaking out about the test. Then the whole thing in the bathroom happened, and I knew you would hate your surprise party. So I figured this would be the safest time," he rambled before handing it to her.

She just stared at it as if it were a foreign life form. She wasn't sure what to say or do. She just wanted this day to end—no more gifts, no more surprises. He silently waited for her to unwrap it. Adela stared between him and the box. Figuring it would be better not to hurt his feelings, she pulled on the loose string. She did not know why it took her so long to open it, but when she did, she could not help the audible gasp that came from her lips. It was a simple heart within a small cage, but it was beautiful. She lifted it out from its place within the box, staring at it.

"I really had no clue what I was doing and my mom kind of helped me, I mean she knew what you would like and all," he rambled again.

She didn't know what taking the necklace would mean. Then again she didn't know what not taking his necklace would mean, either. She cared about Hector but not the way he wanted her to.

"It's just a necklace, Adela. It won't kill you," he muttered awkwardly.

"Thank you, Hector," she told him, surprising him with a hug before backing up and placing the necklace around her neck.

He had just brightened her day without even realizing it. It was like the necklace had brought her good luck. No one or thing bothered her after that. The rest of the day was pretty relaxed. She walked into her other classes, laughed, and smiled with her classmates. She even made Mr. Rheam, her calculus teacher, laugh— and that man never laughed.

As she left school she felt confident. The sun was out and life was good for the rest of the day. To top it off, she planned on eating cereal with chocolate for dinner as she watched television on the couch. Life was looking good.

"Surprise!" She stared at her living room full of people she did not know when she opened the door to her house. In her own glee, she had forgotten about the party, like an idiot.

At least I really did looked surprised, she thought as she walked in, preparing her face for the long night of smiles ahead. She would have a good time, she would smile, and she would laugh because she loved her grandfather enough. She would pretend that life was everything that it needed to be.

Chapter Two

My Brand of Insanity…
… is Better Than Yours

Snapping up from bed, Adela tried to calm herself down. She could not remember her dream but so desperately wanted to. It was on the tip of her tongue, but before she could speak it out loud, it vanished, leaving only a chill down her spine.

"She saw something, Keane," said Principal Pelleas from the other side of her bedroom door.

Adela slid her sheets off of her body and tiptoed over to her door, grimacing to herself as the floorboards squeaked.

"Ellen, we both know that is impossible." It was her grandfather talking.

"We know nothing. She saw something, Keane. I have known that girl all of my life, and not once have I ever seen her as purely terrified as she was in that bathroom."

"It would be better if we discussed this at another time. I am quite exhausted, and you have to be at school in five or so hours." As her grandfather spoke, she felt like he was talking to her and not to Principal Pelleas.

"You're right. It is late. I will see you later, Keane." Hearing their footsteps, she took the opportunity to run back to bed, fighting her sheets until she finally became comfortable once again.

Her door creaked open slightly, she made sure to breathe deeply so that he could hear her. He lingered for a moment before closing the door and walking away. When he was gone, Adela's hazel eyes snapped wide open. She could not sleep any longer. She was worried her grandfather would think she was losing her mind. She had hoped Principal Pelleas would not tell him about what happened at school, but it seemed from their conversation, she had.

He had done more than enough for her. She didn't want him to believe he had failed in some way, shape, or form while raising her. They were all each other had. Yes, she missed her parents, but her grandfather was the best parent anyone could ask for. Smiling to herself, she recalled the first time she had realized all adults were not blind. He opted to teach her himself because she was afraid to leave the house, though she couldn't remember why.

She thought it would be easier to trick him, but she learned very quickly that her grandfather could beat her at her own game. He could sneak up on her without her even knowing. He always knew when she was in the room, no matter how lightly she tried to step. She had even put random things in front of him when he was cooking, and he would simply pick them up and move them. Throwing things at him didn't catch him by surprise, either. He would easily catch them and hand them back to her, telling her to be careful because she could hurt someone. He was the one who wore her out and not the other way around. Thinking about now, she realized she was a pretty awful child.

But she loved it. He just had one rule: never tickle him while he slept. He always kept her on her toes and smiling. She loved him, which is why she didn't want him to worry. Having him worry about her crying in bathrooms was not something she wanted.

"No more weird," she whispered to herself, making a promise. She would not give him anything else to worry about.

It felt like she had only closed her eyes for two minutes before her alarm went off.

"It's Friday, one more day. Come on Adela, get up. You can do it. Just one more day." She gave herself a pep talk. *Why did the world wish to rip me away from my bed at such a young age?*

The older she became, the more she wished she could go back to the magical days of naptime.

Sighing, she found the strength. From where, she wasn't sure. Walking over to the bathroom, she stopped. A trickle of fear up ran up her spine, she didn't know if she could go in. A small flashback tried to force its way back in her mind, but she kept it at bay. She didn't want that image back in her head.

"No more weird," she said, her hands running over the necklace Hector had given her. Marching forward, she stared into her reflection proudly.

No more weird. She smiled when all she saw were her own hazel eyes staring back at her. Today was going to be a better day. Today she wasn't going to let anyone bring her down.

"Good Morning," she told her grandfather as she entered the kitchen, grabbing a simple piece of toast for breakfast.

"What has you so chipper this morning?" he asked, drinking his coffee from his cracked mug.

"Nothing. I just made a promise to myself. From now on I'm going to be a perfectly normal teenage girl." She smiled, pouring a cup for herself. She wasn't a huge coffee drinker, but why not get a boost for the day?

He laughed at her.

"There is no such thing," he claimed.

She frowned. Old people were always so hard on people her age.

"I think I am going to go to school now, before you shoot and kill my good mood. Bye," she told him, grabbing her cup before walking off. She made it halfway to the door when she remembered something and turned back.

"Forget something?" he questioned, turning his head back to her.

"Yeah, this," she answered, placing her cup on the table as she gave him a hug, squeezing him slightly.

"Thank you for everything yesterday. I don't think I said it at all, but thank you. I really did have a good time. The party wasn't that bad either. I can still feel my face." She smiled at him and even though she knew he couldn't see it, she couldn't help it.

"Would you like me to shoot you now or after you come back from school?" He smiled back at her, his eyebrow raised.

"Bye, Grandpapa," she told him, picking up her cup and leaving.

Luckily it wasn't raining; the sun was actually out. Now it felt like fall. That's what she liked about Ashland. In the fall, the tress looked so beautiful; all the shades of gold and red always made her relax. In the fall everything became its best: apples tasted sweeter, and the air was a perfect mixture of summer and winter. Fall was the best season—if you looked past the whole going-to-school thing. But even she could not bring herself to hate school whenever she had a window seat.

She knew she was in a good mood and today was going to be a good day when even the shoving and pushing in the halls of the school didn't bother her. She just walked up to her locker as though she was the only one there.

"What's wrong with your face?" Hector asked her as came up next to her.

"One—never, ever tell a girl that. Two—I opened my locker!" He looked at her as if she had gone crazy.

"Okay," he replied, grabbing his book before walking away.

No, Hector didn't understand. This was proof—proof that today was a good day. She didn't know what happened yesterday. Maybe she had eaten something bad or walked under a ladder. Closing her locker, she simply walked into the same bathroom as the day before, daring anything to try and mess with her today. And just like she thought, nothing happened. No pale hands stretching through the glass. No crying in the stalls. No panic or fear. Today was a good—

"Stare at yourself all you want, the image is not going to change. You're still a freak," Wilhelmina said, her heels clicking against the floor as she walked in, staring at her perfect self in the mirror.

"What is your problem? I've never done anything to you. Why have you chosen me as your punching bag?" Adela snapped, her hands folding across her chest as she waited. She really wanted to know why she was the person Wilhelmina had chosen.

Wilhelmina turned from the mirror to face her, her brown eyes sharpening, boring into her, making her feel insecure and small. But Adela wasn't going to step back and be steamrolled. Out of nowhere, Wilhelmina's face broke out into a smile and she shook her head before turning back to the mirror.

"You are so—" Wilhelmina started as she applied her lip-gloss.

"What? I am so what!" She stepped forward.

"So whiney. Poor me. Big bad Wilhelmina is picking on me. Boo-hoo," she mocked, moving so they were only inches apart.

"Stop caring; they're just words. The only reason why I bother you so much is because you let me. Grow up. I don't care what you or anyone else has to say, so why do you care? Call me mean, but you were crying in the stalls, frightened by your own reflection. That's weird. So therefore I called you weird. Simple." She rolled her eyes and walked past her as if she were nothing.

Adela stared into the mirror again and sighed. She didn't know why she cared so much. That didn't mean Wilhelmina had the right to treat her the way she did. Why couldn't people just be kind? Why was that so hard?

Leaving the bathroom, she realized that she had spent a little too much time in there. She was late for Mr. Watkins's class. Running down the empty halls, she made it to the classroom just as Wilhelmina did, but she couldn't slow down quickly enough, which caused them to slam into each other and tumble into the classroom.

"Will you get off of me?" Wilhelmina said, pushing her off as she rose up off the floor. Adela rolled her eyes, standing up also.

"You both are late," Mr. Watkins snapped from his position in front of the classroom. Everyone's eyes were on them, making her feel slightly uncomfortable. However, Wilhelmina walked on confidently as if nothing had happened.

"Sorry, Mr. Watkins. Adela was having a mini-episode over the mere thought of coming into this class. It took a while, but I was able to calm her down." She smiled, sitting down as everyone just laughed at her.

Adela could feel her jaw clenching. Shaking her head, she sighed. She moved past the smirking teens to take her seat beside Hector. He just stared at her worriedly.

Great. He thinks I am insane too, she thought.

"How kind of you, Wilhelmina," Mr. Watkins told her, rolling his eyes and walking back to his desk to pick up yet another stack of papers. Seriously, the man did not care about the environment one bit.

As the paper made its way back down the row, she read the words bolded and largely printed on the first page. She couldn't help but smile to herself. *Psychics and The Dark Ages* it read. She knew science had something to do with that.

"As you can see, this is not your test," he stated, standing in front of them. Good. She didn't want that test back.

"Everyone basically failed, with the exception of a few." Adela glanced over to Hector. He could tell she was looking at him, but he kept facing forward.

"So I have decided to spare myself from your whining and be nice. Shocker, I know. Instead, you will all be doing an oral presentation and written project on the Dark Ages." Adela wasn't sure if this was any easier than the actual test or why they were going to do a history project in science, but she wasn't going to ruin it for the rest of the class.

"This project will replace the test, but I warn you, you better not even try and slack off on this. I want it on Monday." Every last person in the room groaned. There went their weekends.

This is going to take forever, she thought as she flipped through the pages of questions that needed to be answered.

"Yes, I know, homework on a Friday. Who do I think you people are, high school students? You will be working in groups of three. And since you, Miss White, were kind enough to help Miss Arthur, I believe you two will make a magnificent group. Don't you?" He smirked down at her. She just sighed, leaning back in her chair, glaring.

"Would anyone like to volunteer to be in their group?" he asked around the classroom but no one said anything.

Adela turned to Hector, who pretended to be reading something very important in their textbook.

"Please. Please," she whispered over to him, begging.

"You owe me big." He sighed, his green eyes staring at her sharply through his glasses before he raised his hand.

"Mr. Pelleas, really? Fine. You three are a group," Mr. Watkins said before assigning others to their groups.

"Thank you," she told him. With him there, she could at least maintain a small part of her sanity.

"This can only end badly," he told her, shaking his head. As the bell rang, they all began to pack their stuff when Mr. Watkins called out again.

"Please, I beg of you… I know that it is hard in the post-Internet era we live in, but at least step foot into the library. We have one of the best ones in the state. The least you could do is see it once before you graduate." He sighed hopelessly at us as we walked out his classroom.

"Freak. Boy wonder." *Why was it so hard for her to call us by our names? Adela. Hector. It was not that hard,* she thought, turning to Wilhelmina.

"So when can we work on this because I really can't afford to fail," she told them. Adela took a deep breath, trying to control her anger.

"We can head to the library after school and get most of the heavy lifting out of the way," Hector said softly, not even bothered. She would have to call her grandfather, but he would be okay with it. They turned to Wilhelmina, who thought it over for a moment before nodding.

"Good plan, boy wonder." She smiled before spinning off in all her perfection.

"We have names," Adela muttered.

What happened to her happy, no-weird day? She was not going to let her little hiccup with Wilhelmina bring her down.

Once Adela decided that, the rest of day didn't bother her. She felt fine. She got through first period, which was always her biggest problem. Everything after that was a cakewalk.

While heading to the library after school, she tried to calm herself. The next few hours would be trying. Walking through the doors, she entered the ridiculously large library. Mr. Watkins was right. For a high school, it was really nice. There were three levels, all of which held wood shelves lining the walls, spewing out books. She felt bad for whoever it was that made sure everything was in its place. The large room was bright, on account of the sunlight that was pouring in, making it easy to spot Hector's sandy head hidden behind an unnecessarily large pile of books.

As she reached him, she realized that he had somehow managed to build a fort out of the books he had collected. She snuck up behind him, tip-toeing quietly. He was so far gone in his book, he wouldn't even notice.

"Don't," he spoke out just as she reached him, stopping her attack. He was just as bad as her grandfather.

"How did you know?" Adela asked, pulling out a chair beside him.

"You smell like Jasmines," he said, flipping to another page without glancing up from his book.

She lifted a small end of her raven hair to her nose, sniffing it. How come no one had ever told her this, she wondered.

"What do I need to do?" she asked him, picking up a book from the top of the stack.

"Read until you find something important." He sounded so bored. She really did owe him. He could have done this with some other people or alone, in the comfort of his own home.

"What counts as important?" The book in front of her was at least six hundred pages long. Shouldn't everything in there count as important?

"If it has numbers, dates, or something you have never heard before, write it down." That would take forever. Their notes alone would be able to become a new book. Frowning, she pulled out a pen to copy any random fact that caught her eyes.

One: The Middle Ages is the middle period between the decline of the Roman Empire and the Renaissance. Two: The early Middle Ages are often referred to as the Dark Ages. Three:

The Middle Ages are also referred to as the medieval era. Four: The Doomsday Book was written during this time. Five: The Hundred Years War between England and France was a hundred years long.

They thought long and hard on that name, she thought to herself, rubbing her eyes. She was barely paying attention, skimming the pages.

She had read the same page at least six times, and each time she would fall asleep halfway through. Reading was not as easy as it looked, especially when you did not care.

Frowning, she leaned back in her chair, looking around the library. Time had gone by drastically and there wasn't sunlight coming in anymore. When she had come in, there had been at least one or two other people in the library with them. However, they were now gone as well.

"Where is her highness?" Adela asked, but Hector didn't bother saying anything. He just lifted his hand and pointed upward.

There, Wilhelmina stood on the top level of the library, holding her phone up to the ceiling as she paced back and forth. When had she even come in? Had she been in here the whole time watching them?

"What is she doing?" Adela raised her eyebrow at her.

"There is no cell reception. She came in about twenty minutes ago while you were sleeping," he replied tiredly, flipping again. Angrily she got out of her seat, marching up the wooden spiral staircase until she stood toe to toe with Wilhelmina.

"Help me find a good signal," Wilhelmina said, moving around the deck, searching. In her hand was an overpriced smartphone.

"How about we help Hector instead," Adela snapped, glaring at the girl in front of her.

"Like you were doing, right? What did you find out when you were sleeping?" Wilhelmina replied before bringing her phone and her arm down, moving forward to challenge her.

Whatever anger Adela held within herself disappeared, realizing she was being just as helpful as Wilhelmina was.

"Can we just finish the last of this so we can go home?" Adela sighed, her shoulders sinking slightly under the force of gravity. She was tired and already clocking more hours in school than was healthy.

"After you." Rolling her eyes, Adela just walked back down, only to see Hector now half asleep over the book he was reading.

"Can we just finish this later? Some of us have lives," Wilhelmina said, dumping out everything in her purse as she tried to find the source of the ringing.

She has two phones? Adela thought as she packed up her stuff.

"Do you need a ride?" Adela asked out loud to Hector.

"There's my mirror. Ahh, I almost look as bad as you, Adela." Wilhelmina laughed to herself. Adela just glared back.

She was so tired of Wilhelmina and her cruelty. All she really wanted to do was punch her. Turning back around to Hector she tried to pay attention to what he was saying. However, she was just too annoyed. People like Wilhelmina just got under her skin.

"Adela, don't let her get to you—" He stopped mid-sentence, hearing what sounded like glass shattering.

Glancing down at her shattered reflection, Adela froze. Terror ran through every part of her soul as she stared into the pure black eyes of a lion. It growled, clawing at the surface. She began to back away slowly, unable to speak. She could feel her body shaking and she didn't know why.

"Chill out, you're not that ugly," Wilhelmina said, reaching down to pick the mirror up when suddenly the black head of a snake slithered out, biting the side of her wrist.

Her scream pierced through the room as she fell back, gripping her now-bloody hand.

Wilhelmina froze, the terror that was just in Adela's eyes now replicated in hers. "What? How? Did—?"

The glass began to melt as a black and dark red colored smoke rose from within it and then exploded. A wave of black fire blasted out like whips with such force that it sent the three of them flying backward, their bodies slamming against the wooden bookshelves.

"My head," Hector whispered as he dug himself up. Running his pale fingers over the source of the pain, he felt the hot liquid. Glancing down at his hand, he knew what he saw, but his brain could not process it. Dark crimson blood covered his hands, but they were not the source of the bleeding. Just above his hairline, he felt the gash that was now spilling forth more of the liquid.

"Ahh." His head turned to the small cry at his left side.

There, he saw Wilhelmina's bronze hand stained with blood, sticking out from under the books. He moved as quickly as he could, trying to unearth her from the blasted books. Throwing them every which way he could.

"Wilhelmina.... Wilhelmina!" he yelled down at her. He was panicking; he still did not understand what was going on. Her face grimaced in pain before her honey eyes opened, blinking slowly as she tried to regain hold of herself.

"Ahh," Wilhelmina groaned again, sitting up on the stacks of books as she held her head.

"Please tell me you both see this," Adela's barely audible voice cried out beside them. She could taste the blood in her mouth spilling from her spilt lip. But that didn't matter. Right now nothing mattered except for what was only a few feet from her.

Following her line of vision, Hector and Wilhelmina stared in pure terror at the unbelievably massive beast in front of them.

It was something that couldn't even have been from any of their worst nightmares. It was like someone had merged all of the worst animals they could think of into one beast. It had a dark, fire orange, fur-covered lion's body and head that merged into a black, reptilian scaled neck that ended with a snake's head, its eyes pure black. As if that was not enough, a skeletal, dark goat's head arose from the center of its back, its onyx horns long and deadly. Clawed bat-like wings sprouted from behind the goat's head.

On its place on the table, it angrily roared with hatred, the sound coming from all three of its mouths. Its scream was high and loud, undoubtedly painful and causing their ears to ring in pain. They raised their hands to cover their ears, but it did no good.

"I want to wake up. I want to wake up," Wilhelmina spoke, tears pouring from her eyes as she moved backward slightly.

"This cannot be real," Hector whispered lowly to himself, squinting his eyes. His glasses were long gone, buried under the rubble of the once-beautiful Ashland High library.

The creature—or creatures—moved forward, the wood of the desk cracking under the pressure of its body. Venom from the mouth of the snake dripped onto the table, causing it to hiss, eating through the wood until there was nothing but a large hole.

"Move slowly," was all Hector said as he picked himself up from the pile of books. Each of them moved up slowly, hands extended forward as though that would magically protect them.

The minute they moved toward the door, the beast let loose a heart stopping, blood-chilling screech. Its wings snapped wide as it prepared to pounce.

"Run. RUN! RUN! RUN!" Wilhelmina screamed, as they bolted through the door, running down the empty, dark halls.

The beast, too large to make it through the door, rammed through it, roaring out again, chasing them. They ran as fast as they could, tripping over their own feet. Just as they were about to make another turn, the beast blew a dripping red and orange sphere of fire ahead of them, setting the whole hall ablaze.

"Are you kidding me? It breathes fire? As if it wasn't deadly enough already," Adela screamed as they ran toward the fire escape, spiraling down the stairs.

"This is the reason why I didn't want to be in your group," Hector howled as they continued on. They were on the ground level of the school when part of the ceiling caved in behind them and the creature flew in.

"Really? Because you knew from the beginning that a lion-, snake-, bat-goat from hell would come out of my mirror and try to kill us!" Wilhelmina yelled at him. They were almost nearing the exit when she collapsed.

"Wilhelmina!" Adela screamed, running to her. Wilhelmina was shaking; her body was covered in sweat.

"What's wrong with her?" Hector breathed out heavily, trying to catch his breath. His heart pounded against his ribcage so hard he thought it might escape his chest.

"Watch out," Wilhelmina murmured, pushing Adela slightly as the black snake's head came flying toward her.

The snake screeched in irritation as it pounded against a barrier of what looked to be thousands of shimmering sapphires. It spread until it encased them all within it. The glow of its light was the only thing brightening the halls.

"How are you doing that?" Adela questioned her. Wilhelmina was sitting up slightly, her palms raised in front her.

The light came out of her hands before stretching outward, enclosing them all. The beast against it made Wilhelmina wince before it roared again, backing away. It circled them, its snake-like tail hissing and snapping at the barrier.

"I have no idea. But I can't feel my legs," Wilhelmina whispered softly, her once honey-brown eyes now blue. She was tired and could feel herself fading off into darkness, causing the barrier of blue shimmering lights to flicker.

"You have to stay awake," Hector said quickly once the barrier flickered again. He was trying to think and could not do that without worrying that any minute he could be clawed, burned, or poisoned.

"Your hands," he spoke out softly.

"Yes, I know there is a stream of blue light coming out of them. Thank you, but we can see that," Wilhelmina snapped at him. Her body felt like it was ripping apart.

"Wilhelmina your eyes are blue," Adela whispered, looking back at the girl without a clue in the world how to help them.

"What?" she yelled as the creature's claws struck her barrier again.

"The glass, when you tried to pick it up, it bit you," he told them both, looking between her bronze hands to the black snake behind the wall.

"You think that's why she can do this?" Adela questioned. The snakebite had given her powers? That did not seem right. That beast wanted nothing more than to kill them. She felt her heart drop when the barrier flickered again. The creature tried using its goat horns to ram against it, but that did not work.

"No. Yes. I don't know. I haven't taken 'How to Defend Yourself from Terrifying Creatures 101' yet. It's part snake; some snakes are poisonous, which is why she is like this," he snapped.

"I am so tired guys, I just want to sleep." Wilhelmina coughed up blood onto her lips. Her arms were getting so heavy.

Wiping her lip, Adela whispered to her, "We are not dying here."

"Wilhelmina, keep your hands up, okay. Adela stay close to us," Hector stated, placing one of his hands on the small of her back and the other under her legs, lifting her.

Just as he thought, the barrier stretched out, covering them. Slowly, he began to walk backward; as he did, the barrier moved with them.

"They shall build statues in your honor, my friend," Adela told him as she held on to Wilhelmina's shoulder, keeping an eye on the beast ahead of them.

It slashed, clawed, and breathed out fire, but nothing worked. Adela stared at Wilhelmina's face knowing she wouldn't last much longer. She put her hands underneath her arms, hoping to ease some of her pain. The cool fall air felt nice on Adela's skin. The beast followed them outside. It seemed to know Wilhelmina had seconds left before passing out.

"I'm sorry," Wilhelmina spoke out softly as her hands dropped. The barrier lingered for a moment before it shattered into dust and it was gone.

Had it not been for the beast that was running toward her, she would have frozen in shock over the fact that Wilhelmina White had actually said the word *sorry*. Hector, who looked like he was getting tired from carrying Wilhelmina in his thin arms, broke out running. Adela, right behind him, felt the heat of the fire on her neck as it came closer. But it never did. Right as they reached her car, her grandfather walked in front of the blast.

"GRANDPAPA!" Adela screamed, shielding her hazel eyes from the intensity of the burning light.

When they reopened, her grandfather was standing right in front of the beast, which had now stopped hissing and roaring down at him.

"Grandpapa..."

"Take your friends and go to the house. Do not look into any of the mirrors," he stated calmly to her.

The snake part of the beast whipped toward him, but he lifted his hand and a white flame exploded from it. He dropped his blind cane and she watched as his back became muscular. His fingers grew into large claws. It looked like something was moving underneath his shirt when suddenly large, white-scaled wings ripped through it. He let out a large monstrous-like roar. His whole body began to grow and scale over, until he was nothing but an all-white... a white... she couldn't even say it.

"Did you know your grandfather is a dragon?" Hector said for her.

"Get in the car," she told him.

Chapter Three

We Are Not Ready For The Truth

Adela broke every road law there was to make it back to her home in the shortest amount of time possible. However, she did believe her new, old car had met its maker. Hector laid Wilhelmina on the couch while Adela tore the house apart looking for a first aid kit and anything else she may need. Wilhelmina hadn't woken since the parking lot. They rested Wilhelmina's sweat-covered head on a pillow and gave her a blanket. Because that is what you're supposed to do, right? That's what they did in hospitals and the movies. They gave out pillows and blankets.

Hector lifted Wilhelmina's bitten hand to examine it and was shocked to find out how cold she was. It was like her hand had been in a bucket of ice. It wasn't just her hands, but her forehead as well. Hector stood up, running his hands through his hair. Panic was setting in again. Adela wasn't much better. She was worried about Wilhelmina but she also couldn't get the image of her grandfather out of her head.

"He's a Dragon," she whispered into the silence of the room. She took a seat right under Wilhelmina, pressing against the couch. Her grandfather was a massive, white-scaled, golden-eyed dragon. They had just been attacked by some creature from hell and now her friend—well, someone she knew—was possibly dying.

"We should call someone," Adela said to Hector, who stopped his pacing and looked down at her.

"And tell them what? How do you think that conversation will go? We would all be locked up in a mental institution," he snapped at her.

"We cannot just sit here and do nothing. She is obviously…" She stopped, not wishing to say it, before speaking again.

"We need to do something." Adela rose, yelling at him.

"What can we do then, huh?" he yelled back.

"I don't know. Anything!"

They were both so deep in shock, so afraid and jumpy, that when the door flew open, they grabbed whatever was nearest to them.

"Where is she?" Principal Pelleas questioned quickly when she entered the room. Spotting Wilhelmina, she sped past the two teens who were using a lamp and a remote control as their defense.

Tying her red hair into a ponytail, she touched Wilhelmina's face and hands, searching her over.

"Mom..." Hector started, putting down the remote control he was holding to stand beside her.

"Step back," Principal Pelleas whispered, grabbing a plant near the window, uprooting it and placing it on Wilhelmina's body before raising her hands over her.

Following her instructions, Adela and Hector moved farther away from them. Adela and Hector watched as the vines and roots grew until they connected on her hands and so on. It was like it was encasing her in a cocoon of vines, wrapping over her face and skin. Principal Pelleas touched the living vines and they attached to her hand, crawling up her fair skin.

Principle Pelleas muttered softly under her breath onto the vines, causing them to glisten in an even brighter emerald color until the vines seemed to shatter into small sprinkles of green dust. When it was gone, Wilhelmina looked as if nothing had happened, like she was merely sleeping.

"Did you know your mother was a witch?" Adela asked the frozen Hector at her side.

But before he could answer, she saw her grandfather, newly dressed, step into the room with his walking stick in hand. He seemed fine, but the even the new clothes he now wore could not hide the scratches and bite marks she saw on his exposed arms.

Walking over, he gazed toward Wilhelmina.

"How is she?" he asked.

Principal Pelleas sighed softly, not a word from her pink lips. Her body tensed as she glanced up at him, shaking her head. *What did that mean?* Adela thought to herself. But she knew. People did not just shake their heads at such a question. She wanted to speak her mind, but she feared what would happen if she did so.

"I should call her parents," Principal Pelleas whispered lowly before rising from the ground. The room was filled with a thick silence; it seemed that, just like her, no one wished to speak.

"She's all right?" Hector asked, finally speaking since his mother had come in. "Whatever magic thing you just did is going to make her better?"

Her grandfather did not glance back at them. He did not even speak. Principal Pelleas seemed to be frozen, out of place in their dump of a home with her fancy clothing and expensive cell phone. She held it out in front of her like she was going to make a call but did not know the Whites' number. But that could not be the case. One of the many reasons she was the principal was because she knew everyone, especially the Whites. *How would you not know the number to one of the school's biggest donors?*

Hector stepped up beside his mother.

"Is she all right?" he all but shouted at her.

Finally her gaze broke away from the device in her hands. She looked at him with so much love that Adela could again feel a thud in her heart. The same thud she felt anytime a parent gave their child that look.

"Any sort of an attack by a Chimera is poisonous; however, she was bitten by the snake. They are fatal, and we did not have enough time. I am so sorry." Tears welled in her eyes, but Adela could no longer look at her.

Instead her gaze returned to the girl. The dead girl… the dead Wilhelmina, the girl who had made life harder than it needed to be for her. Part of Adela's mind seemed to be splitting apart. Only an hour ago—if even that much time had passed—they were arguing in the library. Now she was lying on their tattered, depressed, and uncomfortable couch, dead. Adela did not understand. She would not have even realized that she was crying had it not been for her blurred vision.

The white blanket that was being placed over her blocked her view of the peaceful-looking Wilhelmina. Her eyes shifted to her grandfather, who had yet to speak.

"Grandpapa, what is going on?" she asked him, taking a step back.

She was tired, confused, and mostly she was afraid of him, something she had never been in her whole life. But she didn't know him. She didn't know anything at this point. He walked silently over to the front door.

"They are here but I did not call them yet," Principal Pelleas sighed, dropping the phone on to the table.

"Go to your room and take Hector with you," Adela's grandfather commanded.

But she did not move. Hector, on the other hand, did not hesitate. They had just lost someone, and his rational brain told him this was not the time to be defiant. He grabbed Adela's hand and shut the door to her bedroom. She still did not speak; she only leaned against the door until gravity took over and she was on the floor. Her tears fell like waterfalls from her eyes, and even as she wiped them over and over again, they would not stop falling.

"Keane, please no…" she heard the soft murmur of a new voice, it stopped and broke out into dead sobs making her cry even more.

A voice she knew to be Principal Pelleas creaked out, "I am so sorry." It seemed to be all she could say.

"We are supposed to be safe here! No more were to die here. How? I want to know how?" a man yelled angrily. He had every right to be filled with rage.

"A Chimera broke through; we do not know how, Harbin. She fought though, like a true White. She fought, even called forth her light. The light was the brightest type of sapphire, just like yours." Her grandfather tried to comfort him. She was not sure if it did anything, but the yelling stopped and all that was left was loud sobbing.

That sound, that pain, would never wash from Adela's mind. It was permanently embedded, ready to be called forth at any time.

"Was Ms. Arthur hurt?" the man she guessed to be Mr. White, or Harbin as her grandfather called him, asked through his sobs. Why would he care about her? He had just lost his daughter.

"She is fine, thanks to your daughter."

Everything was quiet after that. She heard muttering and low whispers, but they seemed to float to the back of her mind. Hector took her hand. She had forgotten he was even there, but nonetheless it helped. They sat there like small frozen statues, unsure of what to say. Even if they could speak, what would be the point? Neither one of them had any more answers than the other. Sleep finally overtook their bodies; it was not the peaceful type of sleep they wished for, though. It was one filled with horror, fear, and tears.

Only when they felt the stiffening in their arms and legs were they forced to awaken early that next morning. Adela wished it were a dream, but seeing Hector bedside her, she knew she did not hold such luck. Stepping out into the simple living room, both of their eyes went straight to the couch. Wilhelmina was no longer there, only both their guardians, who seemed like they had not been graced with the horror of sleep. They were waiting for the questions both teens were about to ask. However, neither of them knew if they would truly understand or even be able to handle such truths.

"Explain," Adela commanded. She was not going to rest and pretend nothing had happened. In the small, rational part of her brain, she noted how her grandfather was still in the same old clothes as the night before but his injuries were now healed. Principal Pelleas looked over to her grandfather; he just nodded. Slowly, like it did on Wilhelmina, the vines began to cover the walls and windows of the room.

"What in the—?" Adela whispered, stepping back as the vine slithered past her foot.

"Take a seat," her grandfather commanded them. His voice seemed different, more powerful, like it had aged; it held something in it she could not place.

Adela glanced over at Hector, who simply glared at his mother but did not move to sit down. Neither of them wanted to lay on the only vacant seat in the room: the couch Wilhelmina had just been on.

He waited for Principal Pelleas to make her way over. When she nodded, he took off his shades. Like always, his eyes were closed until he rubbed them for a moment before they opened. A small gasp came from her lips when she saw the golden eyes of a dragon staring back at her. They were chilling and they pierced through her.

"As you may have guessed, I am not human." His ancient voice sounded as his eyes moved and gazed at them.

"Are you?" Hector spoke for the first time as he glared at his mother. Sadness glistened in her green eyes before she frowned.

"Yes and no," she stated plainly. Hector shook his head as his jaw tightened. He said nothing more, taking a seat on the arm of the chair.

"It would be best to let us start from the beginning," her grandfather told them. Neither of them spoke. She wasn't sure if any of them were breathing any longer.

"As I said, I am not human. Nor did I originate from here. We are from Cielieu, the land behind the looking glass—what you call mirrors." His eyes watched them carefully, checking how they would react to such news. But Adela and Hector were too shocked to move, let alone speak.

"There are creatures on the other side of our mirrors," Adela spoke out softly as she tested out the insanity of her own words. He just nodded, frowning at her.

"That's where you both are from?" Hector questioned as he glared harshly at the two people…creatures in front of them.

"No, Hector. That's where we are all from," his mother spoke out, staring at him, her own sorrow spilling forth.

"We are monsters too?" Hector's eyes widened as he waited for their answer. *Was that why Wilhelmina was able to put up a barrier?* Adela wondered to herself.

"We are not monsters. We are human, just a different type." Principal Pelleas snapped, sitting up. However, her grandfather—if she could even still call him that— grabbed her arm. She relaxed for a moment before sitting back down; the day was getting to her just like everyone else.

Breathing deeply, she began again. "You know how they say humans only use ten percent of their brains?"

"It's just a myth, we use all of it. It's been proven," Hector replied.

"No, it is the truth. Believe me, I am a dragon." Grandpapa Keane was proving once again everything they knew to be a lie.

"We come from a place called Cielieu, the home of all creatures. Creatures that you have all come to believe are just mythical: dwarfs, fairies, giants and dragons. They are all as real as you and I," Principal Pelleas said to them, glancing over at Grandpapa Keane, who simply frowned. He wanted to protect them, not just physically but mentally as well.

"There was a time when we all shared one world. It was a constant struggle, one that left many dead on all sides due to simple fear. There was a group of humans not like the rest. These humans had somehow unlocked their minds and could create light with a single thought. This light could be used to make anything they wished. At that time, all they wished for was peace, and so together they were able to make a whole new world, one similar to this one but only for our kind. Those humans were called Volsin. We left the other humans their world to fight over. In time we became nothing but folktales and frightening stories, which were once, in fact, simple truths," Grandpapa Keane said to them.

Adela tried to wrap her mind around his words. He wasn't lying—all she had to do was look at his eyes to see that—but her mind was telling her it couldn't possibly be true. Everything she had ever known was a lie.

"Were we even born here?" she whispered softly.

Principal Pelleas simply shook her head. "No, both of you were mere infants when you were brought back here…"

"If this is true, why are we here and not there?" Hector

snapped, pinching the bridge of his nose. He could not believe this as well.

In fact, Hector Pelleas found this harder to believe than Adela did. He had based his whole life on logic. Math, science, the laws of nature, they always made sense to him. How could that all just be a lie? In his mind, his impeccable mind, he could not fathom a world with giants or fairies or even dragons, though he was currently speaking to one.

"You see, each Volsin is different and can use different levels of their mind, so some are more powerful than others. Sixteen years ago the peace we all had enjoyed was disrupted. A very powerful Volsin fully unlocked the levels of his mind. He became corrupted by his power and drunk off his own greed. Then he began to form an army of darkness. Only two Volsin families in all of Cielieu were ever able to become powerful enough to unlock so much of their minds. The Arthurs were one of them." Fire burned in Grandpapa Keane's golden eyes with each word he spoke.

"In order to gain more power to stand against the Arthurs, this dark Volsin murdered other Volsin from different families. He stripped them of their light and then consumed it, adding to his own. But it still was not enough. So he took the light of your father's best friend, your god-father." Grandpapa Keane looked dead into Adela's eyes before speaking again.

What was she supposed to feel? What was she supposed to say? She did not even know if her heart or her mind could take any more of this. She wanted to wake up from this nightmare, but it seemed never-ending.

"There is nothing more evil than to strip a Volsin of his light, the very thing that defines him. By doing so, this dark Volsin increased his own power, only to hunger for more. No one was safe. Death became a familiar thing in Cielieu. No one knew how to stop him—no one but your parents." This here was the truth, something Adela had wanted to know for as long as she could recall. But now in this moment, in the wake of Wilhelmina's death, she was not sure if should know.

"When Cielieu was created, it was meant to be a one-way door for the protection of both worlds. But the only way to keep more lives from being taken was to make a refuge for as many as possible, at least until this dark Volsin could be stopped. The only problem was reopening that door would take an unparalleled amount of light, so much light in fact that it would most likely take the life of whoever opened it." Grandpapa Keane sighed, truly not sure how he could explain this without breaking the young girl. He did not even know if he should.

"Your mother, along with two other Volsin, gave their lives and their lights, Adela, in order to bring as many people over as they could. Meanwhile your father and all those who had chosen to stay fought back the Volsin in the final battle of the Great War. Because of them, Cielieu was not overtaken," he said to her softly, but that did not soften the blow.

Adela had hoped for a split second, dared to dream that maybe her parents were just a mirror away. But that wasn't the case. They were gone. They didn't die in a fire. They never even saw her take her first step. Why had she bothered to hope?

"Your father was one of the Volsin who chose to stay behind," Principle Pelleas whispered to Hector, her green eyes shined as her jaw clutched. Adela felt the boy beside her tense but she did not have the strength to pick her head up.

"What else?" Adela demanded. There had to be more to this. But Grandfather Keane was done talking.

"Adela, we do not know much after that," Principle Pelleas told her. What did that mean?

"I want to go back," Hector stated, shocking no one.

"No," was all either of them said.

Taking a step forth, he glared at both his mother and the dragon before him.

"My father could still be alive. I want to go back," he said.

Grandfather Keane's eyes narrowed dangerously, something Adela would never get used to.

"He is not alive," Principle Pelleas whispered.

"You don't know that. You just said—"

"How do you think the Whites knew Wilhelmina was gone

before I could even call them?" Her question not only froze them both but also added to Hector's depression.

"Emotions, connections like that are all heightened for Volsin. We feel love and hate much stronger then you can even realize. When you lose someone you love, you just know. It is like a bolt of thunder through your heart that rings throughout your soul." Principle Pelleas filled in for her.

"When?" Hector questioned her, stepping forward as well.

"Twelve years, nine months, and twenty-two days ago. I can only guess that your father went into hiding and was found by him," she recited perfectly.

"You cried that whole week." Hector was only a kid then, but he could remember things like that. Adela wondered how many lies he was going over in his head and how many lies she would have to sift through.

"If your father was still alive, you would feel it. You cannot remember the pain of losing him because you were young." She did not need to remember. It would have felt much like it did now.

Hector's whole body was shaking in absolute anger. He could not bring himself to speak, let alone think straight. He stood up and walked over to the root- and vine-covered door, pulling on it until it ripped apart. He left, slamming the door behind him.

Principle Pelleas simply sighed before following her son, leaving Adela with the dragon she had spent all of her life calling Grandpapa.

"This Volsin, what is his name?" Adela whispered.

"He calls himself Prince Delapeur."

Adela simply nodded before going back to her room, locking her bedroom door for the very first time in her life.

Chapter Four

The Straw That Broke Everyone's Back

Adela had not moved all weekend. After Hector had left with his mother, she had spent most of her time in her bedroom. Every mirror was now covered, but she just laid there in bed too afraid to face the world she no longer knew or understood. She hadn't spoken to Hector or to anyone for that matter. Part of her was worried that something had happened to them. Her grandfather, for the most part, had given her space. He seemed too busy anyway, going in and out of the house constantly. The times he left, she would go to the park for a few hours and just stare at all the people. All those people who were carefree, oblivious to the truth. She used to be one of them. She missed being one of them.

But she couldn't hide anymore. Today was the day she dreaded: there was school today. By now everyone must have known about Wilhelmina's passing. She wasn't even sure how they could have school at first, with the school damaged the way it was. However, Principal Pelleas claimed the school was fine. It would have been hard to believe, but under the circumstances, nothing was impossible anymore.

I hate Mondays, Adela thought to herself as she entered her car. Today was going to be hard. Mondays by themselves are always difficult, but today would be a dark day. She wished she could cry more for Wilhelmina. She wished she could openly sob about her like she knew so many would. But she did not know if she had any more tears.

She had cried for the girl who would never turn eighteen. She had cried for the parents who would never watch their daughter grow. She had even cried for the strong, brave, and fearless girl, because Wilhelmina was truly amazing. When she ran out of tears, Adela grew angry at herself. Angry because she was doing the same thing everyone did when someone died. She was remembering all the good that was in Wilhelmina. This angered her because she should have seen it before.

People always remembered the good that was in another after they were gone. But while people are alive, the good is obscured by emotions.

Dressing was easy for Adela; she had limited options to choose from. Usually she wore whatever was somewhat clean and convenient.

Her grandfather was in the living room drinking from his favorite broken mug. His dark shades were placed back on his face, and they seemed so ridiculous now. He was a dragon in sheep's clothing.

She had just reached the rusted doorknob when he spoke.

"I will be at the school today if you need me." Adela felt bad for not speaking to him.

"Okay," she said to him before leaving quickly.

Walking over to the Old Black and Blue as she'd named it, she heaved hard on the driver's door. It screamed loudly in pain before opening to her will.

"Please work," she whispered over it, rubbing her pale hand over the dashboard. Old Black and Blue hacked and coughed like it was dying. It could have been, really. Once more she tried and once more it coughed until it bent to her will. The drive to school was intense. She felt as though her heart was about to cave in upon itself. How could anyone be okay knowing what she knew? Hector was the only person she could speak with, but she knew he would have his own demons to face.

Adela could feel it in the air when she stepped out of her car. The grief was so thick Adela felt as though she was choking.

She wondered if maybe it was guilt causing her to feel this way. It was oddly quiet as she walked through the crowded hallway. It looked absolutely normal, like nothing had even happened. Like she, Hector, and Wilhelmina hadn't ran for their lives just two days ago in these very halls. Ashland High was fine, just as Principal Pelleas said it would be. There were only soft murmurs and hushed whispers as she walked. She was headed not to her locker, but to Wilhelmina's.

But she could not see the red of the locker anymore. It was now covered in everything from roses and hearts to bears and pictures. It seemed to overflow, swallowing Wilhemina's locker whole. There was barely any space for anyone to walk by without stepping on something.

"She was too great for us. Too funny, too bold, too beautiful, so you see we understand. She was too great for us. We weep and we cry, but we understand. She was too great for us. That's the only reason why she is back in the sky." Hector read out aloud the poem that stood proudly under Wilhelmina's class president picture.

Was, Adela thought to herself. Whenever they spoke of her now, they had to speak in past tense. How wrong, how odd.

Hector turned away from the sight before him; Adela just followed him in the opposite direction of the procession of mourners.

"They say she died of cardiac arrhythmia, which gave her a heart attack," he told her.

Why not? A perfectly healthy sixteen-year old girl dying of a heart attack. It could happen. People would believe that. It was better than all the other options that were out there. Walking into Mr. Watkins's physics class, she realized that their group project was due today. It seemed everyone had done their assignment but them.

Did it really matter? Adela thought to herself as she took a seat by the window. The sun was still shining brightly. Didn't the sun know today was a dark day?

The sun needed to be hiding behind massive dark clouds as rain poured out and covered the ground below. The sun should know when to hide. It should be aware of the town's grief. How inconsiderate of it to shine so brightly, how insulting.

Mr. Watkins strolled in with his hastened steps, as usual looking quite disheveled.

"I know today is, ugh... Well, I know it's tough. Let's just take it easy. Who wishes to go first?" he muttered awkwardly, ruffling through his stack of wrinkled and damp white papers. What made them so damp, Adela didn't care.

One by one each group went forward and spoke. It was starting to become redundant; everyone's facts were the same. She didn't even understand why he'd given them this project anyway. This was science, not that she cared that much. Luckily, the bell rang before it was their turn. Walking back to her locker, Adela felt strange, like there was some shift in the polarity of the world.

She began to stumble, slightly bumping into the people beside her. Grabbing her head, she reached her locker before stumbling against it.

"Adela? Adela?" She heard a voice that resembled Hector's. But it was off, like he was speaking to her from underwater or through glass. Burying her head in the locker, she tried to get a handle on the pain scorching through her brain.

"Adela? Adela, are you there?" The further she plunged in the darkness of her own mind, the clearer she could hear the girl's voice.

"Adela, I don't have much time. He's going to take my light." The girl spoke quickly, echoing in the darkness of her mind.

"Who's going to?" Adela cried back. She was running in the darkness. She couldn't see anything. Adela could feel her pain, and it caused Adela's heart to grieve, but she couldn't find the girl. She didn't even know where she was.

"Please, please…," she cried again. Adela held on to herself, falling to the dark ground. She curled up into a ball, trying to stop the pain she felt.

"Who are you? Where are you?" Adela whispered softly. She felt the snow beginning to cover her. It was so cold. Where was she?

Adela's eyes opened. Glancing around, she noticed it wasn't the darkness she'd seen before. She was now on a snow-covered mountaintop. At the edge was girl about the same age as she. She had long brown hair with everything from twigs to dried leaves matted in it. Her eyes were large, and their striking blue color was almost unnatural. The girl knelt in the snow. She had tears pouring down her face. Her whole body looked to be bruised; all over she was covered in cuts and scratches.

"Who are you? Are you all right?" Adela questioned her. She tried to get up, but gravity was weighing her down. It was like a boulder was holding her in place.

The girl's eyes seemed to widen when they saw her. She screamed, but Adela couldn't hear anything. She waved her hands and was screaming and crying, but it was if someone put her on mute. The brown-haired girl began to slowly lift herself off the ground. Then Adela suddenly noticed the girl had a large gash on her side. Whatever caused the wound had torn through the side of her shirt, causing her to bleed. The bottom of her pants were cut as well.

"Don't move! You're hurt!" Adela screamed from the ground. She watched in horror as the blood dripped from the girl's side, around her hand clutching her wound and onto the ground below, staining the white snow.

The blue-eyed girl ignored Adela. Getting up, she shook her head. The girl's tears and sobs couldn't be heard, but Adela could feel them. Her eyes became wet. Summoning all the strength she could, the girl pushed up from the snow. She ground her teeth together and let out a small scream. Getting onto her knees, the girl lifted herself on one foot. From the corner of her eye, Adela noticed a dark boot to her left. She shifted her gaze and saw a man. She couldn't see much, but he was dressed in all black. The only variation in color was his shoulder-length blond hair.

"Help her, please!" Adela screamed, but he didn't turn to her. Instead, he kept walking toward the broken girl in front of him.

She was still crying but seemed somewhat under control now. Her face was expressionless, her back straightened, and she held her head up high. When the blond man reached her, he used his glove-covered hand to wipe her tears. The girl glared, all the hate in the world shining through her sapphire eyes. She whispered something to him, but Adela couldn't hear what it was. The man circled her slowly; he seemed to be speaking as well, but Adela still couldn't hear.

His skin was pale, but his face was unnaturally beautiful, just like the girl's. He looked only a few years older than she was. The girl's eyes connected with Adela's once again. She opened her mouth and mouthed slowly:

"I am so sorry."

Adela watched in horror as the pale man's hand plunged into her chest. The girl's blue eyes widened and began to fade as if someone turned off their light. They dimmed until they were pure black and lifeless. The man pulled his hand out and with that, her body fell to the ground. In the palm of his hand was a small ball of light. It shimmered like a thousand diamonds in the sun. It was beautiful. But slowly it started to fade as the man's palm closed upon it. His fist shook violently, and suddenly the light was gone. He took a deep breath, calming himself before his red eyes reopened and widened at the sight of Adela.

An evil grin tilted his lips, and with one kick of his foot, the girl's body flew over the mountainside, disappearing from her view. He began to walk over to Adela, but once again everything began to shake. He was beginning to blur. He must have noticed this as well, because now he seemed to float over the ground, moving at a greater speed. But it was too late. The vision shifted to darkness and he was gone.

"Miss Arthur!"

Adela's head snapped at the call of her last name.

There at her desk was Mr. Watkins glaring down at her. She glanced around the classroom, every pair of eyes on her tear-stricken, pale face. Hector stared at her, worried. Something was wrong, and it wasn't just because she fell asleep. He could tell.

"Are we boring you?"

Adela's heart was racing; panic set in. That wasn't just a dream. People don't just dream about that type of stuff. This meant something, but Adela wasn't sure what exactly. She was breaking. She had watched another person die. She met Hector's eyes again, directing her attention back to Mr. Watkins.

"Sorry, sir," she replied, grabbing her stuff and walking out of the classroom. There was only one place she could go. That girl's death played over and over in her mind like a dreaded horror movie she wished she could forget. No more… she wasn't going to watch it anymore.

"Adela, wait!"

She stopped in the empty hall, watching as Hector tried to catch up with her.

"Hector," she whispered, shaking her head. Her heart had yet to slow and she felt as if she were going to break down at any moment.

"I can't, not here," she told him.

The halls were empty now, but anyone could walk by at any second. "Principal's office," was all she said before continuing back on her quest.

Hector followed behind her silently. Bursting into the school office, she headed for Principal Pelleas's door in the back of the room.

"Where do you think you're going?" the young office assistant said as he put his body between Adela and the door.

"I need to speak to Principal Pelleas." Adela glared at the older man in front of her. She really didn't have time for this.

"Well, I'm sorry. She's in an important meeting right now," he said pompously. This guy was obviously unaware that she was not one to be messed with. Not today, most definitely not today.

"Hi, Mike, is it? You see, she isn't asking." Hector stepped up behind her, causing Mike to raise an eyebrow at the small teen in front of him. Hector wasn't the intimidating type.

"It's fine, Mike," Principal Pelleas called from behind him, stepping out of her office, her red hair standing out more drastically in contrast with the black suit she wore. It seemed to scream out, *"Yes, she knows a student died. She cares so much she wore all black."*

He nodded and shot a glance at the three before walking off. Principal Pelleas stepped aside, allowing them to enter. Upon entering, Adela saw her grandfather leaning against her oak desk.

"What brings—"

"I saw something," Adela said, cutting off Principal Pelleas. She didn't know how long she'd have the backbone to speak up.

"What?" Hector asked behind her. They all seemed shocked, even her grandfather. He took off his glasses, rubbing his eyelids before his golden eyes met hers. He seemed to be scanning her over.

"Are you all right? Did anything try to break through?" Pushing off the desk and walking over to her, he reached to touch her shoulder, but Adela pulled back.

"In one week I've seen two people die. So no, I'm not okay. I crossed over to Cielieu, I guess, this time." Adela stared up at him. She didn't know for a fact whether she did or not.

Hector grabbed hold of her. "You what?"

"That's impossible, Adela," her grandfather told her, walking back over to the desk.

"I'm sorry, the word impossible has been deleted from my dictionary on account of the monster that attacked us Friday and you being a dragon," she snapped at him.

"Chimera," Hector whispered next to her, causing Adela to glare at him, annoyed.

"Adela, maybe you were just imagining things. All of this may have—"

"I am not imagining this. I watched a girl be murdered in front of my eyes. I stood there and watched...," she started, but she couldn't go on. She'd reached her breaking point. *What is happening? Why is this all happening?*

She hated this powerless feeling.

"Adela, what did you see?" Hector whispered.

"I didn't even know I was sleeping. I thought class had ended, so I gathered up my things and headed to my locker. But the minute I stepped out of the room, I could tell something was wrong. I felt heavy. My head pounded against my skull and it became too hard to walk. Then there was this voice in my head. She told me she didn't have time, that he was going to take her light. I couldn't see anything. It was so dark. I..." She stopped again, trying to gain control.

Hector took her hand, leading her to the chair. "Breathe."

Her hazel eyes stared into his. Nodding, she followed his instructions. She hadn't even realized she wasn't breathing evenly.

Slowly but still shaken, she told them what she saw. The red-eyed blond stripped the girl of her light and kicked her off the mountaintop. The last four words to leave the brunette's mouth were to Adela. Adela spilled forth everything, sparing no detail, to the adults in the room.

She lifted her eyes. Her grandfather's head was down and Principal Pelleas's hand covered her mouth, horror in her green eyes.

"It wasn't a dream, was it?" Adela whispered. She knew it wasn't, but she needed to hear it from her grandfather.

"No," he whispered, sighing softly. His eyes scanned over them.

"He stole her light and therefore, her life," he added softly, walking over to stare out the window. Adela was beginning to notice he did this often. It was then she realized the walls were covered with vines again, just like in her home. They were thicker here, more like branches or roots than vines.

"The man was Prince Delapeur."

He'd looked like any other human to her. In fact, in the split second before she saw the evil in his eyes, she'd thought he looked handsome. Before, Adela would have thought him to be a great cloud of evil, shadow of darkness, or some vile-looking creature that her imagination couldn't even understand. Had she seen the man from her vision on the street or in their town, the only thing that would've made him look out of place would have been his overly fine clothing and red eyes.

"It is a mask. He is such a vain, despicable, loathsome creature. I wish nothing more than to return to him ten-fold what he has done," Principal Pelleas hissed out, stopping herself before her words grew crueler.

"He was… is Volsin, you could say. But evil has consumed him over the years and caused him to… There is so much we do not know. The girl you saw must have had a gift, something very few have alongside their light. It gives her a simple talent that is unique to her. It must have enabled her to connect with others in this realm." Her grandfather spoke, but he had yet to turn around, and it was bothering Adela greatly.

"But why me?" She'd never seen that girl in her whole life. Well, at least she didn't think she had. Then again, who knew?

Principal Pelleas stared at her grandfather's back, waiting. She looked worried, as if she wasn't sure whether or not she should say anything.

Her grandfather's back tensed. "Adela, you are an Arthur. Your parents' names are praised upon. Even if you had half the light they did, who knows what you could do?"

Was that meant to make me feel better? Adela thought to herself. *Was that supposed to mean something? People are dying and some girl believed, just because of my last name, I could do something?*

What could she do? There were so many questions she needed answered. Her grandfather was holding back, and Adela knew that. Her parents had died trying to save the lives of others, yet it all seemed to be in vain. This was much too intense for Adela to handle.

"Adela?" Hector asked softly.

A good ten minutes had gone by since she'd spoken last. She rose calmly from her seat and walked over to the antique mirror on the wall. She stared into her own hazel eyes as the others spoke behind her. There were so many things running through her head at that moment. She feared speaking might break her. She remembered what her grandfather had said, how she was the perfect mixture of her mother and father.

What would they do? Would they have tried to forget all the horror and pain of the last week? Would they continue living on or would they fight back? Would they make the same choice if given the chance?

Everything she wanted to know, everything she needed to know was a mirror away, where her parents died, the place they'd hidden her from. How long would it remain there before it was destroyed? A girl who Adela had never met died today because she wanted to send her a message. She was murdered in front of Adela's very own eyes. How many people, creatures, were going through the same thing? How many were living in fear and terror while she ate popcorn and complained about high school? How many people died? How many were still dying while she stood here?

"I want to go," she whispered.

"I can take you home," Hector offered kindly.

She just shook her head before turning around.

"I want to go to Cielieu," she said, her voice stronger, as she crossed her arms.

"Adela—" her grandfather started.

"I. Want. To. Go. To. Cielieu," she howled, anger clearly flashing in her eyes. No one spoke; they only continued to stare at her as if she were crazy.

"Fine, I'll get through myself," she hissed, turning back to the mirror in front of her. Staring heatedly into the glass, she yelled, "What is it, huh? Open sesame? Bippity-boppity-boo?"

"Adela, that is enough!" her grandfather yelled.

She turned back to him, stepping forward. "I want—"

But he cut her off. "You ignorant, stubborn little girl! You have no clue what it is you're asking. This is not a game or one of your ridiculous fairy tales. This is life or death. Something a sixteen-year-old girl could not comprehend. The mirror is locked anyway. There is no way you can get through." He truly yelled at her for the first time in her whole life.

"Really? Life or death? I couldn't tell. Give me a second to step into the hallway where hundreds of students mourn the death of a classmate and friend. Maybe then it will hit me." Her rebuttal was below the belt. Seeing their faces, she saw just how far below, but it had at least gotten her point across.

"If that man just took her power, then I'm not safe here either. He'll figure out how to message me or even worse, get ahold of me. I'm no safer here than there. At least I can learn over there. You keep saying it's a door. Well, every door has a key. They wouldn't just send us over here with no way of going back."

There was sound logic that no one wanted to admit embedded in her words. If that girl were strong enough to summon Adela, it would only be a matter of time before Prince

Delapeur did the same. Adela knew he'd seen her. His eyes widened and he rushed to her as quickly as he could. If he was heartless enough to not only murder that girl, but to kick her body off the mountain, then Adela didn't want to know what could happen to her. If her family was as strong as they claimed, she was on his list. She had no doubt.

Her grandfather's shoulders seemed to drop. "There is a chance that he may not be able to master it anytime soon. He may have her gift. But it could be years before he could even get to you." He was deflecting, not even trusting the words coming out of his own mouth.

"So what you're saying is that she should just sit around painting her toenails and wait? If and when he figures out how to connect with her, oh well, at least she had a few more years. You said we were safe. Obviously not," Hector snapped angrily in her defense, something Adela was grateful for. But she didn't want him to be dragged into this when he didn't have to be.

"You aren't thinking clearly. You can't just cross over. Yes, there is a key, but it was meant to take us back permanently. Once you step through, there's no possible way to come back. You will be stuck in Cielieu forever. This isn't the time to cling to idiotic fantasies about being a hero," Principal Pelleas told them angrily, which only seemed to anger Hector even more.

"Try Snow White. They have a mirror in that one, right?" He questioned her, turning his back on his saddened mother.

"My job, the one task your parents entrusted to me, was to protect you at all costs. You are not going through. You can have a life here, a loving family. You will be happy here."

All Adela could do was stare at her grandfather. She knew she couldn't stay here anymore. It no longer felt right to do so, but she wasn't a hero either. What could she do if she went to Cielieu? She was and would always be plain Adela Arthur in her mind. But in reality, what did being Adela Arthur truly mean?

"The only way I'll ever know who I am now is by going to Cielieu, by trying to make sense of all this. Knowing what I know now, I could never just go back to my old life," she said to him.

"Hector, you are not going. We didn't go through all of this for you to just walk back in," Principal Pelleas yelled at him, on the brink of tears.

Hector gazed back at her through the thick black frames of his glasses. "I'm leaving, Mom. I love you, but I'm leaving."

"You…" Her grandfather sighed before speaking again. "Once you open this door, Adela, you will never be the same," he whispered, walking between her and the mirror.

"You can't be serious, Keane. They don't know what they're asking," Principal Pelleas cried out, stepping forward.

"They don't. But then again, none of us ever do." He looked over at Adela.

Her mind was set and she wouldn't stop until she was through. Adela was no longer safe here among the humans, and he knew that. If Prince Delapeur had stolen the light of that girl, he could one day grab Adela's mind. He could one day grab all their minds. Grandpapa Keane knew that the best chance for either of them was to learn, and she couldn't do it here. None of them could. He prayed he was making the right choice.

Adela watched as his hand touched the mirror. He stared in each of their faces, and she hoped she didn't seem as scared as she was.

"Do not be surprised if you look different. You're still yourselves; however, your outer appearances will reflect the best you. You must hold hands, and I shall return with you. I will not, however, be at your side when we return. Simply ask to be taken to the Elpida Castle of Light. You will be safe there," her grandfather told them, and Adela wondered who they would ask. And how would they look different?

Hector walked over to his mother, pulling her into a tight hug. Adela wasn't sure what he whispered to her; she didn't wish to know. Part of her didn't want Hector to come along with her, but she knew as much as he was there for support, he, too had questions about who he was and where he'd come from. It was only natural. Hector pulled away from his grief-ridden mother. The black she wore now seemed to match every part of her. Even her green eyes dimmed.

"Hector…" she whispered.

But he simply took Adela's hand and nodded at the mirror, awaiting further action from the dragon in front of them. Adela spared one last glance at the woman behind her. Principal Pelleas didn't look at them. Instead, she found something interesting on the floor below her feet.

Adela thought he would've said some magic words or maybe even shattered the glass. He didn't. He simply touched the mirror with his hands and the reflection of his human self was gone. What now stared back at him was the white-scaled head of the dragon they'd seen him transform into. Her grandfather's—the dragon's— gold eyes began to glow bright, so much so that Hector and Adela were forced to close their own.

"Walk and remember to find Elpida."

She heard him speak, but it was deep, more ancient sounding, like when they were first attacked.

Blinded, they took a step forward. Once they did, the hard surface beneath their feet disappeared. It was as if something pulled at them. For a quick moment Adela felt like she was floating, until her body connected with the ground.

Chapter Five

The Gate To Nowhere And Everywhere

When Adela rose from the ground, she wasn't quite sure what to expect. But she knew for a fact that she didn't count on the large number of eyes that were upon her. There she was in the heart of a large, crowded city square that was made of nothing but shaded stones. You would think she'd no longer be surprised by anything anymore, but that didn't seem to be the case. Before her were what looked to be small creatures. They were about the height of dwarves, with long, sliver-white hair covering every inch of them, except their large noses, which all had moles at the tips. They walked upon the stone sidewalk alongside humans, Volsin, as if nothing were out of place.

Spinning around, she noticed it wasn't just those creatures that were odd. There seemed to be people with bushy tales peeking from under their coats. Fox-like tails, she would call them. However, their facial features looked human, if the whiskers and pointed ears were ignored. There were even a few ghosts, all of whom seemed fabulously dressed as if heading for some fancy dead dinner party, walking right past her like she was nothing but another person in their way.

"Um, Adela?" Turning around, she expected to see Hector; however, the teen before her couldn't be the same person.

Adela blinked a few times, trying to make sure her eyes were working. Hector had grown at least five inches; he was now standing at a little over six feet tall. Hector was so toned and muscular that the tiny clothes he wore had ripped. He stood there in front of them with only his shorts on. His toned chest was exposed to the world. His hair was now a light brown, and he even had what looked to be a little five o'clock shadow going on. He wasn't old, either. He was just unrealistically *handsome*. A word she would never have used for Hector before. He placed his black glasses on and off his now- straightened nose, frowning slightly before finally deciding to leave them off.

"I just bought these too." He sighed, glancing at Adela, who just stared, stunned. "You look…like you, but…"

Hector was right. Adela, for the most part, looked completely the same. Her hair may have grown an inch or two and her skin was perfect, but she was still the same old Adela, and to Hector that was beautiful.

"Volsin. I shall never understand them," stated a goat-man just before he pushed past them, his hooves clicking away on the dark stone road as he walked. His goat's tail wiggled in annoyance as he continued down the town road with a bag of liquid in one hand and scratching his head with the other.

"I'm not sure, but I think he was a satyr." The new Hector spoke.

"Can you two get out of the way? Jeez, you're holding up traffic here." There on a bicycle was what looked to be another, much larger satyr with a group of others behind him. The horns on his head were larger, curling over at the sides.

Stepping to the side, the new Hector stammered out an apology before allowing the group to pass. On the backs of one of the riders was some sort of leaf, which had been made into a backpack to hold a small beast child with only tiny horns on its head. In his hands was a small wooden flute. Meeting their gaze, the child stuck his purple tongue out at them before disappearing in the distance.

"This wasn't what I expected," Adela muttered to herself. What she had expected, she didn't know, but this definitely wasn't it.

"We should get on the sidewalk," Hector stated. Behind them there seemed to be a pub or bar of some sort. Creatures came in and out of its door, each one ignoring the sick, gray, skeletal-looking creature sitting right outside.

The creature was hunched over. Its head was much too big for its little body. It looked like a starving, tailless, gray squirrel. Its hand was raised, but the creatures just walked by like it was nothing.

"It's Gollum's long-lost cousin." Hector smiled as they approached, causing Adela to smack his arm. New appearance, same Hector.

Spotting them, the creature lifted its skeletal hand to them "Deeta? Please, deeta?"

She didn't need the genius by her side to explain that deeta was some sort of currency.

"I am sorry...," she spoke, but the Gollum creature hissed at her before it looked on to the next person.

Stepping into the pub, it was more of the same: a large bar with unknown drinks and creatures. Behind the bar was one of the white-haired dwarf creatures standing on a stool and pouring some sort of dark sludge into a glass. Taking a deep breath, they walked forward and, oddly enough, no one stared at them. They seemed to blend right in. How such a thing would be possible, she didn't question.

"Uh... excuse me," Hector asked as politely as he could over the noise. But that didn't seem to get the creatures' attention.

"Excuse me." He tried again. Still no one paid them any mind.

Frustrated, tired, and on the brink of insanity, Adela slammed her fist on the polished countertop.

"Can we please get some help here?" she shouted, causing the white-haired creature to turn, though she wasn't sure if he could see her through his hair or not. The dwarf wasn't the only one; everyone seemed to stop and the once-noisy pub now became absolutely silent.

"Is there a reason you're screaming like a banshee, Volsin?" The white creature spoke now.

Lowering her voice, she spoke again. "I am sorry to interrupt… that. But if you could direct us to the Elpida Castle of Light, we will be on our way."

Again, no one spoke. All she could hear were different sorts of breathing. All of a sudden, the entire pub broke out into laughter. Each and every one of them laughed hysterically, spilling their drinks upon one another. Others simply shook their heads and rolled their eyes, or eye, at the pair.

"I don't think they know," Hector muttered down at her. She was assuming that much on her own.

"You all must be the dumbest Volsin in all of Cielieu. One cannot just go to the Castle of Light. You must be chosen and then guided there." They laughed again at their stupidity.

"Look, my grandfather told us to go to the Elpida Castle of Light, which means I was chosen. Now how do I get a guide?" Adela questioned them as they laughed even more.

"I am sorry, but I simply do not know nor care. If you want you can sit there and wait until your grandfather comes, oh chosen one. Would you like some Lacdul or maybe some Maligros?" Once again, they guffawed.

"Adela, we should just go," Hector said.

However, before she could answer, a voice broke out from the laughter. "Did you call her Adela?"

They turned to face a pale-skinned woman with a head full of green snakes. Considering their current history with snakes, understandably, they took a step back from the woman.

Her dark eyes gazed at them, waiting for them to reply.

"Yes, my name is Adela. Adela Arthur."

At her words, the laughter and voices stopped. It became deadly silent as once again all eyes were upon her. The woman's dark eyes widened and each of the snakes on her head turned to her, all of them varying shapes and sizes.

"Adela Arthur. *The* Adela Arthur? Only child of the great Lliam and Kaila Arthur?" the woman asked, taking a step forward as they, in unison, took a step backward.

Adela had heard her parents' names spoken only in passing, but never in the way the snake-haired woman spoke of them. She said their names with so much care, so much hope, Adela was left to wonder who these great people were.

"Yes," Adela replied, causing a range of gasps throughout the pub.

The snake-haired woman reached for Adela, but Hector pushed her behind his new large frame.

"I never thought I would live to see another Arthur." She smiled happily.

"An Arthur! You shouldn't be here. How did you get back?" The white hair-covered dwarf lashed out from behind the counter. Everyone seemed to be speaking at once, some excited and others terrified. Adela stopped paying attention to the creatures that surrounded her, realizing maybe it wasn't a good idea to answer the woman's question so honestly.

"Enough! All of you old buggers," the snake-haired woman said, walking around. "Leave the poor Volsin alone." The hair of snakes also hissed at them while she continued. "Go about your business. Now go on. I said get."

Facing them, she smiled. "Follow me." She led them to a crowded table. However, as they neared it, the table cleared, each one of the creatures giving her a small greeting.

"I am Athelina," she told them kindly.

"Hector Pelleas," Hector told her.

"You really are Adela Arthur?" she asked.

Adela simply nodded. "I am."

"They say you're the only one who can defeat him. That it is your destiny. That's why you're back, right? You came back to save us, to stop him," she whispered happily.

"I… I…"

"We're just trying to get to the castle," Hector said, trying to change the topic.

"A baby Roc will be sent out, hopefully one of a deans are close by. You can't get to Elpida Castle without one." She smiled graciously.

"Thank you," Hector told her. He seemed uncomfortable, but then Adela would be too if she had to sit and wait without a shirt.

But he didn't really look that much out of place. Every now and again a new creature would walk in, looking even more odd than the one before. Neither of them had to speak to know what ran through the other's mind. This truly wasn't the sight either one of them was expecting. They believed they would be walking into a war zone or a grief-stricken society. It surely didn't look so. The creatures laughed, drank, and then laughed some more. Adela found it somewhat of a relief. Every once in a while, it would grow quiet as people would turn to stare at her. She would wave, give them a smile, and once again it would become rowdy.

Adela didn't know how long they had been sitting in the corner of the local pub when a tall figure wearing a long golden cloak stepped in. The person dropped her hood when she entered, giving Hector and Adela a better view of her face. She was a much older and expressionless woman with dark black and gray hair pulled into a tight bun on top of her head. Not one strand could be found out of place. Yet that wasn't half as strange as her eye color. They seemed to be as gold as her cloak.

Athelina, the woman who had snakes for hair, stepped forward to speak to the woman. She said something that couldn't be heard from Hector and Adela's position in the corner. She then pointed over at them, and the older woman glanced up gracefully. She lifted her small hand and waved them over.

Hector stood. "I think our tour guide is here."

Had it been any other day in any other town, Adela would have joked sarcastically to lighten the mood. However, today she simply rose and walked toward the woman in gold. Before Adela could speak, the woman flipped up her hood and walked out the double doors. Stepping outside, Adela noticed that not only was the gray skeleton creature gone, but so was every other creature that had crowded the streets earlier that day. Sunlight was fading, and Adela couldn't see the sun anywhere in the sky.

Instead, she saw the moon about one-third full. But this information came second to the sight of the black unicorn with massive wings standing before them. The creature looked to Adela, then simply returned its gaze to the hooded woman.

Petting the dark unicorn, the hooded woman turned to them. "This is a Noxecus. You both shall ride him until we reach Elpida."

She simply walked in front and a golden light began to glow from her small hands. With a small flick of her wrist, a golden disc of shimmering light formed. It lowered to her feet, hidden by the length of the cloak as she stepped on it. Glancing at the teens behind her, the woman waited, raising a dark eyebrow at them.

Adela turned toward the Noxecus, who seemed to be waiting for them as well. The winged unicorn dropped its wings onto the ground and stared at them. Hector walked forward, testing the weight of his foot on its wings. The Noxecus didn't even flinch when he climbed on top before taking a seat upon its back. When Hector finally sat down, Adela followed, walking on its feathered wing before taking a seat behind Hector.

The floating woman before her moved slowly through the town square. Adela noticed everyone was hurrying to his or her home at this point, just as the moon above became fuller. Each shutter was closed, and doors were locked. Before either Hector or Adela could think more about it, the Noxecus took a mad leap and sped forward.

"What's happening?" Adela questioned, even though she knew her friend wouldn't have an answer.

The golden-cloaked woman was much farther ahead, moving at a greater speed than before. Stone townhomes seemed to blur together. The winged unicorn ran faster and faster toward what Adela noticed to be the edge of a cliff. It came closer and closer, and even though she knew the horse had wings, a small fear began to set in. Grabbing Hector's torso, Adela took a deep breath.

With a giant dive, the winged unicorn went down, causing both their eyes to widen and a scream to break free of their lips. The dark waters below crashed harshly on the rocks, and just before they reached the shore, the Noxecus pulled up. Its wings spread out wide before flapping quickly, and slowly they began to rise up over the water.

"Let's not do that again," Hector said.

Apparently the Noxecus could, in fact, hear him and broke into a hoarse laugh. Hector glanced back at Adela, who just shrugged and laughed along with the horse. What did she really know? She did notice that the moon was now full and seemed much larger than usual. It stood out in the pure black sky, not a star in sight.

The golden-cloaked woman floated proudly in front them on her golden saucer of shimmering lights, not saying a word. The moon provided enough light for Adela to see the hooded woman's small hands embedded together behind her golden back. She tried to take in everything around her. In the dark sea below, Adela noticed large fins flipping up before crashing down upon the water.

In the middle of the sea stood a large boulder upon which was a dark stone archway leading to nothing and preceded by nothing. It was merely a stone arch upon a rock, looking completely out of place. However, this seemed to be where they were headed. The Noxecus flapped its wings two more times before it dove down, gliding quickly through the stone arch. Somehow, in the four or five seconds it had taken to get through the archway, a bridge appeared on the other side. A very dangerous, high bridge with the sea they had just been flying over hundreds of feet below. The archway they passed through was still behind them, except now it stood before a forest.

Neither the woman nor the winged unicorn flew again. Instead, they both walked on the narrow brick bridge toward a massive fortified castle. It seemed to go on for miles along the side of the mountain to which the bridge connected. The castle was enormous, with long waterfalls flowing from some of its windows into the sea below. There were garden balconies covered in various plants and flowers. The castle was intimidating and beautiful all at once. It stood high and proud, as if it knew the power of astonishment it held.

The entrance was so high that Adela almost broke her neck trying to look up at it. There were large hooded statues standing guard, which began to move. They used their hands to open massive gates to allow Adela, Hector, and the hooded woman through. The second the gates were open, two figures stepped forward. One was in a cloak of emerald and the other of sapphire. The hooded figures waited for the winged unicorn to come to a full stop in front of them before dropping their hoods and stepping down the stairs. The figure in the sapphire cloak was an older woman with long blond hair and large blue eyes. The figure in the emerald cloak was a man with bronze skin and striking green eyes.

Adela heard whispers. Glancing up, she saw the faces of many young men and women staring at them. They lined the castle verandas, men on one side and women on the other. With heightened curiosity, each one stuck his or her head out the windows. All had one of four eye colors: green, blue, gold, or red.

"Lady Hellebore, I was not aware you had gone," said the man with green eyes and an emerald cloak.

The woman spoke as Adela came down from the Noxecus. "Yes, well, Lord Myrtus, when your baby Roc comes bearing the message that Adela Arthur has returned to Cielieu, you must make haste."

Upon hearing this, there was a gasp throughout the whole castle, making Adela feel very uncomfortable. Both cloaked figures stared at her completely stunned, but not as much so as the young men and women above. They whispered and gasped, and some left only to return with more people. This caused Adela great discomfort.

"Surely you are mistaken, Lady Hellebore. This cannot be." The blonde spoke softly, just a step above a whisper.

The woman in gold, whom Adela now knew to be Lady Hellebore, simply walked forward, closing the gap between the two cloaked figures before speaking again. "Look at that child. Tell me I am mistaken."

Both glanced at Adela, and before long a small frown played on their lips. With a small sigh and sad eyes, the woman in sapphire stepped forward.

"Hello, my dears, I am Lady Fern. You both must be tired. Please, do come in," she said politely.

As they stepped into the dimly lit castle, Adela was hit with a sense of nostalgia. The hall they walked through was lined with many hooded statues similar to the giant ones that had opened the gates for them. In the hands of these statues were dark purple flames that seemed to hover, not even flickering in the air. As the hall continued, it led out to a grand foyer, within which was a grand staircase. The staircase divided into a double stairway leading to even more foyers at various levels of the hall. The balcony above held more onlookers gazing at Adela and Hector with their colorful eyes. None of them spoke a word. The silence caused Adela and Hector's footsteps to echo resoundingly.

"All those not in their dormitories will be cleaning Dragon's Landing at first crescent," stated the man in the emerald cloak.

By the time Adela and Hector made it to the staircase division, the entryways were cleared, the last of the onlookers exiting through the nearest door or hallway.

"Miss Arthur will stay in the Golden Hive and Mr. Pelleas in the Emerald Den," spoke the green-eyed man to the woman in blue. Lady Hellebore had long since vanished.

"How do you know my name?" Hector questioned, causing the man to direct his attention toward him. "Mr. M—I mean, Lord Myrtus," Hector stammered under the heat of the man's glare.

"We will also need to get him a suitor elf. The poor boy will freeze without a shirt."

Adela bit her lip, stifling the laugh that threatened to break out. Lady Fern glanced at her before directing her to follow, leaving Hector alone with the man in green. Each hallway Lady

Fern led her through seemed to lead to more stairs. Adela was certain she would have no clue how to navigate these halls.

"You are sixteen, correct?" she whispered. The hall had gotten much darker, save for the small sapphire flame in the woman's hand.

"Just recently, yes." How she had known that, Adela didn't want to know. The woman stopped again, turning to face her, the flame of sapphire light causing her blue eyes to stand out even more.

"The Golden Hives are split up by age and gender. All you must do is open the door and it will lead you to the place you need to be." The woman stepped aside and waited for Adela to pull on the ring handle shaped as a bee.

Adela, glancing back, said to her, "You aren't coming in?"

"I am headmistress of the Sapphire Falls. Only those of a golden cloak may enter. Your mother belonged to the Golden Hives; thus, you are free to enter."

Adela thought about that for a brief moment. Her mother had stayed in these rooms.

The woman turned and began to leave. She seemed to float down the hall away from Adela. "Your dorm-mate is already waiting. She will lead you to Grand Headmaster Elderberry in the morning."

Adela could barely see the headmistress's light within the darkness of the massive hall.

Adela entered the Golden Hives and was immediately taken aback. The rooms were ornately decorated, everything in gold. And there was a girl sitting on a large couch, staring at Adela with sleepy golden eyes, just as Lady Fern had said. As Adela walked closer, she could see more of the small girl. She was somewhat short with frizzy brown hair. She wore gold-colored pajamas.

"Hi. I am Fallanita Foxglove, and I'm very tired right now so please, do not hold any of my words or actions against me. I'm not even sure if I'm truly awake." She yawned and, like Lady Hellebore, formed a golden disc of light. But she made two. Stepping on one, she waited, looking at Adela to step on the other.

"Well, come on," she said. "I'm mere seconds away from falling asleep here."

Nodding, Adela stepped on the shimmering saucer of gold as it hovered over the ground, and all too soon both she and Fallanita began to rise.

It was then that Adela noticed the balconies above. Each one spiraled until reaching the top. It actually resembled the inside of an enormous beehive. Adela wobbled upon the plate as they made their way to the balcony of their room. The gold underfoot disappeared, dropping them softly on the landing. Fallanita pulled back the golden curtain and stepped inside. Once again, everything from the soft carpet to the bedding was the same color: gold. Fallanita walked to the bed on the far right and fell upon it. Sitting on the second bed, Adela tried to grasp what was happening before lying back. Today had marked the longest day of her life, and she knew it was just the first of many.

Chapter Six

The Man With The Very Long Name

"You cannot keep her to yourself, Fallanita. It is quite unfair," said one girl wearing a golden cloak.

"How come Lady Hellebore chose you?" questioned another.

"Will you all leave? It is quite rude of you to enter our room," responded Fallanita.

"Oh, Fallanita shares a room with an Arthur and now she thinks she's better than everyone," retorted the first girl. "This is absolutely preposterous. I am so much better with my light than you are."

Unbeknownst to the three teenage girls bickering in the den of the golden room, Adela was wide awake. She sat upon her canopy bed, watching amusedly. *So this is what it's like to have siblings,* she thought to herself as she peered through her sheer golden curtains.

"That is absolutely absurd," said the taller girl with chocolate skin.

Adela could see Fallanita far better now. She seemed to have more energy. Her round face was held high, a sign she wouldn't permit the others to come any farther. If they truly wished, they could easily pick her up. Even so, she waved her finger at them, making her look like a mouse trying to hold back a herd of elephants. The mere thought caused Adela to break into a loud laugh that, in return, caused three pairs of golden eyes to turn in her direction.

"Now look what you did!" Fallanita yelled up at them angrily.

Knowing she could no longer hide in the comfort of her bed, Adela pulled back the net and walked forward. She stepped down the stairs she didn't remember climbing last night. All the surrounding gold threw her off for a moment, but she recovered, looking to the smiling girls.

"Hi! I am Tara Saltsgiver. If you need anything, I am only two hives over," said the taller girl, the one with chocolate skin.

She walked beside Adela and, before she could reply, another girl appeared beside Tara. The second girl was just a few inches taller than Fallanita. She had a very round face with a small birthmark on the side of her lip and freckles. Her eyes, just like every other girl in the Golden Hives, were bright gold. This, however, wasn't what confused Adela. She was curious as to why, at the mere sight of her, Adela felt as though she'd found the true meaning of Christmas.

"And this," Tara said, pointing to the star-struck, freckled face girl beside her, "is Faye Burdock."

"Hi, I'm Adela…" She hesitated, not wishing to hear the gasps that would ensue as a result of her last name. But before they could speak, Fallanita blocked them with her small body.

"Okay, you all have met. Now you have to get out or I will call Lady Hellebore."

The girls glared at Fallanita before sighing and taking their leave through the window.

The short brunette, Faye, turned to her. Smiling very cheerfully, she walked over and gave her a massive hug, and Adela learned to not be fooled by her small size; the girl was almost unnaturally strong.

"I need my arms," Adela told her, causing her to break away quickly, golden eyes wide.

"Oh, I am sorry," she said kindly with a smile on her face.

Adela returned the kind gesture. "It's fine."

Fallanita walked back up the stairs leading to the beds before taking a seat.

"I cannot believe you are here," Fallanita said, smiling, something Adela was realizing Fallanita did a lot—unless she was half asleep.

"I'm not sure why that's so hard to believe," Adela told her.

Fallanita frowned.

"You're an Arthur," she said, as if that should provide a sufficient explanation.

Adela understood that her parents helped many people, but she didn't understand what caused everyone to say her name in such a manner. Instead of pressing further, she changed the topic.

"Why are everyone's eyes gold?" Adela questioned.

Again, Fallanita frowned, somewhat confused.

"Our eyes reflect our light. The better you get, the shaper the color becomes," she explained, as if it were common knowledge.

I guess it is, Adela thought.

Suddenly, Fallanita's golden orbs widened and she hurried off the bed, reaching for the golden cloak in the den area.

"I am to take you to see Grand Headmaster Elderberry." Fallanita had moved from the golden dresser to the golden trunk at the foot of her bed; Adela hadn't moved from the bed but watched the brown-haired girl with the uttermost curiosity.

"Grand Headmaster Elderberry?" Adela questioned her.

"Lord Elwin Alfred Carnell Alvar Elderberry V has been the Grand Headmaster of the Elpida Castle of Light for the last sixteen years. He became the youngest Grand Headmaster ever at fifty-five," Fallanita recited perfectly, without hesitation, as she continued her search. This left Adela to wonder how anyone could pass down a name such as that, not once, but five times.

Finally, she pulled out a small black box. When she opened it, Adela saw a black whistle.

"You will need a suitor elf for your clothing. I would give you some of mine, but I doubt they would fit," Fallanita told her before blowing the whistle.

Adela knew she'd seen Fallanita blow the whistle, but she didn't hear a thing.

"Is it broken?" Adela questioned her, walking closer to the small girl.

"What? Oh, no, it works fine." Fallanita giggled.

Adela walked into the golden den. It the first time she'd gotten the chance to truly take in her surroundings.

Like everything in the Golden Hives, the den was varying shades of gold, some lighter, some darker. The sofa was a darker gold while the pillows upon it were lighter. The coffee table was the same dark gold as the fireplace. Each brick was a medium tone, carefully laid out. Once again, Adela felt out of place. Everything was too lavish for her. She felt as though she were bound to break or ruin something.

"Finally!" grunted a tiny voice. "I have been waiting for days."

There on the mantel above the fireplace, was a man no more than five inches high. Walking over, Adela picked him up by his tiny brown jacket.

"What in the world?" Adela laughed softly, staring down at the tiny person.

"What! What are you doing? Put me down this very instant!" he yelled, surprisingly loudly for someone of his size.

"Sorry." Adela laughed, placing him back on the mantel.

"He is a suitor elf." Fallanita smiled. Walking over to him, Adela noticed his pointed ears. One ear had a ring pierced through it.

"My humblest apologies, sir, for making you wait." She tipped her head toward him.

"You know I hate to be woken up early, Fallanita. This is a busy time and I have a lot of work to do. I need rest." He frowned and turned his attention back to Adela.

"Well, turn," he said, shaking his hands at them, waiting.

"I'm sorry, what?" Adela turned to Fallanita.

"You need clothing, correct?" the elf questioned Adela,

who hadn't thought about it. But now that she did, she couldn't expect to wear the same jeans every day.

"Clothing and shoes, that is what I do. Now turn," he stated again as if it were the most common of things.

Adela looked at him skeptically. "You make clothing?"

"And shoes. You aren't spinning." He huffed again. Following his orders, she began to spin.

"Slower," he directed. Adela was again trying her best not to laugh as she turned more slowly for the small man.

"You have small feet," he told Adela, and she frowned.

"I do not," Adela said defensively, looking down at her feet.

"I have seen a lot of feet, and yours are small," he stated again. Turning and walking, the elf went straight through the golden wall. Adela touched his exit but couldn't figure out how he passed through.

"Pay no mind to him," Fallanita said. "He enjoys his job, no matter how much he may fret over it. The bathroom is through there. We must hurry and be off." Fallanita walked over to the closet behind the door that Adela had failed to notice.

Adela went to the bathroom. It took a moment to figure how to work the bathroom, but once she did, she made sure to get ready as fast as possible. The last thing Adela wanted was for Fallanita to get in trouble.

"You ready?" Fallanita questioned as she tied her golden cloak around her neck. The cloak fell to the ground, stopping at the perfect length, which must have been hard for someone so small.

Adela nodded, for she was much too nervous to speak. They both now stood at the balcony of the Golden Hive. The name made even more sense during the day, when she could see the entirety of the massive hive. Fallanita and Adela were somewhere in the middle, but it was still a long way down.

"Higher levels are for the oldest. The best rooms are given to the last years. They all live in the massive Hive Heart. The balcony all the way at the top it is for twelfth years and those waiting on the CBLs. I can't believe, after everything we go through here, we still have to take those." Fallanita sighed, expecting Adela to understand what she spoke about, but Adela hadn't a clue. She hadn't grown up in this new world where anything seemed possible with a flick of a wrist.

Fallanita seemed to understand her mistake. "CBL stands for the Cielieu Bureau of Lights. After we graduate from here, in order to use our light outside the castle, we have to pass whatever test they give us. But do not worry. That is still two and a half years away. By then you will know everything you need to know."

Adela smiled and nodded, but she still didn't speak. She wasn't trying to be rude, but she was beginning to understand just how big her situation was and how much she had to learn. *Is it even possible to learn a whole civilization's worth of knowledge in two years?* Adela thought. *Will I even last that long?*

Fallanita created the same disc of shimmering light as before. With a deep breath, Adela took a step upon it.

"So you all have never used your light before?" Fallanita questioned. She didn't seem to understand how people could get from one place to another without the aid of floating discs. For Adela, such things were left to cars and planes or Adela's personal favorite, her own two feet on solid ground.

"No, never. We only recently found out about magic," Adela replied, causing both of them to freeze just a few feet from the ground floor.

Fallanita simply frowned once more. "Light is not magic and magic is not light. Only the weakest of us will ever use magic. It is a desperate device that depends on tricks, and it must always balance itself out. That will often end in pain for either the person using it or for anyone they know. Light depends on you, nothing else." Adela nodded and Fallanita continued their descent.

Adela made a personal note to self: *Magic and light are not the same thing.* Fallanita seemed to be very passionate about it, and Adela didn't want to be scolded by the smaller girl again.

Adela couldn't have been more relieved when her feet finally touched the ground. Her heart, however, still needed to calm down. Opening the door, she felt a small twinge of dread. To make things worse, she now stuck out more than ever. In the hall, Adela was surrounded by teens of all ages, each one staring at the only girl not in a uniform and cloak. Red, green, blue, and golden eyes all stared at her, parting the like the Red Sea as she walked by. It was the red eyes that threw her off the most. They seemed so unreal and frightening.

"How ill at ease you must be." Fallanita looked like a child compared to the older, more mature people she'd seen.

"I'm fine." Adela lied. Fallanita glanced up at her. Apparently she needed to work on her lying skills.

Walking among the massive crowd of teens were younger children that weren't wearing any of the four colored cloaks. Instead, they wore white.

Adela could tell where she was now. The castle had been dimly lit before, but she knew she was in the same hall that led out to the grand foyer, near the grand staircase that divided the room. Adela walked up the stairs behind Fallanita until they reached a large oak door with two statues of kneeling angels. The angels weren't gazing at each other; both were facing down as if weeping. Adela reached out to touch one of the angel's shoulders and the moment she did, the marble angel's head snapped up to glare at her.

"I…," Adela stammered, unable to find the words to say.

The angel tilted up his head, a frown upon his lips, before returning back to his original state. This time, however, the angel moved his wings forward to encase his body, protecting himself from view or touch.

"Note to self: do not touch anything," Hector whispered. He seemed to come out of nowhere. Beside him was a boy of the same height draped in a cloak of emerald.

"They only weep when someone is in trouble," the newcomer said to them.

"I'm sorry. I didn't know…," Adela started to say before Fallanita hit the teen in green, who was beginning to laugh.

"Ryker, that isn't funny! They don't know you're joking." Fallanita glared at him.

"I'm sorry, I couldn't pass it up." He laughed. "I am Ryker Saltsgiver. Hector has told me all about you."

Adela glanced at Hector, who simply turned his attention to the weeping angels in front of the door.

"Wait, did you say Saltsgiver?" Adela asked him, remembering the run-in she had with Tara only a few moments ago.

"Oh, yeah, Ryker is Tara's twin brother," Fallanita said, causing Adela to do a double-take.

For twins, Ryker and Tara looked nothing alike. Tara had beautiful chocolate skin, dark brown hair, and golden eyes while Ryker was as fair as Adela was with blond hair and green eyes.

But before she could speak, the massive door before them opened on its own to reveal a tall, warrior-looking man with dark hair. His eyes were two different colors; the one on the left was a piercing red and the other a stunning blue.

"Thank you so much, Mr. Saltsgiver and Miss Foxglove for escorting our guests. You may rush off now before you're both late for class," the man said. He had a very gentle and kind voice, neither too soft nor too loud.

"Yes, Lord Elderberry." Fallanita nodded, and her little legs were soon skipping down the hall.

Adela hoped her face didn't look as shocked as she felt. Fallanita had said that Headmaster Elderberry had been in charge for sixteen years, but the man before her didn't look to be much older than forty. She would have thought it to be impossible, but then again, everything in Cielieu should be impossible.

Lady Hellebore's face hadn't changed since the last time Adela saw her. The older woman once again looked bored or maybe tired. She didn't smile or frown. She was just there, which Adela thought was quite odd.

Glancing over at Hector, who now was wearing a simple shirt with the same jeans as the day before, Adela felt better. She was no longer the only odd one out.

As Hector and Adela walked into the room, she realized they were in a large office library. The walls were lined with shelves of books separated briefly for the window overlooking a colorful garden maze. The surprisingly young-looking Headmaster Elderberry stood in front of his wooden desk. In the corner was the stoic Lady Hellebore of Gold, Lord Myrtus of Emerald, and Lady Fern of Sapphire.

"Please sit," said Headmaster Elderberry. Adela looked around the room, confused, then looked to Hector for advice.

"Where?" Hector asked, his thoughts seemingly on the same page as Adela's. Other than the large oak desk near the window and the piles of books, there were no seats.

"My apologies. Yet again it has escaped me that you are unaware of your abilities."

At the snap his pale fingers, two chairs formed out of sapphire lights in the center of the room. Adela touched hers, unsure if it was even possible to sit upon. However, it was strong and sturdy just like the hovering disc. She felt as though she were in trouble, but this wasn't Principal Pelleas's office.

"So a Pelleas and an Arthur have returned to Cielieu." He tilted his head to the side, staring at the two sitting before him. Even though the tenderness in his voice hadn't vanished, he didn't seem very happy about the words he spoke.

"As you must have grasped by now, I am grand Headmaster Elwin Alfred Carnell Alvar Elderberry. You may simply call me Lord Elderberry. This is how you will refer to your teachers."

Adela didn't think it was wise to speak, for she still felt like she was in massive trouble.

Lord Elderberry turned away from her and Hector. Staring at the books on his side, he questioned, "Why, in all good logic, would you dare to come back here?"

Adela wasn't sure how to answer such a question. She just felt she needed to, that there was no other choice. Her parents would have wanted her to come back. So she told him, "I felt…" For some odd reason her words wouldn't form.

"We needed to. We just needed to find ourselves. Find what was missing." Hector answered for her.

"Not a suitable reason." Lord Elderberry sighed. Frowning, he turned back to face them. The frown on his lips looked foreign to him, as if it wasn't something he often did.

He warned them, "This castle will fool you. It will make you forget about the darkness that sleeps just outside these walls. It will make you doubt there is even evil. That is what the castle is meant to do—allow the children, not as lucky as you once were, to have joy and peace. And it allows them to grow, to cling to hope, and to laugh."

Lord Elderberry sighed once more and shook his head. His sapphire and ruby eyes seemed to pierce into the teens, causing them to shift. Before any one of them could speak, the door behind them suddenly opened.

"We lost two more to him today," cursed a woman in a red cloak. She had short red hair with bangs that failed to hide the painful-looking scar on her face. The scar ran from the tip of her hairline, through her left eye, and down her cheek. Her footsteps were hard against the ground as she walked toward Headmaster Elderberry and continued.

"We went into the Stygian Forest to search for her, but," she hissed out angrily, "the blasted dogs made it to them first."

"Lady Datura," Lady Fern whispered loudly—as loud as a whisper could get, anyway. The woman's head snapped around. At that moment she noticed the teens sitting in the chairs before Lord Elderberry, who didn't seemed surprised by her intrusion. Now that Adela could fully see the woman in red, she noticed how severe her face looked, as if she'd never smiled.

"I understand your frustration, Lady Datura. However, this is not the side we wish to show our visitors yet," Lord Elderberry said sternly. The *yet* at the end of his sentence didn't go unnoticed.

With a deep, angry huff, Lady Datura turned from him. She walked over to stand with the other headmasters in the corner, thus completing the full set of colored cloaks. Even with her distance, Adela could feel Lady Datura's anger rolling off her in waves.

"Why did they come back?" she hissed, arms crossed.

"They wished to find themselves," Sir Myrtus mocked, still wearing a lowly frown on his lips.

Lord Elderberry walked slowly behind his oak desk before forming a chair of blue to sit upon. He sighed once more and looked over at the four in the corner. Adela could see he was debating something of grave importance. Siting up straighter, he nodded, and Lady Datura walked forward toward the center of the room. Her red eyes looked angry, and this gave Adela a bad feeling in her stomach. She felt uneasy under the heat of her gaze.

"What color is your light?" Lady Datura questioned, directly focusing on Adela.

"What color is my light?" Adela repeated, not knowing how to answer. She knew what it meant, but she didn't know if she even held any within her.

"Your light," the woman hissed at her.

"I do not know," Adela answered truthfully.

Lady Datura's back straightened as she glared down at them. "What is your plan, then?" She sneered.

"We don't have one," Hector replied, beyond frustrated with her. They hadn't thought of anything more than just getting here.

"You travel to the land behind the mirror that you know nothing of, the world in which your parents never wished for you to dwell, all so you could find yourself?" Lady Datura nodded to herself, summarizing the information she'd gathered.

"Neither of you realize the depths of the darkness into which you have stepped. You are even worse than children. At least children know their light." She merely extended her hand, and a large book flew from its shelf. It came around beside her, encased in shimmering red light. The book levitated right toward the palm of her hand.

"Lady Datura, that can wait." Lady Fern spoke sadly, the small amount of peace remaining on her face now shattering.

"Two Volsin have lost their lives. They graduated from here no less than a year ago. This is the world we live in once we leave this castle. And these two have willingly come back here, sealing their fates. Their eyes need to be opened." Lady Datura glanced back at Lord Elderberry, who merely nodded at her.

Each page of the book glistened with the red light until it was flipped open to the back. The book floated from Lady Datura's hand toward Hector and Adela. Neither of them knew what exactly they were looking at.

"Marion Wynn, son of Rena and Jonah, age nineteen. Nereida Dunn, daughter of Freya and Uncas, age eighteen." The words she spoke were autographed onto the page in red shimmering light. The light around the book faded and it descended into Adela's open hands. She ran her fingers over the last two names Lady Datura had read aloud. The red ink stained the parchment paper like blood. Above those two names were many more, each one stating the name, parents, and age of a deceased student. Adela touched the dry paper before flipping the book to the pages behind it. Thousands of names, thousands of people, thousands dead. Some of them her age or younger were recorded in the book. The book could only fit one more name before it was finished.

"You have made your point, Lady Datura," Lady Fern told her. Her voice, for the first time since Hector and Adela had met her, was above a whisper. She seemed to be the only person concerned with what they were shown.

Lady Datura stepped back. It seemed, however, that their lesson wasn't over. Shimmering gold and emerald lights covered more books as they flew from the shelves, powered by Lord Myrtus and Lady Hellebore. Each one landed directly in front of the duo, each opened book filled with more names. Hector and Adela realized at this moment that the room in which they sat was no library; it wasn't even an office. It was a memorial room for every Volsin who had died.

"Now she has made her point." Lady Hellebore spoke for the first time.

The books glowed once more in Hector and Adela's hands before they were ripped away. One by one, each book was returned to its respective place on the shelf. Adela sat uneasily on her sapphire chair, unsure of what to say.

"Yes, you've made your point, quite clearly, in fact. This isn't a game. We knew that before we came. But you aren't the only ones who have lost someone," Hector stated angrily.

He's right, Adela thought. They weren't the only ones losing people.

"That's enough. It's settled. They are here now and no amount of howling will change that. They understand," Lord Elderberry said, glancing around the airless room. It seemed as if no one was breathing, or if they were, they were doing so very softly.

"Make the others aware so they may impart knowledge as well. They shall be taught everything while they are here," he said, shocking not only Hector and Adela, but everyone else in the room as well.

Sir Myrtus stepped forward. "You wish all of us to teach them five years' worth of knowledge?" He looked to Grand Headmaster Elderberry, green eyes narrowed angrily.

Lord Elderberry spoke simply. "Teach them of their light and then the older students will fill them in on all the rest."

"Great, high school all over again," Adela muttered under her breath.

This wasn't what she had been expecting at all. No, not high school, this is worse than high school. Now they were freshmen. They were at the bottom of the food chain. High school was a lot easier and more fun when you weren't freshmen. No one wants to go back to high school after leaving, unless they were given the option to be seniors. Then they know everything they need to know; they don't have to worry about classes. This was going to be bad. Adela could feel it.

"At least there's less of a chance that a Chimera will come out of nowhere in this school," Hector whispered.

Though it was a whisper, he was loud enough that all eyes were on upon them. Adela sighed. She just wanted to be anywhere but the dean's office, no matter what realm she was in.

Lord Elderberry stood up abruptly, his red and blue eyes staring at them, more surprised. Walking around his desk, he moved toward them.

"You faced a Chimera and yet you're still alive?" He questioned them, confusion written all over his face. Both Hector and Adela stiffened. It was too early to talk about it, too soon to speak of it. They'd only just lost her.

"We did. But our friend wasn't so lucky," Adela whispered. Her head hung low, causing her to miss the shocked and confused glances around her.

Lady Datura spoke, her voice no less harsh or cold despite her intention not to be cruel. "How is it possible a Chimera broke into the lesser realm?"

Adela wanted to ask her how it was possible her eyes were red, or how she and Hector were sitting on chairs made of shimmering light.

Hector spoke this time. "We don't know. It was only a few days ago. If it weren't for that or Adela's vision of the dying girl, we would have never known of Cielieu."

Adela turned and glared at the brown-haired teen beside her. He had said that in the worst way possible. How a genius could be so stupid was beyond her.

Sighing, she turned to meet the eyes she was certain were awaiting her. For the third time this week, she retold the horror she had witnessed. It seemed much harder to get the words out now, but she managed to tell them anyway. Adela told the headmaster of how she'd watched the brown-haired girl with the dazzling blue eyes die, her light ripped from her chest by Prince Delapeur. By the time she finished, Lady Fern ran from the room so quickly that Adela had to blink a few times. Lord Myrtus's bronze face-hardened before them, and he took his leave. Lady Datura didn't move. Instead, she simply used her light to pull out another book before handing it to Lord Elderberry and then walked out. Adela glared at Hector once again before facing Lord Elderberry, whose eyes seemed to shine with sadness and pain.

Opening the book, he softly spoke. "Esthella Lamorak, daughter of Mira and Axel, age eighteen."

Adela could see the sapphire light shimmering as the name appeared in the book in his hands.

"Lady Hellebore, will you please have someone retrieve Jeremy for me," said Lord Elderberry to the plain-faced woman who simply nodded before taking her leave.

"As for you two..." Lord Elderberry began as two scrolls glowed with a blue light. They flew through the air before falling into Hector and Adela's laps. "You two will begin here as students after the Welcoming Ball. You will wear cloaks of white until you gain your light. It would be wise not to slack off, for you are very behind."

"What about my grandfather?" Adela whispered. She hadn't seen him since she'd gotten here. Granted, it had been just two days, but to Adela, it felt like two years.

"I am aware of your situation with Elder Kreon. Sadly, adult dragons are only permitted near the castle during emergencies. He will have a message sent soon, but for now, you must go with your dorm-mates who are waiting outside for you. Be mindful to use them. They are the best in their respective lights," he said simply.

When Hector and Adela stood, the chairs they had been sitting on faded. But before Adela left, she turned back to the middle-aged man who was no longer paying attention to them.

"I promise we'll work as hard as possible," she said.

"Hopefully that is enough, Miss Arthur," Grand Headmaster Elderberry said.

Chapter Seven

In Need of a Volsin Dictionary

"They are alive." Fallanita laughed when Hector and Adela stepped outside.

"Just barely." Hector exhaled as he began to unroll the scroll that Lord Elderberry had given to each of them, but before he could, Ryker took the paper from his hand.

"Believe me, mate, you do not want to open that. The book keepers hate that," he said to Hector as they began heading toward their hall.

Adela stared wide-eyed at the scroll in her hand. "The what?"

"The scroll lists all the books you will need to borrow from the library. The book keepers read it better when they are kept rolled up," Fallanita replied, not sure where Ryker had lost them.

Adela could hear Hector asking more questions, but she felt odd as they walked through the hallways. There weren't as many people around now as there were this morning, but there were enough to make her feel uncomfortable. Adela felt as though she had a giant sign around her neck that read, "I am an extraterrestrial." The students all seemed to stare and then run out of their way. Nothing bothered Adela more than being the center of attention. She wasn't good at it. Whenever there were eyes on her, she seemed to completely embarrass herself.

She noticed the same hooded statues she'd seen the night before no longer had purple flames hovering over their hands. Instead, the flames were a very light blue, and the moment she focused in on one, the flame shifted to green. A much younger student, who had to be at least eleven or twelve and was dressed in a white cloak, arose immediately at the change in the flame color. He gathered his books as quickly as possible and ran down the hallway.

"Ugh, I hated when I had classes at green light." Fallanita groaned as they began to descend the stairs.

"Oh, don't complain until you have had Lord Silverweed's History of the Screaming Arts at blue lights. Never will I make that mistake again." Ryker frowned at the memory.

Adela looked over to Hector, hoping he would be as confused as she was. However, he seemed to be following along perfectly. Hector didn't look in any way confused, surprised, or overwhelmed. It was like he'd known about all of this already, like he already fit in. She tried to shake it off, but Adela couldn't deny how homesick she felt, how out of place.

"Adela? Are you all right?" Hector called out to her, pulling her out of her thoughts.

"Yes, why wouldn't I be?" she asked him simply before turning toward the door at the end of the hall.

"Is that the library?" she questioned Fallanita. The door seemed abnormally large, growing with every step they took toward it.

"You mean the second home of all the Emerald Dens? Yep, this is it. We call it the green room," Fallanita joked.

"Funny, but that is a gross exaggeration," Ryker said simply, rolling his emerald eyes as he pushed open the door only to reveal a sea of green cloaks.

"See, what did I tell you?" Fallanita laughed, but she was the only one due to the fact that both Adela and Hector were frozen at the door.

Yes, on all five levels of the library were books engulfed in emerald lights. Books flew across the room. There were many students inside, but they seemed to be floating on a sea of green cloaks. The library truly seemed to be the second home of the

Emerald Dens. Some were in packs, while many of them had just chosen a corner to silently read by themselves. But that didn't bother Adela or Hector. They were truly shocked by the giant green worms with glass eyes and glasses that crawled through the stacks. These worms lifted books with their heads and placed them upon shelves with ease.

"So those are the book keepers," Hector said softly, glancing up at the giant green worms as one of them came toward them.

Adela eyed the giant beast as it came closer and closer to her until it was less than a foot away from them. Its glass eyes turned down to them with anticipation.

"Your list," the worm prompted. Adela jumped slightly and then lifted her scroll up as high as she possibly could. The worm— book keeper—came down and bit the edge of the scroll before sucking down its throat.

"And yours?" The worm turned toward Hector.

He tried to pretend his arm wasn't shaking, but to Adela, it was quite obvious. Some people hated spiders. Hector Pelleas hated worms. But she knew that fear had more to do with how, when they were children, Adela would put worms in his socks. They weren't real ones, but he didn't know that at the time.

After ingesting Hector's scroll, the worm turned and headed back to the rows upon rows of books.

"They are Cartus Worms," said Ryker. "After the Great War, most of their homelands were destroyed. Many of them became book keepers here at the castle for safety. They are very friendly but prefer to be left alone. They ingest the scrolls because, to them, each class has a different flavored book," Ryker finished as they headed over to a table at the far-east corner of the room.

Adela enjoyed the fact that no one seemed to pay attention to her as they walked to a table. These students all seemed much too preoccupied with their books to give her the time of day.

"We were told about Prince Delapeur," Adela said when they sat down. This change in topic set Fallanita and Ryker ill at ease, both frozen, uncomfortable.

"What?" Hector asked, looking between the two.

"We do not say his name here. We wouldn't want to give him that pleasure. I need to get a book," Fallanita stated angrily. She rose from her chair and escaped down the hall.

"I'm sorry…" Adela began.

"Don't be." Ryker sighed. "Many of us have lost someone we care about because of him. There is this myth that he actually becomes stronger each time you say his name. He wants us to say it often and with as much fear as possible."

"Fallanita lost someone?" Adela whispered, trying to search for the tiny golden-cloaked girl amidst the green ones.

Ryker looked over his shoulder before leaning forward. "She lost her older sister and mother. No one knows for sure, but everyone says that Fallanita's dad become a reaptor in order to keep her safe."

Before Adela could reply, two of the massive worms crawled over with a mountain of books on their heads. Ryker backed away from them as the worms bowed down, placing the books on the table before Adela or Hector could even stand.

"Thank you," Hector said to them. The worms simply nodded, crawling away again. On the top of both stacks was a scroll that looked a lot like the ones the worms had swallowed moments before.

"Do we even want to know how we got these back?" Hector asked, eyeing the scroll carefully.

"I believe not." Ryker laughed.

"What are reaptors?" Adela whispered softly, leaning back in. She couldn't get Fallanita out of her mind. She didn't know what it was like to have a mother or a sister and then to just lose them. How could Fallanita even smile after that?

Ryker just frowned. "After the wars, it was said that Prince… he lost and was hurt badly. As a result, he lost a lot of power and followers…"

"Why would anyone ever want to follow him?" Hector asked angrily.

"When it truly looked like he was going to win the war, some Volsin began to pledge allegiance to him. In exchange, he gave them power, so much power that it corrupted them. As Volsin, we are only meant to handle our own lights and power. Anything more than that and our bodies will begin to break down. The amount of power that he gave them was enough to cause them to morph into hideous monsters with just one desire—to feed. There are three different types of reaptors. The first are those who still have humanity. They are marked with tattoos. The more visible they are, the longer they have served under him. Then there are the pale-skinned ones with all black eyes. They understand little of what Volsin say and can barely speak. Lastly, there are those so far gone they are nothing but skeletons in cloaks. At night they terrorize and feed off the creatures of Cielieu," Ryker whispered.

"So reaptors are a cross between vampires and zombies," Hector said, more to himself.

"What are those?" Ryker asked, puzzled, his green eyes wide.

"They're not important," Adela said. "These reaptors, they steal the lights of Volsin just like Prince… he does."

Ryker simply shook his head. "Yes and no. If they come after a Volsin, they are usually very weak, but all the underage Volsin are here. You have to be at least a tenth year to leave the castle during the year, and you must be back before nightfall, when the moon is full. Most of the reaptors stay away from stronger Volsin. Stealing that much power would only destroy them. Instead, they take only what they need to survive for the day."

"That's why the whole town shut down on our way here," Hector whispered.

"What are we talking about?" Fallanita asked. Each of them sat back quickly. Hector stared wide-eyed, like a child caught stealing a cookie.

Adela simply rolled her eyes at him. "We were just talking about vampires and zombies. Did you find your book?"

Fallanita, just as confused as Ryker, shook it off. "No, I didn't need a book. I just wanted to leave for a moment," she said, shockingly honest.

"Okay, well, I don't know about you, but I'm starved. Can we head to the dining hall before we see the suitor elves?" Ryker said, encasing half the stacks of books in emerald light and lifting them with ease.

"Why do we need the suitor elves again?" Adela asked them.

Fallanita did the same with Adela's books, making both Hector and Adela feel like foreigners on a different planet once again. Back home, neither of them truly fit in. Hector was the genius that everyone used, while Adela was simply the poor girl that had bad clothing. It was hard to believe, even with all the creatures and things within this castle, they were still the oddest things there.

"Your uniforms and outfits for the Welcoming Ball," Fallanita replied. "But don't freak out. It is mostly for the younger kids. We just have to dress nice and show up."

"Can't you just blow the whistle again?" Hector asked them.

"We could, but they hate being called by slates." Fallanita laughed.

Adela sighed. There was another term she was going to have to learn. It was like they were all speaking another language. Every time she felt like she was beginning to grasp it, another term was thrown in. How could she possibly remember what all these things were?

"What are slates?" Hector asked, following her thought pattern, as they climbed up the stairs.

"We all call those in white cloaks slates because they are blank until they gain their light," Ryker said.

The walk back to the door seemed so much shorter than Adela remembered, but then again, she still had no idea how to get around the castle. All she knew was they had made a left, then a right, followed by another right and then went up a flight of stairs, reaching the magical door at the end of the hall.

"So we're going to be referred to as slates?" *Basically*

freshmen, and no one ever liked freshmen, which explained the elves, Adela added in her mind.

"Just think of it as motivation to find your light quicker." Fallanita grinned as she pushed open the door.

Stepping to the dining hall, if it could be called that, Adela and Hector almost dropped the books in their arms. It wasn't a dining hall at all. They had somehow stepped right into the middle of the forest. It was massively beautiful, with trees more than 150 feet high. Swinging from some branches were two-headed silverback monkeys along with what looked to be small dwarfs walking in and out of the trees. There were tiny people, who Adela believed to be fairies, all with wings that flapped so quickly it almost looked like they were floating. But that wasn't it. No, that was just the beginning. There were also deer, many with six to ten branches sprouting from their antlers. Also present were little green men that fell off of leaves and onto the backs of butterflies. They rode them, using them as though they were cars.

In the midst of all of that chaos were four enormous round tables: red, gold, emerald, and sapphire. A fifth table stood out from the rest. It was straight and long, for the lords and ladies in front of them all. Somehow, all the students were able to sit at their respective tables with space to spare. In the center of the round tables were mountains upon mountains of fruits, nuts, berries, roots, and small game. It was as though any food that could be found inside the forest was now being served.

Every last Volsin stared at them as the Hector and Adela entered the forest. They didn't have cloaks or uniforms and their eyes held none of the bright, vibrant colors of any of the other students. Everything about them screamed outsider. Adela felt more than uncomfortable.

"Wow, this is awkward," Fallanita whispered over to Adela.

"Where do we sit?" Hector asked Adela as though she would know. She figured she would follow Fallanita and sit at the golden table, but what about Hector?

"I'm going to head to my table." Ryker smiled, waving at the Emerald Dens. "Hector, are you coming?"

Adela turned to him. "It's fine. You should hang out with them."

"Or you can sit with the cream of the crop," stated a tall, golden-haired beauty with deep, red eyes. She was walking across the grass clearing as though someone were spilling roses at her feet.

"Excuse me, but when did the Red Diamonds become the cream of the crop?" Fallanita snapped, glaring up at the beautiful girl.

Her red eyes narrowed dangerously as she glared down at the tiny girl. Diverting her attention, she turned to Adela.

"I am Scarlet Danewort of the Red Diamonds, and I wanted to personally welcome you, on behalf of all the Diamonds, to the Elpida Castle of Light. Our families were close, and I believe you would like to spend time with a light of higher stature." She sneered toward Fallanita with the last part of her statement before smiling at Adela once again.

Adela had to hold Fallanita's arm with one hand, gripping her books with the other, in order to keep her from attacking the beautiful blonde. "Thank you, but I think I'll just sit with the Golden Hives." Adela smiled politely.

Scarlet simply frowned. "Suit yourself, but remember you are an Arthur. You don't have to lower yourself to their standard. You are special. Golden Hives are not."

"My mother was a Golden Hive. I think she was special, so if you would excuse us, we have a table to get to," Adela said, dragging Fallanita away from the red-eyed girl and the gasping tables of Volsin behind.

"There has to be a queen bee everywhere." Hector sighed as they made their way to the round golden table.

"Faye and Tara, right?" Adela asked as she and Hector took a seat, placing their books on the table.

Tara smiled brightly, moving over to give them more room. "Yep. I hope my brother wasn't too much to handle."

"Brother?" Hector asked, grabbing an apple from the table in front of them.

"Yeah, Ryker and I are twins. You must be Hector. He told me all about you this morning. I am Tara and this Faye," she said, smiling, and then she pointed to the shy girl on her right who waved quickly at Hector before grabbing food from the center of the table.

"Hello. Ryker told me he had a sister, but he made it seem like you were his younger sister and not his fraternal twin." Hector laughed before basically eating the apple whole.

"Of course he did. Just because he is a few minutes older, he thinks he is more mature than me." She sighed, shaking her head before grabbing a bowl of nuts and handing it to Adela.

"Bell nuts." She smiled.

Adela stared at the normal-looking nuts before taking a bite. She wouldn't have anticipated the experience of flavors she never tasted before. She opened her mouth to speak but instead let out a chime, causing everyone around her to laugh. Once again, Adela tried to speak, but couldn't. Instead, a loud ring came out.

"Bell nuts are amazing. They just come with side effects." Fallanita snickered as Hector took some as well. He tried to speak, but instead, all that could be heard were the sounds of a doorbell.

"Does all the food come with side effects?" Adela asked when she was finally able to speak again, dropping the nuts onto the table.

"Only the forest food does, but not all of it," Faye whispered, speaking for the first time since Adela had met her. She had a soft voice that reminded her of Lady Fern of the Sapphire Falls.

"Try the apple," Fallanita said, causing Adela to stare at the fruit with skepticism.

"I'm not going to fall into a deep sleep where only a true love's kiss can wake me, am I?" she asked, glancing around.

The only person who seemed to get it was Hector. Sighing, she took a bite into the forbidden fruit. It was just as sweet as the nuts, yet it didn't taste like an apple. It tasted like cotton candy, which only made her want to eat more.

"It's really good," Adela said, except now her voice was unreasonably high. She sounded like... well, like Hector did before his major makeover.

Hector couldn't stop laughing. "You sound like you sucked down a whole tank of helium."

"Thanks, Hector," Adela squeaked, causing her to laugh at herself. "Now I'm afraid to eat anything else. Bell nuts, cotton candy-flavored helium apples... What's next?"

"I think I know," Hector said, staring wide-eyed at his orange hands. "I only ate like two or three berries."

It was Adela's turn to laugh. "I don't know what they are, but I'm calling them Oompa Loompa berries." She smirked.

Grabbing the cup in front of them, she didn't even think twice before gulping it down. She waited, but nothing happened.

Tara and Faye laughed at her.

"It's just Cielieu juice." Fallanita joined in the laughter.

"Yeah, what's an Oompa Loompa?" someone asked from the other side of the round table.

It was odd. Even though the table was large, you could hear and see everyone around the ring. The mountain of food in the middle didn't block anyone's face, and there had to be at least a hundred students at this one table alone. The person who sat on the other side of table was just slightly older, but it made Adela aware that people were still watching her. She was grateful for Tara, Faye, Hector, and Fallanita for taking her mind off it for a moment, but now she was back to reality. Well… as much reality as anyone could have in the middle of a magical forest.

"Oompa Loompa are little orange men with green hair who work in a chocolate factory," Adela said a little too seriously, getting a rise out of Hector.

Each and every one of them gave her their attention and began to ask her questions one at a time.

"What is the other realm like?" said one.

"Is it true no one has light?" said another.

"There are no other creatures but humans?" questioned another student farther down the table.

"How do you defend yourselves?" asked the first one again.

"Do you *have* to defend yourselves?" inquired another in quick succession.

"I thought the lesser realm was scary!" stated another party.

"Everyone, hush!" Fallanita yelled, standing from her seat. She was so tiny, however, that her attempt to be bigger was amusing. Nevertheless, all the students listened to her.

"Thank you," Fallanita said more softly before taking her seat again.

Hector and Adela both just stared at her in shock. Who knew someone so tiny could demand so much respect?

"There goes our little warrior." Tara laughed, taking a bite out of some more fruits.

"The lesser realm is completely different from here, and I'm sorry I can't explain it better. All I can say is the people there wouldn't believe this place unless they saw it with their own eyes," Adela answered. "No, we don't have light, but no one really needs it. If there are any other creatures there, I haven't seen them. And we have many different ways to defend ourselves, but we also have people who take care of that. And I forgot the last one," Adela replied, trying to answer all of their questions.

"No, the lesser realm isn't scary." Hector reminded her. "Some of the people are, but those are usually the Justin Beiber fans."

"What's a *beiber*?" asked one of the younger kids.

Adela couldn't help it; she broke out into a fit of laughter. Sadly, only one other person understood, but she couldn't help that. Hector laughed along with her, and everyone else simply went back to his or her own conversations.

"Thanks," Adela whispered to Hector, who simply smiled and nodded before grabbing his scroll in order to hide his face in the books.

"Such an Emerald Den." Tara laughed.

Faye simply frowned. "You can't know that. When I first came here everyone thought I would be a Sapphire Fall. Some people still do."

"She has a point," Fallanita replied, taking another bite of her food.

"True. What are your classes, Adela?" Tara asked, already grabbing the scroll.

"Hey, you're in the same class as Fallanita and I." Faye smiled. "We both have Archery and Defensive Intelligence with Lord Levi Silverweed."

"I have that class too," Hector replied.

"Who is Lord Silverweed?" Adela asked, looking to the long table of lords and ladies.

"You see the scary-looking Volsin with the long red hair and the scar across his face?" Tara whispered.

Adela followed her gaze, spotting at the far end of the table the man with a painful-looking scar that ran from the top left of his face to the bottom of his right cheek. There was also a tiny monkey on his shoulder whom he seemed to be feeding. It reminded Adela of a shipwrecked pirate.

"What's up with the monkey?" Hector whispered, and the moment he did, Lord Silverweed's red eyes glanced up, causing them all to look away.

"No one knows, but it's always around. Like always. Last year a twelfth-year Golden Hive tried to steal it and Lord Silverweed wanted him expelled, but he couldn't make that happen, so now he hates all the Golden Hives," Fallanita whispered.

Great, that's going to help my cause, Adela thought to herself.

"The next class you have is Basic Weeds and Needs with Lady Armina Dusseldorf. She's the Emerald Den with the long neck and big ears. Then your next class is Aerodynamic Light and Flight with Lady Gwen Fern, whom you have met, along with History of the Lights with Lord Herdock. That one is going to be a total nightmare. He is the very short man with a strong stutter, but don't worry, even though he isn't supposed to favor Golden Hives, everyone knows he does."

As she spoke, Adela looked for him. She saw the small man in the golden cloak up front. He was just as tall as Fallanita, and that wasn't tall at all. He was bald with only a few sliver hairs coming out of his head. He looked as though he were pushing one hundred and something.

"Oh no," Tara and Faye both said at the same time as they stared at her scroll.

"What?" Adela asked them quickly. But none of them answered. Instead, they rolled up the scroll and placed it back on top of the books.

Adela reached to unroll the scroll. She quickly read the only name they hadn't read out loud.

"Natorbi practice with Lady Zara Datura."

That was the blonde Red Diamond who wanted to tear Hector and Adela to pieces earlier that morning.

"Oh no," Fallanita added.

"I have that too. Why is that so bad?" Hector asked, glancing around at the girls who surrounded him.

"Nothing. Natorbi is the most treasured and beloved sport to Volsin all over Cielieu," Fallanita said, all but jumping out of her seat with excitement.

Adela calmed down, only slightly. "So Natorbi is a game. Why is that so bad?"

Both Tara and Faye looked away to hide their laughter.

"Bad move," Tara whispered to her.

"Natorbi is not a game! Natorbi is a hardcore life-changing sport. You can't even play until you're fifteen. That doesn't even matter because you have to be chosen to be one of the five to actually lead your team. Natorbi takes ninety percent skill, four percent agility, and six percent luck. Natorbi today, Natorbi tomorrow, Natorbi for life, and this year we are not coming in second place," Fallanita said. Four other Volsin around the table cheered alongside her.

Adela leaned away, staring wide-eyed at the crazed-looking girl in front of her. She didn't know whether to run or laugh. Faye and Tara seemed to think laughing was the best option. They were almost falling upon themselves, tears pooling in their golden eyes.

"So I take it you're on the Natorbi team?" she asked her.

"She is this year's youngest and only female Natorbi player. There hasn't been a female Golden Hive player in, like, eighteen years," Faye replied, holding on to her round cheeks in order to keep from laughing.

"Okay, we get it. Natorbi is serious, but why did you all say *oh no*? Where I come from, that means something bad," Adela asked as Fallanita sat proudly.

"You have it with Lady Datura. You see how serious Fallanita is? Lady Datura is ten times worse. At least you only have that class once a month, otherwise you may need to invest in Wolfgang for the bruises you will get," Tara said, making them all worry.

"All the lords and ladies love Natorbi, but the only person to ever best Lady Datura is Lord Elderberry—but he is the master of everything," Faye replied, glancing up at the middle-aged man at the center of the white table. He almost looked like a king at a royal feast.

"Can you all explain that to me? I thought Ryker told me he was, like, seventy-something?" Hector replied, glancing back up.

"What do you mean?" Fallanita asked.

"Shouldn't he be, well, you know…?" Hector paused, not wanting to offend anyone.

"What he means is, shouldn't he be old? Like with wrinkles and a long beard or something?" Adela finished for him.

"Oh, when you have mastered your light as well as Lord Elderberry has, your body actually ages slowly. He is only one of two Volsin in all of Cielieu still alive who can achieve that," Tara whispered. The way she spoke along with the frown that spread across her pale skin made them both aware of whom they were speaking.

Prince Delapeur.

Chapter Eight

The Welcoming Ball

When Adela walked out the magical door to the Golden Hives, she came face to face with Ryker, Tara, Faye, and Hector. All of them except Hector were dressed in their respective lights, from the green tie Ryker was sporting to Tara's and Faye's golden dresses. Just as with the cloaks, Adela and Hector would stick out because of their clothing.

"Um…" Hector coughed. "You look nice."

"You don't look too bad yourself, but you know me and dresses." Adela smiled as the door behind her opened and shut once again, this time allowing Fallanita through. The tiny girl pulled and tugged at the sleeves of her golden dress before giving up and glaring at them.

"I hate these things," Fallanita hissed, sharing the same thoughts as Adela.

"I thought you said it wasn't a big deal, just something for the younger students." Ryker joked, causing Fallanita's golden eyes to narrow before she stomped past them.

"She could so take you," Tara whispered to her brother.

"I know." Ryker grinned. "Are we ready?"

Faye nodded. "Yes, please, the faster we get this over with, the faster we can get ready for classes."

"Why does everyone hate the welcoming ball?" Hector inquired, as Adela would have asked had she not been so busy trying to walk in her heels.

Do not trip. Whatever you do, Adela, don't trip, she thought to herself. Her dress was nothing fancy but beautiful nonetheless. The last thing she wanted to do was embarrass herself.

"We don't hate it, but it's always the same," Tara said. "At the beginning of every year we have to listen to all the overexcited slates—"

"No offense," Faye replied, cutting off Tara before she could continue.

Tara glanced over at them before rolling her eyes. "They don't count."

"Should we be happy about that?" Adela laughed while holding on to the side of her white dress.

"You know what I mean." Tara sighed. "The welcoming ball is just boring."

"How about we meet up when all the talking is done?" Ryker suggested. He looked just as excited as his sister, which wasn't much at all.

When they all agreed, Adela took a moment to look around. As more and more students flooded the halls, she noticed it was the younger students who seemed excited. Meanwhile, the older ones couldn't care less. Adela wasn't sure why that was, but she did make sure to stay close to her group. At this point they were all just following the herd, slowly moving toward the guarded doors. These were similar to the gates protected by the two cloaked statues she'd seen open the doors the night they came to the castle. These guards came to life as well. Reaching down and opening the doors, they allowed a rush of music to fill her ears. Adela gasped when she saw the ghost above her flying into the shining ballroom.

Everything was extraordinarily beautiful. Adela wasn't sure where to look first. There was a stockpile of food located in the corners and so much light above their heads that the ceiling seemed to glisten with a million stars moving across the night sky. All the lords and ladies stood in the front of the room as the ghosts above them danced. The music was provided by instruments in the corners, which seemed to play on their own accord. Before her eyes, Adela saw a tiny blue butterfly flutter by, wings flapping along with the music as if part of the orchestra. The blue butterfly wasn't the only thing that filled the air. Shifting her gaze toward Hector, Adela realized that he, too, was amazed at the magic filling the air.

"Ladies and gentleman, it is my pleasure to welcome you to the 663rd annual Welcoming Ball of the Elpida Castle of Light," Lord Elderberry stated from the very front of the room.

The younger students cheered as the older ones simply clapped. None seemed to be in the mood to attend such trivial things as this ball. Adela noticed they all looked somewhat solemn, and she couldn't understand why. To her, this was happy. She didn't mind something happy.

"We are all born with light. Some of us hold it within ourselves and it dims, for light is not meant for ourselves alone. But here, in this castle, each one of you is expected to share that light with one another so it may grow and get brighter. Even one light in the dark is helpful," Lord Elderberry stated as the star-covered ceiling above them dimmed until only one solitary star remained.

"And when there are thousands of lights in the darkness, you forget there is darkness at all." With each one of his words, another few stars among the thousands began to shine brighter. This encouraged cheers from the audience.

Lady Fern stepped forward, glancing over the students with the brightest smile on her face. She began, "For the

Sapphire Falls, the Praesuls are Colton Ashwater and Bethany Wahs from the ninth years..."

"What are Praesuls?" Adela whispered, leaning over to Hector slightly. "I don't know. It wasn't in any of the books I've read," he whispered, watching as the next two names were called.

Ryker turned back and said, "Two upper-class students, one male and one female, are chosen from each class and light to speak on behalf of that year. So there are eight students for each class, but really it is all about the twelfth years. Last year, I was the Praesul for the ninth-year Emerald Dens. Once the Praesuls are chosen, they must welcome the new slates."

Adela nodded, only understanding about half of what Ryker said. She figured it had to be like student council back home. Adela was beginning to understand why the older students were so bored. Listening in nice but uncomfortable clothing as names were called could really become annoying after a while. However, when Lord Myrtus called Ryker as the Praesul for the tenth-year Emerald Dens, he grinned brighter than anyone else in their group. Tara just hugged her brother before he was given room to make it to the front.

One by one the Praesuls were chosen. However, the air in the room changed when Lady Datura called out, "Scarlet Danewort and Jeremy Lamorak."

It was as though death had walked into the room. Not a single person dared to smile, laugh, or cheer. Things were only made worse when the beautiful blonde stood up front without Jeremy.

"Where have I heard that name?" Adela whispered to herself.

Lord Elderberry stepped forward once again, in his eyes a reflection of the sadness felt in the students' hearts. He allowed the silence to fill the air before finally speaking again.

"Believe us when we say we all feel your pain. Loss, no matter how well you know someone, is loss. And we have many, too many in fact, that we have lost. The darkness that lives outside these walls is often so real we can only hope to see a brighter day… a hope that begins in all of you. Hope, even in the darkest of times, is something you may find strength and comfort in. Not only in yourselves, but in the hope of those around you. Hope keeps you moving forward.

"There is a story of a young boy who once had to face a giant one on one. Everyone, even his family, didn't believe he could make it. He, however, had hope and his small light, and he was able to bring the giant to his knees. This year, find your inner giants and do the same. You all are more than strong enough to do so. Do not let this loss halt you, but rather, let it push you further. Tonight is not a night to grieve because you are all…?" he asked them.

"Students of the light," everyone replied, and suddenly the death that Adela had just felt throughout the ballroom was gone. Even with the older students, it was as though his words were enough. Maybe they were. Adela wasn't sure, but she was pleased to go back to the happy atmosphere that had been the general mood of the evening.

When Lady Datura finished calling off names of the new Praesuls, they, just as Ryker had said, began to welcome all the first-year students. Whenever their names were called, the students would erupt in cheers and claps, making each one feel either very embarrassed or overjoyed by the attention.

Adela watched as Ryker smiled at Hector and her before calling, "Hector Pelleas." With that, everyone last one them turned back to applaud him. Adela grinned as well, turning to her best friend and clapping obnoxiously, causing him to glare at her.

"Welcome, Hector Pelleas!" She joked.

"You do know this means they're going to call your name too, right?" He smirked when her eyes widened.

Before she could speak, it was too late.

"*The* Adela Arthur."

There was a gasp just before cheering, and every last student began to stare. Even the lords and ladies turned back to her. The fact that the Praesul who had called her had managed to add *the* to her name wasn't lost on her. She knew that shouldn't have been there. *The* meant that she had done something, which she hadn't.

"Welcome, *the* Adela Arthur." Hector joked beside her.

It felt like a full two minutes had passed before music erupted in the ballroom and students returned to chatting loudly amongst themselves. Adela noticed a few of the other tenth years coming her way. She took her chance to get away as quickly as possible, leaving Hector to handle all the questions. She escaped through a side door hidden between two pillars. Adela followed the soft voice she recognized to be Faye's until the freckle-faced girl was in view. Faye was sitting with some other students; she was the oldest among them.

These students studied on the other side of the castle, if Adela remembered correctly. Their side was mostly for the younger students, those with no light yet. Adela wondered how bored they must have been. Nothing in the Welcoming Ball applied to them yet. Adela began to listen to Faye speak in the corner of the hall, right under one of the statues with a yellow flame burning in its hands.

"What else is in the lesser realm, Faye?" a young boy asked, his front tooth missing, making his words come out choppy.

Faye looked them all over, feigning seriousness before smiling. "Are you sure you can handle it? It is a secret, you know," she told them.

"I am the best at secrets!" one little boy boasted, jumping to his knees with a wide grin, and the chorus erupting behind him agreed.

"I don't know…" Faye teased.

"Please, Faye, we won't tell anyone," another child begged.

"Fine." Faye sighed to their amusement. "It was a dark, stormy, ogre-filled night when the worst battle of the Great War took place. Parents gathered their children all over Cielieu in order to make it to the lesser realm. The great families of Arthur, Lamorak, and Elderberry created three passageways to enter the other side. In this way everyone would get a chance to escape, but they would not be able keep the passageways open for long. Some parents jumped in with their children, and some fell in without theirs, unintentionally leaving them in Cielieu." Faye smiled sadly.

Adela realized that all of the small children in front of Faye thought their parents were back in the human world, not dead. They believed they were trapped somewhere else, not by choice. Adela wanted to believe that as well, but her practical mind wouldn't allow her. There was no way that their parents could be on the other side. They weren't even born when the Great War took place.

"But there is no light in the lesser realm. Are they safe?" the boy with the missing tooth asked her.

"Of course!" Faye grinned. "Yes, there is no light. But there are no wars, no one ever gets sick or dies, and best yet, parents and their children are always together. On every street are fairies in disguise giving out flowers. And in the air there are invisible dragons soaring through the sky. No one bothers each other because everyone is happy."

"Always?" one child asked.

"Always," Faye replied with a confidence that would have fooled Adela if she hadn't lived there. She only wished that was true, but there was no point ruining it for them.

"Now all of you head back into the ball or Lady Datura will have you cleaning Dragon's Landing," Faye commanded. This caused a group sigh before the children raced back, past Adela, into the door she'd walked out of.

"That was a nice story," Adela said to her.

Rising from the ground, Faye dusted off her golden dress before smiling again. "Yeah, I know that isn't what the lesser realm is really like, but like Lord Elderberry said, it is good to hope."

"What really happened to their parents?" Adela asked.

Faye frowned. "*He* has been hunting down Volsin after losing the Great War in order to gain his strength back. The other side of the castle shouldn't even be here. Before everything happened, you had to be at least eleven to enter the Castle Of Light, but with so many kids displaced, the lords and ladies traveled all over Cielieu to bring children back. Whenever they hear something has happened, they bring them here and this becomes their new home."

Adela was almost afraid to ask, "Did they bring you here?"

"No, I still have my mom." Faye smiled. Her voice was softer when she spoke again. "I lost my dad in the war, though. He was a Red Diamond and felt like he had to fight. My mom is a sapphire and tried to escape with me to the lesser realm, but the door closed with her arm in it. She lost her arm and my dad, but I still have her, so that's good."

"I'm sorry," Adela whispered.

"Don't be. It's not your fault. Some people are just evil," Faye replied. Just then the door swung open and a laughing Tara and Fallanita fell out. Behind them was a very sour-looking Hector along with Ryker.

"What happened to you two?" Adela asked them.

"You mean after you ditched me to deal with the pack of wolves?" Hector glared.

Adela grinned. "Yeah, after that."

"My sister and Shorty here thought it would be hilarious if they told all the girls that we loved to dance," Ryker snapped over at the two girls who only laughed harder. "The only problem was that neither of us knew the dance steps because they weren't real!"

"So there we are dancing in the middle of the ballroom like monkeys on pine needles, while everyone's snickering, completely oblivious to the fact that we were being set up," Hector continued, not happy at all.

Adela tried to hold back her laughter, but she couldn't help it. This was too funny not to laugh.

"It's not funny!" Ryker snapped again.

"It's a little funny." Faye smiled.

"It was even funnier seeing it." Fallanita laughed. "How did you, oh wise Emerald Den, not realize it was a joke?"

"He was distracted by Miss Bethany Wahs. Was that the reason you were so excited to be a Praesul?" Tara grinned at him, causing Ryker to flick a pebble-sized emerald light at her.

"Tara!" he yelled.

"Ouch!" She glared, already prepared with light of her own.

"Before we get into trouble, how about we all calm down and drop the light," Fallanita said, getting between the dueling siblings. It didn't work, as they could both see clearly over her head.

"I say he is free to take two cracks at the both of you," Hector muttered under his breath but loud enough to be heard.

"Fine, we are sorry. Can we go to the gardens now?" Tara sighed.

"It would be better if you really meant it, but fine," Ryker replied, storming off, leaving the rest behind as he walked past the last statue in the hall.

"Come on." Fallanita smiled as she slightly lifted up her dress to run after him.

Adela turned to Hector, smiling at their newfound friends. "Do you think we made the right choice coming here?"

"It doesn't matter. We can't go back. All we can do is look forward. Bring on the dragons, werewolves, goblins, and mermaids." He grinned, running after them.

For once, Adela just stopped thinking and ran after them. Tomorrow was the first day of class, and she would worry about it then. But even as they headed towards the gardens, Adela still felt as though she was Alice in a whole new type of wonderland. That feeling only became stronger when she stepped into the gardens.

There stood stone giants and fairies all tending to the trees, flowers, and bushes with no care in the world that students walked in the field underneath them. They picked leaves overhead, allowing them to fall down like rain over the students below, much of them younger then Adela herself. They danced under it and a few even laughed as they sat on to the giant's feet. With each lift of their massive legs, it would take them further into the gardens, saving their tiny Volsin little legs the trip.

"Mollis giants," Hector whispered over to her. "They are very kind to Volsin as long as they aren't bickering or fighting, which agitates them. The also like to garden in the nighttime."

"Why at night?" Adela questioned as one of the stone giants made his way over to them.

"I'm not sure. Maybe you should ask him." Hector replied, and when he did, the stone Mollis giant reached down his hand for them to climb on.

Adela glanced back at the rest of their friends to find that they were all already riding alongside giants and enjoying themselves. Stepping forward, Adela stood in the palm of his hands, as did Hector, before he lifted them up onto his shoulders. Adela wobbled and gripped his stone ear to keep from falling as the giant went back to his duties tending the trees. Hector just sat back and relaxed. It was like he was made for Cielieu and the Castle of Light. But in a way, Adela realized he actually was, and so was she. They were both made for Cielieu. So Adela just took a seat on the shoulder of a giant and enjoyed herself.

Chapter Nine

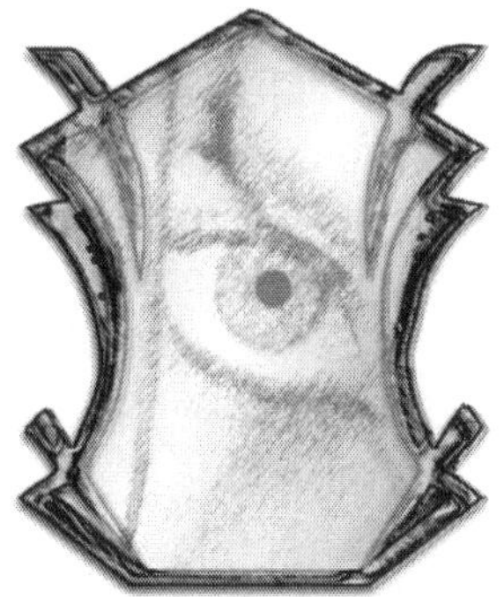

Every Hector Has His Day

Adela picked up both the golden tie and the bow tie in confusion. She had never worn either and had surely never had a uniform. She could handle the white button-down shirt, the gray sweater, and the sweater vest with the letters GH embroidered on the breast. What she couldn't handle was the skirt. Adela Arthur loved jeans. The last time she'd worn a skirt was so long ago she couldn't even remember. She knew it was sometime before she'd found out her grandfather was a dragon and there was another world living behind her mirror.

She felt odd wearing it, as though she were pretending to be something she wasn't. Adela did look like a student at the Elpida Castle of Light now, even if she didn't feel like one.

She'd spent the first five minutes after she woke up this morning mentally preparing herself for the day. But she knew nothing could prepare her. Adela grabbed her white cloak, seamlessly perfected by a suitor elf.

"You look like one of us now… Well, minus the cloak, but still," Fallanita said excitedly, standing beside her in the mirror.

"Thanks, Fallanita… I—" Before Adela could finish her statement, a tiny bird with large golden feathers and bright red eyes flew into the room. It left streaks of shimmering red light behind as it flew.

"Message for Miss Arthur," the bird sang so softly Adela almost missed it.

"It's a baby Roc," Fallanita said. The bird flew around the room as if it were searching for something.

"It won't leave until you either accept the message or deny it," she informed Adela. The only person… well, creature that knew she was here was her grandfather.

"I accept," Adela replied. The baby Roc froze and plucked out one of its own feathers and let it fall to the ground before flying out the window, leaving red shimmers in its wake.

Fallanita picked up the feather before it touched the ground and handed it to Adela. The moment Adela's hands came in contact with the feather, a familiar voice rang out clearly.

My Dearest Adela,

"I miss you greatly, but now that you are in this world, this castle is the safest place for you. I know it must be difficult for you, waking up one morning and finding your life forever altered. The Elpida Castle of Light has existed for generations with one goal in mind: to make the invisible visible. They teach young ones, like you, to bring forth their truest selves even in the darkest of times. You, Adela, have wanted to carry the world upon your back since you were a little girl. Before you even realized anything else, you wished to make others smile. It is quite a difficult thing to do at times, especially now. Such a goal can wear us down, taking away even our ability to find peace.

"You are here now. There is no going back, so enjoy your life. Enjoy being sixteen. Enjoy stage one. It truly is the best stage of all. Do not let the world you now live in become too much for you, and never forget that all is not always what it seems. Always keep your ears, eyes, mind, and heart open to the light.

With Love,

Grandpapa Keane"

Adela blinked for a moment, rubbing her ears to clear the ringing.

"Who was it from?" Fallanita questioned from the other side of the room, about to leave. Adela wondered how long she'd been standing in one spot.

"You didn't hear him?" she asked, placing the feather on her bed. Her grandfather had spoken as loudly and clearly as he always did.

"No, it was a private message. Only the recipient can hear it," she explained while clasping her golden cloak around her neck.

"Oh, well, it was from my grandfather, who happens to be a dragon. It's complicated. Apparently my parents gave me to him before they died," Adela whispered, more to herself than to the short girl across the room.

"That makes sense. Dragons are the strongest creatures in all of Cielieu. They are rarely ever seen, but everyone knows not to mess with them. Parents will do anything to protect their kids," Fallanita whispered, like Adela, speaking more to herself.

"Fallanita…" Adela began.

"No, it's okay. I know what Ryker told you. It's true. My father made a deal with him and became a Reaptor. I know everyone talks about it behind my back, but I don't care. A lot of kids here are orphans. My dad is alive. He loved me enough to do what he did. I would rather have my dad alive and a Reaptor than gone forever. I am going to become strong enough to figure out how to help him," she said proudly. Looking at her now, seeing the passion and drive in her golden eyes, Adela believed her friend.

"If anyone could do it, it would have to be you." Adela laughed. She grabbed her books as Fallanita made two discs of light. As Adela stepped on, they made their way down the hive.

"Does it take a lot out of you to make this thing?" Adela asked, referring to the golden plate she stood on.

Fallanita just shrugged. "My first year here, I fainted every time I used my light. Now I don't even notice. It's like an extension of me, as easy for me as picking up those books was for you. I just think and it happens. Sometimes I'll get a headache if I use my light too much, but that's the same as any other part of you. It just takes time and training."

"I am so behind." Adela sighed.

They reached the ground level and jumped off the discs. How was she supposed to work in these classes when she didn't even have light? Now she understood what all the lords and ladies meant in Lord Elderberry's room.

"Don't worry, we'll help you, I promise. You will get this down in no time." Fallanita encouraged her as they left the hive and found Hector and Ryker already waiting. Hector, too, had a uniform and white cloak.

"Morning, guys," Adela said to them. "I'm surprised you aren't already at the dining hall for breakfast."

Hector simply sighed. "Our first class is in five minutes. You don't have time for breakfast."

"I know." Adela laughed. She was never big on breakfast, so she didn't mind. She knew he was just trying to be kind and he was just as nervous as she was. When Hector was nervous, he over-prepared for everything. It was insane.

"Do you have Archery and Defensive Intelligence?" Adela asked Ryker. His emerald eyes were running through a book faster than Adela thought possible.

"Yeah, I just wish it wasn't with Lord Silverweed." Ryker sighed.

"He doesn't like Emerald Dens, either?" Hector asked as they walked.

"Nope. Just the Red Diamonds." Fallanita frowned, stopping at one of the open windows to glance up at a group of Red Diamonds on the grounds outside.

Adela walked up beside her and watched as one of the Red Diamonds made a bow and arrows of shimmering red light. He hit the same spot on the tree, over and over again, until the tree toppled over, not pausing even when it did. One by one, Red Diamonds unleashed their arrows until all that remained of the fallen tree was firewood. Lord Silverweed walked out of nowhere with his tiny silverback monkey on his shoulder. He was clapping at the students' achievement.

"Wow," Hector whispered as he watched them.

"Please don't tell me that is our Archery and Defensive Intelligence class," Adela whispered as she watched them wide-eyed.

"Okay, we won't tell you." Ryker laughed. "But we do have to get down there. The last thing we want is to be late."

"How are we supposed to do that if we don't have light?" Adela worriedly whispered as they walked down the spiraled tower.

Fallanita simply shrugged. "I am not sure. Just be nice to his monkey."

"Yes, because that's the key." Ryker rolled his eyes as they made it to the ground floor.

None of their reactions made Adela feel comfortable. She knew she had to learn, but they were simply throwing Hector and her into the deep end. She had no idea how to learn to use her light; she didn't even know where to start. Adela could feel herself panicking as more and more people reached the ground floor around her. However, she couldn't hear any of them. She simply took in everything around her. Everyone was so upbeat and cheerful, as far as Adela could tell. She and Hector were the only ones in white cloaks, making them stick out, like normal.

No matter how nervous she was, Adela was grateful she didn't look like Hector. Even with his makeover, he was still the same guy on the inside. When old Hector didn't know how to do something, his arms would start to shake. Adela could tell that was happening now. He was learning to hide it better, though.

"Hey, guys!" Tara smiled, all but hopping toward them and giving Ryker a brother-smack before turning toward the others.

"Nice to see you too, Sis." Ryker sighed, rubbing his arm.

"Where is Faye?" Fallanita asked, trying to look over the taller people around her.

"Here I am. Sorry, I tore my cloak and had to find my spare," Faye replied from behind her. Her face seemed flushed as though she had just ran.

But before Fallanita could reply, Lord Silverweed stepped in front of the group of students, causing immediate silence.

"All of you know who I am," the red-haired and red-eyed man hissed out sternly before his gaze fell on Hector and Adela. "All of you with light, that is."

His words caused every last student to stare at them for a moment and even a few to snicker.

"Miss Arthur and Mr. Pelleas, seeing as you do not have your light and we cannot place you with the rest of the slates, you will be helping me demonstrate this lesson. Come forward." Lord Silverweed sighed, already annoyed with them.

Adela glanced over at Fallanita, who mouthed, *"I'm sorry,"* as Adela walked forward with Hector. Lord Silverweed's red eyes looked them over with nothing but disdain. Adela wanted nothing more than to glare back at him. Even his monkey looked like it hated them, but she knew better than to cause a problem, especially on her first day of classes.

"Everyone, get into your lines," he yelled out to the students behind them. "You two, follow me."

Lord Silverweed walked farther and farther away from the students and to the forest before stopping before a large tree.

"You both will stand here. Do not move." He walked back to the group of students and made a chair of red light to sit upon. "Each one of you will hit the target over their heads," he stated, causing both Hector and Adela to gasp and stare at one another before glancing upward. Sure enough, there was a small red disc above them.

"Lord Silverweed…" Adela began.

"Don't worry, all of the arrows will be nonlethal. They only use safety lights," he stated, interrupting Adela and giving his attention to his monkey.

She met the golden eyes of Fallanita, who stood first in line for the Golden Hives. On her right side were the Sapphire Falls, then Emerald Dens, and on her left were the Red Diamonds, each waiting to take aim. The first row pulled their arms up as if they were holding a bow and arrow. Some took deep breaths and their lights began to glow. They glowed and shimmered until forming the weapon they needed, each weapon matching the colors of their eyes and cloak. Adela met the gaze of Scarlet, who simply smirked at her with an evil expression.

"Sapphire Falls," Lord Silverweed called out. With his words, a shimmering sapphire arrow came flying toward them. However, it missed both teens and grazed the tree at the far left.

"Elbow down, Miss Wahs, elbow down." Lord Silverweed sighed, rolling his eyes at the brunette. She didn't seem bothered, though. She smiled widely before walking to the end of her line.

"Emerald Dens," Lord Silverweed called next, and again a shimmering arrow flew toward them. Luckily, the student was a better shot and was able to hit right over Hector's sandy head.

"Good one, Farrell!" Hector shouted up to the boy with red-brown hair and green eyes. The boy thrust his fist in the air before going to the back of his line. Adela noticed Hector was making a lot more friends here than he did back on the other side of the mirror. She called it that, *the other side of the mirror*, because she wasn't sure if she could call it home anymore.

"Golden Hives," Lord Silverweed ordered.

Fallanita turned to face Adela. She took a deep breath, stuck out her tongue, and took aim. Her golden arrow hit its mark perfectly, hitting less than an inch over Adela's dark head.

Thank Goodness, Adela thought. You never knew what would happen when Fallanita took aim.

"Red Diamo—" Lord Silverweed began to call, but before he could even get the words out, not one, but two red arrows were shot toward Adela. The first hit its mark; the second hit her right in the arm, burning on impact.

"Ah…" Adela grunted out angrily. She grabbed her arm and, through furious eyes, glared up at the beautiful blonde who'd taken aim.

"Scarlet, one arrow would have sufficed." Lord Silverweed scolded her. He had yet to move from his self-made chair.

"Sorry, I did not even mean for the second arrow to hit her." She smirked, her sharp, bright eyes narrowing.

No, she meant for both of them to hit me. Adela glared. The arrow itself was like static shock, but knowing Scarlet Danewort had it out for her made Adela want to fight back. Scarlet was ten times worse than Wilhelmina. At least Wilhelmina never tried to kill her. Scarlet was basically queen. When she walked through the halls, the students parted and when she spoke, no one else did. To top it off, she was one of the best in everything.

Adela regained composure and waited again for Lord Silverweed to call the next round of archers. Each person had to go twice. It really wouldn't take that long if everyone hit their mark and if Lord Silverweed didn't stop to give advice. He never did get up from his seat. Everyone took their first shots and neither Adela nor Hector were hit again, but all too soon it was once again Scarlet's turn. Adela knew for a fact she would aim at her.

"This is going to hurt," she mumbled under her breath, closing her eyes as she waited for the shimmering red arrow to hit her.

"Red Diamonds," Lord Silverweed called.

Taking a deep breath, she waited, but the pain never came. Instead, she heard a massive gasp ring out through the field. Peeking out from her closed eyes, she too gasped. Opening her eyes wider, Adela stared at the green barrier of light that now covered her! But she wasn't the one doing it. Turning to her side, she looked over at Hector, whose green eyes seemed to shimmer brightly. He had his muscular arm extended in front of himself. He seemed just as shocked at what he was doing.

"I'm not sure how to make it go away," Hector told Lord Silverweed, who was out of his chair for the first time and now at Hector's side.

Lord Silverweed's red eyes glanced over the boy before glancing over at Adela.

"What made you form it?" he questioned.

Hector looked over at Adela before turning back to Lord Silverweed.

"Uh, I knew Scarlet would try to hurt her again and I didn't want her to," he muttered under his breath.

"Well, look then, Miss Arthur is fine. You did what you intended. Simply pull back."

Hector thought over Lord Silverweed's words. He seemed to understand what he meant. Once Hector did, the barrier shattered into dust around him.

"Welcome to the Elpida Castle of Light, Hector Pelleas of the Emerald Dens." Lord Silverweed smirked, patting him on the shoulder before walking back to his chair.

Once he did, all the Emerald Dens in line broke out into a mad dash, screaming madly as they came to him. One minute Hector was standing, the next he was on the grass under a pile of Emerald Dens.

"Emerald Dens! Emerald Dens! Emerald Dens!" they chanted, laughing on the ground, with Ryker leading the pack. Adela backed away, giving them room to celebrate their new member, and walked over to Fallanita. Seeing Hector laughing and being cheered as if he were some star athlete made Adela smile. He was all but dragged by the group up the tower, where their screams faded into the distance.

"They aren't going to sacrifice him, are they?" Adela joked to Fallanita. Everyone had broken away into their respective groups.

Tara smiled. "No, they are most likely taking him to Lord Hopper Myrtus, the headmaster of the Emerald Dens. Who knows where after that..."

Adela barely heard her. Instead, she shifted her gaze to Scarlet, who seemed to be glaring at her as she made her way to a group of Red Diamonds behind her.

"I don't get it. If all the lights are equal and none is better than others are, then why do the Red Diamonds think they're superior?" Adela frowned.

"They have been the Natorbi champions since, like, forever," Fallanita complained angrily.

Glancing around, Adela noticed the field they were on was almost cleared. Odd since class was yet to be dismissed.

"So is class over?" she questioned.

"On account of Hector's light, yeah. That or Lord Silverweed's baby monkey needed a nap." Fallanita smiled as they reached the tower.

"I cannot believe he found his light in such a short amount of time. Do you think Lord Silverweed planned that?" Faye said softly as they walked, causing all of them to stop for a moment.

Adela stared, shocked. "You think Lord Silverweed knew Scarlet would try to hurt me in order to get us to bring out our light?"

"It makes sense. Many us found our lights out of necessity. I first used my light while I was falling out of a tree when I was eleven," Fallanita replied.

Tara simply nodded. "Ryker and I got ours when we were

seven. There was a large storm one night and we were scared. All of sudden we were protecting each other."

"I don't remember when I had mine. It just happened," Faye added. "But that is the only reason why Lord Silverweed would make us take aim above his head."

Adela didn't say anything. She just let their words sink in, and they began to walk once more. She wanted to be happy for Hector, but right now all she felt was pressure. She didn't even know if she had light, yet Hector did. She saw it with her own two eyes. Hector was trying to protect her just like Wilhelmina was trying to protect them. But she should have protected herself. She needed to stand up for herself, and she wouldn't be able to do that until she found her light. She had promised Lord Elderberry.

"Your next class is in the Enchanted Wing, isn't it?" Tara questioned as they turned the corner, snapping Adela out of her trance.

"That's the wing with all the ghosts, right?" Adela thought for a moment, remembering what Fallanita had told her about the castle the night before.

"Yes. Those don't bother you, do they? They don't really see us. Technically, we are the ghosts to them." Fallanita laughed.

Each one of the ghosts looked as if they were living, breathing Volsin. The only difference between the dead and the living was the cloaks. The ghosts of Elpida were all dressed beautifully, as if they were going to some royal's party. They moved around at their own pace as if no one was there. Some held wine glasses in their hands, and others ate small bites of food. The fact that everyone could hear their private conversations made things strange. It was quite amusing when the ghosts were laughing amongst each other. However, when they were angry, they seemed to morph into the most terrifying people. They screamed loudly and even threw objects. Luckily for the teachers here, they never seemed to enter a classroom. They either lingered in the fancy decorated halls or spent time on the stairwells.

"This is it, Adela. We will see you later." Fallanita smiled and pointed her to the door.

"Thanks, guys," she replied, waving them off before walking inside.

The very first person she noticed, was their teacher, Lady Armina Dusseldorf. She was hard to miss. Lady Dusseldorf had a long everything. She had a very long neck, which matched her long face, which held her long nose. Her fingers were also very long, and she had large sapphire eyes and overly frizzy black hair.

"You must be Miss Arthur. Welcome!" Lady Dusseldorf smiled brightly, pulling Adela into a quick hug. Adela could hear a few snickers amongst the class as a result.

"Hello, Lady Dusseldorf," Adela whispered, pulling away.

The long-faced women leaned in close and whispered, "Do not worry. You do not need light for this class."

Adela simply smiled and nodded. She wanted to get away from her and find her desk. She almost didn't recognize the Emerald Den sitting next to the open desk. He was covered in flowers and plants.

"They placed one of those on you quickly." Adela laughed at the brand new emerald cloak now draped over Hector's shoulders. He looked good, almost like he was born to wear it. Well, if she understood Fallanita's explanation of how the light worked, he kind of was.

Most Volsin's eye color came from their parents' lights. This meant that one had a high chance of having the same color as one of his or her parents. But every rule had an exception, and Fallanita was one of them. Her mother was a Red Diamond and her father was a Sapphire Fall. All of the lights were within. It was just who you were at your core that made one of the lights come forth. That light was yours to control and shape, something Adela couldn't figure out.

"You're not angry, are you? I mean, I hate that now everyone will be staring at you more because you're the only one our age wearing a white cloak. I really don't even know what I did," Hector told her once again, saying the truth in the worst possible way.

Adela's lips formed into a thin line before she glared. "I wasn't before, but now that you put it that way… Thanks a lot, traitor." She couldn't hold the anger on her face long before smiling at him. "It's fine, Hector. You should be proud. Emerald Dens, congratulations!" she told him, which made him rub the back of his blond head.

"Miss Arthur, what is the name of this plant?" Lady Dusseldorf questioned in her soft voice. That was a feature Adela noticed all those who belonged to the Sapphire Falls had. None of their voices ever seemed to rise over a small whisper.

Adela stared at the beautiful baby purple-and-white flowers. They looked so delicate and soft. They'd sprouted from the soil like little upside-down umbrellas. Adela hadn't a clue what type of plant it was.

"Wolfsander," Hector answered for her.

Lady Dusseldorf's blue eyes widened as if she finally noticed the newly cloaked student in the room. She tilted her long face to the side.

"Harmless or toxic?" she questioned him.

He leaned forward slightly, taking a closer look before speaking again. "Toxic," he said.

Those are toxic? Adela looked back at the little purple upside-down umbrella flower. How could something so beautiful be so dangerous?

"Thank you, Mr. Pelleas, but please wait to be called on," she whispered as she chided him with a smile on her long face. "And congratulations," she added, nodding to his cloak.

He smiled widely again, and more students gave him their congratulations as well. Today was most definitely Hector's day. Adela was happy for him.

Chapter Ten

Hidden In The Deepest Corners

"How do you not feel even a little bad for eating this?" Adela questioned Fallanita, who was staring at the assortment of fish and other odd-looking seafood on the golden table. Even after two months, Adela still wasn't used to the oddness of the Castle. Tara and Faye glanced up from their mountains of food, giving Adela an odd look. None of them seemed to understand how eating anything would make them feel bad.

Adela again stared at the dining hall, if it could even be called such. Most dining halls are in some nice-looking ballroom, but not here. Such a thing was too simple for the Elpida Castle of Light. Here the dining halls, Adela realized, marked what they would be eating. Since today was some type of seafood, they were dining underwater. Yes, underwater, something Adela wasn't even sure was possible. The Red Diamonds, Sapphire Falls, Emerald Dens, and Golden Hives were now sitting on the sea floor.

It didn't feel like water at all. Tara tried to explain that they weren't really in the sea, that it was just a moving picture of what was happening at that exact moment. Adela would have believed her if it weren't for the skillful swimming mermaids that swam by. They didn't notice the students. They had long fin-like tales and miniature tentacles resembling strands of hair that flowed gracefully in the water. Sometimes they would swim directly over the table of food or behind her back, yet Adela never touched them.

The menu of the day matched where they ate. So today, various types of fish and clams—or what she believed were clams— were offered. She'd never seen a red and green clam before, but there one was, just lying on the table. Adela thought she could be eating one of the mermaid's siblings without even knowing it.

"You do not like fish either?" Kalliden questioned her. Kalliden Caraway was a very attractive teen, just like everyone seemed to be. He had short brown hair, a perfectly symmetrical and smooth face, and golden eyes. He was a nice enough guy who never ran out of questions for her.

"Never mind." Adela sighed, grabbing a drink.

All of a sudden Fallanita ran into the dining hall wide-eyed and breathless; "You will never believe who I was in the hall with today."

"Are you all right?" Tara questioned her, looking at her quizzically.

"Jeremy Lamorak has finally come out of his room!" she blurted. Tara and Faye gasped. Kalliden frowned and Adela sat there confused. She didn't understand why that name seemed so familiar to her.

"It's been two months," Tara stated, shocked.

"Yeah, he hasn't said a word, but then again, you know Jeremy doesn't talk to anyone anyway," Fallanita replied, grabbing a few fish.

"I'm sorry. I'm confused. Jeremy Lamorak, he's the Praesul for the Red Diamonds, right?" Adela questioned. Once she did, they all stopped and stared at her in amazement. Adela remembered him from the Welcoming Ball, or better yet, the lack of him. No one had ever given her the details that night.

Kalliden rolled his eyes once again.

"He is the most handsome sixteen-year-old Red Diamond. No, scratch that. He is the most handsome guy ever!" Faye replied and Adela laughed. How the castle could be so... paranormal and so much like a regular high school simultaneously was beyond her.

"That is not important and you know it," Kalliden muttered under his breath before he looked back over at Adela. "You don't remember?" Kalliden asked her.

Adela looked at him oddly. "Remember what?" she questioned. They all stiffened.

Fallanita spoke up softly. "You were the one who told Lord Elderberry you watched his older sister getting her light stripped from her."

Adela froze. Just like that all the memories of that day came rushing back. She remembered every painful detail and knew she always would. But how did they know what she saw?

"When they told him, he locked himself in his room. He is now the last Lamorak. Esthella was all he had left. Both their parents and their older brother were all stripped of their lights by Prince…" Kalliden explained.

Adela's heart broke for him. He had lost everything.

"The only Volsin allowed into his room was Lord Elderberry," Fallanita whispered softly.

Adela was currently fighting and losing the mental battle with this memory. She didn't want any of it. Such a thing was too painful to remember.

"Adela," Fallanita whispered beside her.

Glancing up, Adela noticed everyone's golden eyes upon her, each one seeming more worried than the last.

"I am fine, honestly," she told them, but once again, little Fallanita seemed to know better. Her eyes narrowed skeptically.

"Is Jeremy okay?" Adela whispered. It was a dumb question really. Of course he wasn't okay. He'd just lost the last member of his family and locked himself away.

"It's hard to tell. The Red Diamonds only really talk to other Red Diamonds. Jeremy barely even talks to anyone. In fact, the longest sentence I've ever heard him speak contained two words," Tara stated.

"Yep. *Please move,* if I remember correctly." Fallanita laughed, trying to lighten the mood. It did, however, displease Tara.

"Shut up! At least he can see me. He didn't even notice you until you jumped up, and he still didn't say a word." Tara teased.

Fallanita stood up defensively, which didn't help. She only made herself look smaller. "Why does everyone make fun of my height? I am not that small."

It was a lie. She really was that short.

"Well, you hang around tall people. If I spent all day with short people, I would be called a giant," Faye stated logically, trying to help but failing to do so.

"You're just mad because you know Scarlet has basically claimed him." Fallanita changed the subject. The battle between them broke into uproarious laughter.

Ignoring them both, Adela watched a school of fish swim by. They were tiny little guys that looked like miniature flames. They swam in circles, chasing after one another while avoiding the mermaids.

"They are called firefly fish. They are the mermaids' favorite dish. If we touch them, though, they burn our hands," Kalliden informed her randomly.

"Are they really on fire?" Adela, trying to get a better look, asked.

"Yes and no. If you take them out of the ocean, the flames disappear," he replied.

"You have been studying with the Emerald Dens, haven't you?" Tara asked him. He glared. Adela couldn't help but shake her head at them. They always did know how to lighten the mood.

Before Adela could get a word in, the doors thundered open. Striding in calmly was probably the most attractive guy Adela had ever seen in her life. Even from where she sat, she could clearly see his bright red eyes and dark hair. His hair was scruffy and cut short, layered with some strands scattered across his forehead. No words were spoken. It seemed like everyone was holding their breath. The way he walked through the water made him look like a demigod.

His piercing red eyes scanned over the tables as he looked for someone. At the corner of her eye, Adela watched Scarlet smile brightly. She pulled out her ponytail, letting down her golden hair and allowing it to fall in small waves. Scarlet stood up, making her way to the gorgeous teen. His eyes locked with Adela's, and she impulsively looked down.

"Too late for that now. He saw you. You're kind of hard to miss, with your white cloak and all," Fallanita whispered.

"Shut up right now," Adela hissed back at her. She didn't dare to look up.

"You're Adela," the smooth voice stated behind her.

"Yeah…," she replied, turning to face him. He was emotionless as he stared down at her. Adela lost her inner struggle, swallowing softly under his stare. He took her hand gently and guided her out of her seat. Adela looked up at the tall man before her. He continued to stare at her carefully with his red eyes.

"Did you need something?" she questioned softly. She could feel everyone's eyes on them.

"Yes," he replied, pulling her lips to his.

Adela stared at him in utter shock, unable to think. He continued to kiss her passionately. She felt something tug at her mind. She closed her eyes and the world around them disappeared. He broke away slowly, but they were no longer inside the dining hall. Instead, they seemed to be on a snowy mountaintop.

"Where are we?" she asked. She glanced around the hilltop until she looked forward and froze. Adela was looking at herself. There she was, lying on the snowy ground, something she remembered vividly. "No," she whispered timidly. She took a step forward. However, he walked softly to where Esthella Lamorak stood, bloody. He walked right in front her, shaking his dark head.

"You idiot! You stupid bloody idiot!" he yelled at her as a sob broke through his lips. Adela realized he was about to watch his sister be murdered.

"Stop, don't look!" She ran over, pulling at him. He ignored her. He just stared at his older sister, tears pouring from her large blue eyes, through his own unleashed tears.

"You shouldn't see this." Adela pulled at him, but again he ignored her. She wasn't sure he could even hear her.

The man dressed in all black, Prince Delapeur, appeared. Adela now recognized him as he walked over slowly, saying something she still couldn't hear.

"Jeremy, this will not change anything," Adela whispered to him. This was the past, and he was somehow living it through her.

She didn't want to watch this again while she lay on the ground helpless. Even now, as she was free to move, she couldn't help Esthella.

I am so sorry, Esthella mouthed again. Adela released the teen in front of her and stepped back.

Adela realized it wasn't her that Esthella had apologized to, but her younger brother. Esthella had known he would have figured out a way to see this. She knew her brother would end up watching her die. She was apologizing to him for the pain this would bring him.

The tears in her eyes fell as Adela watched Prince Delapeur's hand reach into her chest and strip Esthella's light. Her lifeless body fell upon the snow, and Jeremy fell to his knees beside her. He stroked her brown hair softly.

"I am the one who is sorry," he told her, then kissed her forehead. Rising, he turned to Prince Delapeur, who was crushing her glistening light in the palm of his hand. And Adela remembered something.

"Make it stop! JEREMY, MAKE THIS STOP!" Adela screamed frantically. He couldn't see what was about to happen.

Jeremy turned to her, unheeding, before glaring back at Prince Delapeur. She didn't know what to do. *How am I supposed to end this? He can't see this.* She didn't want him to suffer any more then she knew he already was.

"You son of a—" But he stopped when he saw what she knew would break him. She hung her head down low, knowing how this would play out. After Prince Delapeur crushed her light, he walked over to Esthella's body and kicked it over the mountain as if she were trash, disposable.

"I will kill you. I swear by it. I will hunt you down like the monster you are and I will rip you limb by limb!" he yelled at the top of his lungs, but Prince Delapeur couldn't hear him. The scene faded into darkness just as Prince Delapeur began to fly toward her.

Once again she felt Jeremy's warm lips on hers. She pushed away. When she did she saw they were back inside the dining hall, and every last person was staring at them. Looking down at the sea floor, she ran out of the room. She kept running. She could feel the tears cooling in the wind. She didn't know where she was going. She just kept running downstairs, upstairs, dashing from one hall to another.

Finally she burst through two large oak doors that led her to some small meadow. The ground seemed to form a sea of lavender flowers. In the far corner Adela saw a large tree that looked like some massive giant had either stepped or leaned upon it. It was bent over, and its pink leaves seemed to hang like an umbrella.

With her finger she traced her lips. She could still feel the warmth of his kiss. He had stolen her first kiss and tainted it. He went into the deepest part of her mind and forced her to watch, not only his sister suffer again, but him as well.

She hurt for him. Her heart broke for him. He had no one left. He'd just watched his sister die. And if she couldn't get the memory out of her head, how could he? She felt like it was her fault; she should have been able to do something. She should have stopped him. But she didn't even know how. Every time she blinked, she could see them both—the pain that ripped through them, the love they had for each other. They were family. She hadn't even realized how much they looked alike at first. Esthella was a Sapphire Fall and Jeremy was a Red Diamond, two extreme opposites, but that didn't matter because they were family.

Were. Past tense. So many things were becoming past tense. One man had wiped out Jeremy's whole family. How could he breathe? How could he even go on each day? She'd never hated someone as much as she did Prince Delapeur. She'd never wanted to inflict pain on someone so badly. She thought about how much he had taken. How many lives were shattered by his evil? She wanted nothing more than to repay him. What good was it to be a member of a powerful family if you couldn't make a difference? What good was it if you were powerless?

Stupid, she thought to herself, wiping the small tear from her eye.

"You didn't even know her," Jeremy said, now standing in front of her. Adela jumped, not sure how he managed to find her. He was right, though. She hadn't known Esthella. She stared at the beautiful teen in front of her, trying to figure out what to say.

"But you did," was all she could come up with.

"And you do not know me. I came to apologize. Now let Lord Elderberry know when he asks," he said before turning to walk away.

"I will help!" Adela yelled out to him.

He stopped and turned back to her. "What?"

"I will help you avenge your family and mine too," Adela replied, standing up.

"I didn't ask or want your help. You don't even have light," he retorted before he left, shutting the door behind him. There was nothing she could really say to that. She fell back to the ground.

Taking deep breaths, Adela tried to get a hold on herself. She meant what she said. She was going avenge them all. She would do anything to make sure she did. Right now she needed to find her light. Rising from the ground again, she walked out the door and headed toward the only person she believed could help her.

She wasn't sure where or how to get to his office. Truthfully, navigating the whole castle was confusing to her. She had no idea where she was going and was about to panic until she saw the weeping angels. She wasn't sure if she should knock or not, but she made up her mind and walked in to find Grand

Headmaster Elderberry and Lady Hellebore in a heated discussion. The moment she stepped in, they both turned to stare at her. Adela had a feeling they were speaking about her.

"Miss Arthur—" Lady Hellebore began.

"I need my light." Adela interrupted. Lady Hellebore simply shook her head in amazement.

"I do not disagree," Lord Elderberry replied, closing the book in his hand and placing it on his desk.

"I've been here for two months and not even a twinkle. Everyone claims I'm the daughter two the great Arthurs, but I can't even do anything. I feel like..."

"A sixteen-year-old girl who is placing too much on her shoulders," Lord Elderberry finished for her, nodding over to Lady Hellebore who simply sighed before leaving, shutting the door as she left.

"Please sit," he said, creating a chair of shimmering blue light.

"I don't want to sit," Adela muttered. His red and blue eyes stared at her, waiting for her to sit down.

Adela sighed, exasperated, taking a seat. "Happy?"

"Very. It's always tenth and twelfth years." He smirked to himself.

"There are tenth and twelfth years who don't have light?" Adela asked, misunderstanding.

He shook his head. "No, they always give me the most trouble."

"I'm sorry." Adela frowned, feeling all her energy leave her body. She was so inspired to do something, and now that she was sitting, she felt grounded.

"Why did you come?" he asked her.

Adela wasn't sure. "I need to find my light."

"Did you think I was hiding it from you?" he replied, leaning against his desk.

"No, but—" Adela answered.

"No, but you were hoping I would tell you some shortcut to make it easier. You want to learn five years' worth of light in two months." He interrupted her. Adela was anything but calm.

"Hector found his within two days!" she responded, rising from the chair of light.

"That is grand for Hector. However, you are Adela, and your light is dependent upon you," he replied.

"I have to do something. That's part of the reason I came back. I wanted to do something. Prince… he needs to be stopped. He is a monster."

Lord Elderberry frowned. "Prince Delapeur. His name is Prince Delapeur, and if you feel so adamant about your cause, you should not fear saying his name. He is a Volsin with power that no one can understand. What we cannot understand, we fear, and that is how he gets his power, because we all give him fear to feed upon."

"Fine. Prince Delapeur! There, I said it and I hate him. I want nothing more than to destroy him..."

"Enough!" Lord Elderberry yelled. "You have no right to hate. Do you think you are the only one to watch those you care for die? Do you think you are the only one to feel pain and anger? You know nothing of it. This anger you have, this pain you feel will not help you. Prince Delapeur conquered that long before you were born. Just as you cannot destroy fire with fire, nor stop a flood with water, you cannot battle hate with hate, especially when it is not your battle to fight."

Adela glared furiously at the man before her. "Then why I am I here? This has always been my battle from the moment I was born. Just because I was sent through that mirror doesn't make it any less so. I was meant to be here. I believe that. I just need to find my light."

"You are just as infuriating as your parents. Why do all you Arthurs make it your personal mission to save the world?" He sighed, calming down drastically.

His words also caught Adela by surprise. Hearing about her parents was like hitting below the belt and now she felt... She didn't know how she felt. She wasn't like her parents.

"Adela, your only duty right now is to enjoy yourself. I understand Jeremy's actions have caused you great pain, and I have told him to apologize. However, darkness and pain find us often enough. You do not have to search for them."

That explained why Jeremy apologized so quickly, even though it didn't seem sincere.

"You don't get it. Everyone thinks I'm supposed to be this great Arthur. You don't know how that feels. You're the great Grand Headmaster Elwin Alfred Carnell Alvar Elderberry," she whispered.

"The fifth," he added, causing both of them to laugh.

"I'm sorry, but I can't say that twice." Adela smiled.

Lord Elderberry simply smirked. "It is quite a mouthful. But I add the fifth because I also know what it is like to live under the shadow of another great name, Miss Arthur."

"Yeah, well, you seem to be doing just fine," Adela replied as she fidgeted with her hands.

"Did you honestly expect it to be easy?"

Truthfully, Adela wasn't sure what she expected. She didn't want to say that, though.

"No, but I wasn't expecting it to be so hard, either. I've tried meditating, reflecting, and getting angry. None of it has helped. Sometimes I wonder, maybe I don't have light. Maybe you guys found the wrong Adela Arthur," she admitted, returning to her seat.

"Maybe you're right," Lord Elderberry replied. "Maybe your grandfather watched the wrong mother use the last of her strength to protect her daughter. Dragons are not often wrong, but it could be possible. Maybe you are not the same Adela Arthur who, at two years old, used her light to learn how to walk."

Adela's head snapped up immediately. "What?"

"You are aware that few Volsin have abilities besides their light, correct?" he replied.

"Yes, but I never used light," she replied.

"When Jeremy was searching your mind, he came across a very determined young toddler with light who desired to walk more than anything in the world. But she kept failing. Frustrated, the young two-year-old figured out she just needed something to hold on to. She made handles of light floating in thin air to help her walk."

Adela searched her mind over and over again. She couldn't remember any of that.

"That can't be true," she whispered, more to herself than to the middle-aged man before her.

"Did you ever think to ask your grandfather why he homeschooled you?"

And just like that, Adela remembered all the times she wanted to go to a normal school, with other kids her age, but her grandfather told her she wasn't ready. She'd always believed that he had done that because he wasn't ready to let her go.

"You have light, Adela. You have always had light. As you grew up, you stopped believing you did and simply called it your imagination. Now it is time to believe again. Sadly, believing in ourselves is often too much for most of us to bear. Many fear themselves and what they could possibly do." Lord Elderberry exhaled. Raising his right hand, a book covered in blue light flew toward him. He opened it quickly before sending it over to Adela.

"What is this?" she inquired. The book fell into her hands.

"The yearbook from your mother and father's twelfth year at the Castle of Light. You may open it when you exit," he instructed as she eyed the large white book.

"Thank you," she said, walking toward the door.

"Anytime, Miss Arthur."

When Adela walked out, she took a deep breath and closed her eyes as the door closed behind her. When she reopened them, she wasn't expecting five pairs of eyes to be upon her. There they were, the whole gang: Hector, Fallanita, Tara, Ryker, and Faye.

"Are you all right?" Hector asked, his newly vibrant green eyes checking her over.

"Yes, I'm fine. What are you all doing here?" she asked, even though she was grateful to have so many people who cared.

"We all saw what Jeremy did...," Ryker started.

"It's fine. He just wanted to see his sister," she explained. She wasn't angry anymore, just tired.

Tara smirked. "We got that part after you ran away. I am just confused as to why he kissed you to do it."

"That jerk didn't have to kiss you. All he had to do was take your hand. When I find him I am going to…" Hector began to threaten.

"Wait, what?" Adela asked, tightly gripping the yearbook in her hands and interrupting Hector before he could go on.

"Jeremy Lamorak's ability requires him to touch someone and his choice of contact was a kiss," Ryker explained with a grin. Everyone but Hector and Adela seemed to find it funny.

"I am going to kill him," Hector hissed.

"Hector, that's wrong. He just lost his sister," Faye stated.

"He should have thought about that before he assaulted a girl." Hector seethed.

Tara laughed. "Overreaction, check."

Adela really didn't want to deal with any of that right now. She just wanted to look at her parents' yearbook. There was already enough drama in her life to fill a novel. The last thing she needed was to deal with this as well.

Chapter Eleven

Clash Of The Olympians

Adela searched high and low for the room with the leaning tree and lavender flowers in order to be alone. But no matter how hard she tried, she couldn't find it. So she gave up and took a seat on the windowsill overlooking the entire castle, with her parents' yearbook in hand. Yearbooks at the castle were quite different from any other yearbooks Adela could have ever seen, of course. When she first opened the white book, she didn't find anything odd. That was until she touched one of the pictures. The minute she did, the image leaped off the page and came to life over the book, like a movie.

Grandpapa Keane was absolutely right. She did look like a perfect mixture of her parents, and they were beautiful. As she ran her hand over her mother's photo, she watched as her dark hair moved in the wind. Adela could even hear her mother's laughter as she grabbed at snowflakes until her father threw snowballs at her. It was funny. Of all the times she'd pictured her father, she'd never thought of him as a blond. Flipping the page, Adela found both of them again. This time when she touched the picture, the image of them dancing rose. Her mother was wearing this beautiful golden dress, her father a green tie.

"Adela," Hector called out behind her, causing her to jump. Fallanita hopped up onto the windowsill, glancing down at yearbook.

"You guys scared me." Adela jumped, snapping the book closed.

"Sorry," Hector replied at the same time

Fallanita complained. "I was watching that."

"We don't have class until the flames are yellow," Adela said, pointing to the hooded statues on the other side of the hall. The flames in their hands were still green.

"We know. We just came to check on you," Fallanita replied, grabbing hold of the yearbook and reopening it.

"I don't need to be checked up on. I'm fine." Adela sighed.

"We know," Hector replied quickly.

"You look like your mom." Fallanita smiled at the photos. "But you have your dad's smile."

Adela shifted to look at the book as well. "Thank you."

"Adela!" Fallanita yelled even though she was right beside her.

"Geez, Fallanita, I'm right here," Adela responded.

"Sorry, but, come on, you have to see this." She apologized.

The smaller girl yelled, handing the book to Hector before grabbing hold of Adela and running down the hall. Adela tried to pull away, but the girl had a surprisingly strong grip.

"Fallanita, where are we going?" Adela yelled as they ran up the stairs.

"You'll see. Come on!" she yelled back.

Adela caught the golden eyes of Tara, who simply shook her head and kept talking to her brother. Adela almost fell over when Fallanita abruptly stopped at a large wall covered in trophies and medals. Fallanita pointed to the medal engraved with the name of Adela's mother.

"Your mom was Natorbi champion all four years! She won the Natorbi cup her twelfth year, and the Golden Hives have not won again since she left. She was the last female to ever play Natorbi for our light, until I gained a spot!" Fallanita yelled, all but jumping out of her skin. She was so excited it almost made Adela want to jump.

"This is amazing, Fallanita." Adela laughed, reaching up to touch one of the many plaques bearing her mother's name. Truthfully, it was almost like a shrine to her mother.

"Hector, where did you go?" Fallanita asked the gasping teen as he reached them.

"Where did I go?" He gasped. "You ran… no, you basically flew to the other side of the castle. What are we even looking at?"

"Big shoes…," Adela whispered softly. This wall was her mother's legacy, and it was just making her shoes harder to fill.

"Whoa, your mom won all of these?" Hector asked, looking up at the massive wall.

"Yep," Adela replied.

"Here she is," Fallanita replied, grabbing the yearbook back from Hector and opening it to the page with more of her mom's victories. Touching the photo, the image came to life and Adela couldn't control her smile as she watched her mother jump up and down in a full bodysuit, dripping wet head to toe, kissing the trophy.

"Your dad is there too. He came in third." Hector pointed to her father in his own full bodysuit. He looked so proud of her mother as the Golden Hives all lifted her into the air.

"Natorbi today. Natorbi tomorrow. Natorbi for life," Fallanita whispered with a smile. "You're definitely trying out."

"Fallanita, you don't understand. I'm horrible at sports. Ask Hector," Adela said quickly, pointing to the brown-haired teen who just laughed at the thought.

"She really is bad." He grinned.

"Can you swim?" Fallanita asked her carefully.

"No...," Adela lied, causing the small girl to step forward and glare at her. "Yes, I can swim." Adela sighed.

"Then you can try out. Lady Datura holds tryouts on the first days of Natorbi classes. If you gain a spot, then she will not hate you as much." Fallanita grinned as they walked toward the dining hall.

"Thanks for reminding me." She sighed as they walked. At first she wondered why people didn't make discs and float everywhere. Then she found out that using light was strictly prohibited in the halls and dining rooms. That left only the dorm rooms and classrooms, which made sense because you needed light get into the rooms in the hive.

"It's true and you are going to be great. After all, it's in your blood. Can you imagine an Arthur back on the Golden Hive Natorbi team? I love all the guys, but having another girl on the team would be amazing." Fallanita smiled, already in dreamland.

"No I ca—" Adela began.

"Adela, are you all right?" Hector asked.

She was completely frozen, staring at the red-eyed teen that was on his way into the dining hall.

"I'll meet up with you guys," Adela said to them, walking away before either could speak.

He was walking with a group of Red Diamonds, one of them being Scarlet, but he didn't seem to be paying attention to any of them. Jeremy looked as though he was living in his own mind. He didn't even seem to be aware of where he was or where he was going. In fact, he didn't even notice Scarlet trying her best to start a conversation.

Adela walked right up to him and said, "Sorry, you're missing lunch today."

"What?" He glared down at her.

"You owe me." She glared back.

"What is wrong with you? His sister died. He doesn't owe you anything," Scarlet hissed.

"He wouldn't have known or seen that if I hadn't come here," Adela replied, not breaking contact with his red eyes.

"Do you want me to say thank you?" he replied angrily.

"Not really, but I need your help and, seeing as you owe me, it works out," she replied, standing tall.

"I only speak to and help Red Diamonds," he hissed before walking around her. Scarlet smiled, walking around her as well.

Adela knew she was about to aim below the belt, but she had started to understand the Red Diamonds. Diamonds were created under high pressure and extreme heat. The only way to get to them was to pressure or anger them.

"Maybe that's why your sister called me instead of you." The moment the words left Adela's lips, she regretted it. She wanted to pull all the words from the air and stuff them back into her mouth, but it was too late.

Jeremy turned back to her, his red eyes blazing like fire. His hands began to light up like fireworks. His nose flared as though he was trying to breathe again and his jaw tightened.

"Is there a problem here, Mr. Lamorak?" Lady Hellebore asked, stepping beside him.

"No," he stated, taking a deep breath. "No, there isn't any problem. Adela and I were just talking about a favor I owe her."

"Really, now?" Lady Hellebore asked, her golden eyes now focused on Adela. "What favor is this, Miss Arthur?"

"His father was my godfather. I just wanted to know about him," Adela said quickly, causing both Lady Hellebore's and Jeremy's eyes to widen.

"Very well, then," she said simply before walking toward the dining room door. But she stopped before entering. "Miss Arthur, is the whole group needed for this favor?" Lady Hellebore asked, glancing around at the group of Red Diamonds along with Hector and Fallanita.

Everyone seemed to understand and walked toward the door. Both Scarlet and Hector hesitated, though. When they were all alone, Jeremy walked toward her, stopping only an inch from her face.

"That was wrong," he hissed.

"So is kissing someone in order to invade their mind, especially when you didn't have to," she replied, not in the least bit scared.

"I..."

"I really don't care. I was angry at first and I don't know why you did it, but it doesn't matter now. I need you to help me get back into my mind again. I want to see the first time I used my light. You told Lord Elderberry you saw it..."

"Can I get a word in or are you always this demanding?" he snapped. Adela eyed him carefully before nodding. "I kissed you because that was the only way I could actually be in your mind. If I had just held your hand, I would have only seen it, not experienced it, and I needed to experience it. I never told Lord Elderberry anything. He simply told me to apologize, which I did," Jeremy replied, ignoring Adela's confusion.

"They said—"

"Which is why I never pay attention to the *theys.* They never recognize the facts." He cut her off.

"Oh," Adela whispered, dropping her head.

"Yeah, oh," Jeremy replied. "But I will help you anyway."

"I feel like an absolute jerk right now. Why would you do that?" Adela asked him.

Jeremy simply shook his head. "Because if my sister believed in you, then so can I, at least for now. Although, I doubt she knew how conceited you are."

"I am not conceited," Adela said as they began to walk once again.

"You used my dead sister in order to force me to use my ability for your gain. You are conceited," he repeated.

"Look, I'm sorry. I know that was…"

"Don't bring her into this. Let's just get this over with," he replied, stopping at the door Adela had been searching for the whole morning. The door with the leaning tree and lavender flowers.

"You're kind of a jerk. Did she know that?" Again, Adela wanted to take the words back the moment she said them. Sometimes she wondered where her filter was.

Jeremy simply smirked. "Yeah, she knew that, but she just blamed it on the Red Diamonds."

"She was smart," Adela whispered, inhaling deeply in order to take in the scent of lavender.

"She was," he whispered. "Now stand still and relax."

Adela nodded, but when he came closer to her she couldn't help but laugh.

"I'm sorry." She laughed. "But you look so angry. Last time I didn't see it coming, but would it hurt you to at least look like you don't want to kill me?" She smiled.

"But I am starting to want to kill you." He sighed, more than annoyed with her already.

"Fine. Just trying to clear the—" But before she could finish speaking, he kissed her once again, and when they broke apart, Adela was back in her home.

"What is this place?" Jeremy asked, glancing around the pink room with flower-covered walls. Adela remembered those walls. It had taken her five days and three coats of teal paint to cover them up.

"It's my room. My childhood room," she whispered, glancing at the small princess-style bed with her favorite stuffed dolphin—the one she wouldn't admit she still had hidden in her dresser. Hearing laughter streaming in from outside her door, she moved past her bed and opened the door widely. There she saw the two-year-old version of herself with short black hair, clapping at her grandfather. To her surprise, her grandfather wasn't wearing sunglasses. To the best of her knowledge, he'd always worn his dark shades to cover his eyes.

"Come on, Adela, you can do it." Her grandfather smiled at her childhood self. He was seated on the other side of the floor with his arms outstretched.

Jeremy snickered beside her, causing Adela to glance at him. "It's ironic because he's a dragon."

Rolling her eyes at him, she simply took a seat beside the younger version of herself. She watched as the younger Adela pushed herself off the ground, her chubby legs wobbling under her weight. She took a step forward and then another, then immediately fell back again. At this, she began to cry. Her grandfather came to the rescue, lifting her up.

"It's okay, bumble bee. You will get it next time. Do you want food?" he said before placing her back on the ground.

"No!" The younger girl pouted before taking a deep breath and glaring at anything in sight.

"What are you doing?" Jeremy whispered.

Adela turned to him before turning back to herself. "I have no idea, but I look like I am trying to give myself a headache." Adela watched in shock as her younger self created a long horizontal bar of golden light. With her tiny hands, she grabbed onto the bar and began to use it to walk to the other side.

"You little cheater," Adela told herself with a grin on her face.

"Unconventional, but it gets the job done," Jeremy replied.

"Adela Arthur, what are you doing?" her grandfather asked, wide-eyed, as the tiny girl kept walking toward the other side of the room.

"Walk, Papa," she said, then turned around once again to walk back to where she first started.

"You little cheater." He laughed when she came back to him. "That was good. Now, no light."

"'kay," the little girl replied.

Just like that, the image of her and her grandfather disappeared. Now they were in darkness for a spilt second before returning to Adela's room once again.

"What just happened?" Adela asked, rising from the ground.

"We're in another memory," Jeremy replied, looking around the room again. Everything was exactly the same, except her bed was slightly bigger.

"I now know how Leonardo DiCaprio felt in *Inception*." Adela sighed.

"How who felt in what?" Jeremy asked, even though it seemed like he didn't care all that much anyway.

"Never mind," she replied just in time to watch a much taller and better-walking version of herself barge into the room before slamming the door behind her. The five-year-old appeared to be crying as she jumped onto the bed.

Seconds later there was a knock on the door. "Adela, can I please come in?"

"No, go away," the girl yelled, throwing her dolphin at the door.

"So you've always been demanding," Jeremy replied, causing the older girl to glare at him once again.

"I don't remember this, but it's my memory," she whispered.

There was another knock at the door before finally her grandfather simply walked in. This time he did have on his sunglasses. Adela watched as he pretended to stumble slightly as he walked toward the bed and sat down.

"Adela…"

"Why did you stop me from telling that kid the truth? There are fairies and dwarfs living on the other side of the mirror in Cielieu. You're a dragon, and I'm a Volsin. I didn't make it up. You told me so." The young Adela sobbed.

"Adela, those were just bedtime stories. It isn't real and I'm not a dragon," he whispered to her. Adela watched as he lied to her.

"But I have light…"

"Adela, that is just your imagination…"

"No! I have light and you saw it. You said you saw it, Grandpapa," she cried.

"I am so sorry, bumble bee, but I didn't. You are a special little girl, but you don't have light and there are no such things as dragons or dwarfs," he replied, pulling her into a large bear hug.

"I have no light?" The little girl whispered in confusion.

This time when everything faded to black, she could feel Jeremy kissing her again. When she broke free, she took a deep breath before stumbling backward to control her spinning head.

When she turned back to Jeremy, she found him wiping blood from his nose with his sleeve.

"What happened?" she asked, getting back up quickly to see his face.

"Nothing, I am fine. I paid my debt," he replied, breaking free in order to walk toward the door. But before he could, she grabbed him again.

She sighed. "Just sit down. If I knew this was going to hurt you, I would never—"

"I'm fine," he replied, taking a seat under the tree.

"Sure you are," Adela muttered as she sat next to him. She allowed herself to just breathe and remember everything she'd seen.

It was odd how they were her memories, yet she couldn't remember. She understood she was young then and she understood why he had to lie to her, but it still saddened her. Adela missed her grandfather. At first she thought maybe she missed the world she grew up in, but now she was realizing she never fit in there either. She'd told herself she didn't have light for so long that she honestly believed it. She did have light, though, and all she had to do was bring it out of her. Staring at her hand, Adela tried to envision it. She thought about herself wanting to walk and how dedicated she'd been. She was just as dedicated now. Now she knew it was possible.

"You look like you're trying to give yourself a headache," Jeremy said, pulling her out of her trance.

"I'm trying to—"

"I know what you're trying to do. You're just doing it wrong." He rolled his eyes.

"Do you have a better idea, Lord Know-it-all?" She glared.

Jeremy sighed. "If I help you, will you leave me alone?"

"Sure, Jeremy. If you help me I will leave you alone so you can continue brooding and glaring at the world." There was something about Jeremy that brought out the worst in her and she didn't like it.

Jeremy said nothing. Instead, he turned to her and raised his hand, creating a small ball of red light.

"My sister taught me this trick," he replied. "Let it hover over your hand and try to change the color."

Adela had never felt anything like it before. It was like holding a small light bulb in her hand. The light was warm and heavy. It was as if her hand and the light were opposite sides of magnets repelling one another.

"We're not supposed to use light outside—"

"Stop talking and concentrate." He cut her off.

"I am concentrating." She glared.

He sighed and the light over her hand disappeared before he stood and began to walk way. "No, you're not, and I am done helping you. You keep huffing and puffing about wanting your light, but the truth is you're scared. You don't want to use it or find it. You couldn't avenge a baby Roc, and you do not deserve to be an Arthur."

Suddenly the lavender flowers he walked through all began to die and the petals were blown off the tree. In less than a few seconds, the whole room became a barren wasteland and thunder roared in the clouds above. Adela didn't notice any of it; all she really wanted to do was punch the teen in front of her.

"Take it back," she yelled at him.

"No, you're a nightmare," he yelled.

Adela wasn't sure where it came from, but she knew she was no longer in control of herself. One minute she was fine; the next she had what seemed like a golden thunder bolt blazing in her hand.

"Take it back!" she hissed again.

"Poor little Adela Arthur with the hard life. You make it seem like everyone here should be grateful to you or something. We were better off without you," he replied.

Without a second thought, Adela threw the golden lightning bolt at him. However, Jeremy didn't even flinch. Instead, he simply created one of his own and threw it back at her. The two bolts of light collided upon impact with an ear-piercing scream.

"And you act like a pompous prince! *Look at me. I'm Jeremy Lamorak. I lost my sister.* You aren't the only one to lose someone!" she yelled at the top of her lungs, again hurling lightning bolt after lightning bolt at him.

"You don't know me and you didn't know her. I don't have time to deal with scared little girls. I have lost everything!" he snapped, creating a shield to block the bolts of lightning he couldn't deflect before returning her assaults.

Copying his shield, Adela made another one out of gold. "Well, guess what, I'm scared and I have a right to be. I lost my home, my friend, and my grandfather. Not only did I lose everything, but I found out my whole life was a lie! You aren't the only one hurting here."

"ENOUGH!" Lord Elderberry yelled as the doors to the room exploded open.

Both Adela and Jeremy froze, staring at the older man who seemed to have an army of teachers behind him. Adela tried to speak as her shield of light disappeared and she felt extremely exhausted. Before she knew it, the world around her faded into darkness.

It felt like a second to her, like she'd taken a very long blink. However, when she reopened her eyes, she found herself lying in a white hospital bed with an odd taste in her mouth and a raging headache.

"You chose a convenient time to faint," Jeremy muttered, more than annoyed with her.

Adela rubbed her eyes before sitting up. "Where am I?"

"Where does it look like?" He sighed, sitting up from his chair.

"You know, Jeremy, you are a—"

"Think wisely, Miss Arthur, before you finish that statement," Lord Elderberry replied as he entered the room. It was then that Adela noticed they were all completely alone.

"I stayed with her until she woke up. May I leave now?" Jeremy sighed.

"No, you may not," Lord Elderberry answered. "Not until I hear Miss Arthur's version of the events."

Adela looked between the dark-haired men in front of her, unsure of what to say. What was Jeremy's version of the events?

"I asked him… I used him to get into my memories. I watched myself use light and then we got into a fight," Adela summarized, looking intently at her hands.

"I see." Lord Elderberry sighed.

"I am sorry. I…," Adela began.

"Both of you have detention for the next month."

"Lord Elderberry, a month!" Jeremy complained.

Lord Elderberry's mismatched eyes narrowed dangerously. "No, now it's two months. Not only did you both lie to Lady Hellebore and enter a student's mind after I specifically told you not to, but you entered Avalon's Field and destroyed it using light you were not permitted to use. Be grateful your detention isn't for the whole year."

"Yes, sir," Jeremy groaned.

"As for you..." He sighed, causing Adela to jump. "Welcome to the Elpida Castle of Light Adela Arthur of the Golden Hives."

"Thank you, sir." She smiled.

He simply nodded before walking toward the door again. "When you are feeling up to it, Mr. Lamorak will follow you back to the dorms and explain how we do detention here."

When the door shut, Jeremy sighed angrily, pinching the bridge of his nose before turning to glare at her.

Adela almost ripped the sheets as she jumped out of bed. "Can we call a truce?"

Instead of replying, Jeremy simply grabbed his cloak from the chair and walked away. Sighing, Adela grabbed her things before following him. Neither of them said anything as they walked. Adela noticed the flames in the hands of the hooded statues were now a deep red. She had missed her two classes today. She wasn't worried about Archery. She was more concerned about missing Natorbi with Lady Datura. The next time she had that class, Lady Datura would definitely make her life harder.

"Good night," Adela muttered as Jeremy walked through the magical door. She sighed and walked into the Golden Hives. Once the door shut, a dozen golden-cloaked students accosted her, all cheering and laughing.

"Ladies, let's give her a Golden Hives welcome." Fallanita laughed as they surrounded her, each one jumping higher and higher into the air.

"Golden Hives, Golden Hives, hoo-rah!"

Chapter Twelve

The Joy Of Dragon's Landing

Adela stared at the shimmering golden light hovering over her hand. She was trying to get it to spin like Fallanita had shown her last night. All Adela could get it to do was hover. Though she was happy she now had the light, Adela was learning a valuable lesson about herself: she was never satisfied. Ever since she was a little girl, she'd wanted to do it all. She wanted to be the doctor, lawyer, dancer, singer, movie star, and princess. She wanted to be the best at everything and often beat herself up when it didn't happen. It was a blessing and curse, something she loved and hated about herself— mostly hated.

So instead of being excited about her light, Adela was already trying to figure out how to form something with it.

"Don't think so hard. Just breathe." Fallanita laughed.

"I am breathing!" Adela replied, her newly golden eyes never leaving the orb of light in the palm of her hand. The moment she blinked, she lost it and the orb shattered. "Dang it. I can't breathe," Adela said, grabbing her golden cloak. Lady Hellebore had placed it on her shoulders the moment everyone stopped cheering.

"Oh no, you don't," Fallanita said, snatching it. "Today is Natorbi tryouts. That means no cloaks, just suits."

"It's my first official day as a Golden Hive and I can't even wear a cloak," Adela groaned. The suits weren't as tight as Adela thought they would be when she first received hers. They were much different than the ones she'd seen her mother wear in the photos. The new and improved Natorbi suits were all black, with the exception of the long white strip running down both sides from her shoulders to her ankles.

"Come on, we're going to be late," Fallanita yelled.

She threw a pair of boots to Adela, who couldn't bring herself to rain on the girl's parade. Fallanita was so excited. In fact, she was more than excited. She was beside herself. Adela wasn't even sure if the small girl had slept.

"Do you want to create the disc?" Fallanita asked from the top of the balcony.

Adela glanced down before taking a deep breath. She created the orb of light, forcing it to spread in her hand before slowly allowing it to fall to their feet.

"Adela, that's amazing. It took me nine and a half months to do that." Fallanita smiled.

"It took her nine months. It took the rest of us a year." Tara and Faye laughed as they came down from their hives as well. They stood on their discs of light, dressed in their Natorbi suits.

All their discs were stable, but hers flickered every few seconds, making Adela a little worried she wouldn't be able to maintain it.

"Come on, Adela," Fallanita calling out from her disc.

She nodded and took a step out. When it held her up, Adela let out a large sigh of relief.

"You are so amazing, Adela. I can't believe it." Faye smiled, flying over to her side.

"Thanks," she muttered. "But how do I go down?"

"Just give in to gravity and allow yourself to fall," Tara replied.

Taking Tara's word to heart, Adela just gave in to gravity, releasing her mind and body. The moment she did, her disc and body went plummeting down the hive. Adela screamed at the top of her lungs. The disc stopped only a foot from the ground. Her heart beat rapidly. She couldn't relax and the light under her shattered. She fell to the ground. "When I said *give in to gravity,* I meant slowly." Tara laughed as they all reached the ground level.

Faye ran over to help her off the ground. "For your first time, that was really amazing, Adela! We all fall."

"Thanks, Faye." Adela laughed. "Truthfully, it was kind of fun—minus the whole hitting the ground part."

"You're bleeding," Faye whispered to Adela, wiping the blood from her nose.

"I'm fine. I promise." None of them seemed to be convinced. "I'm fine, guys."

"Okay, then can we please go? Adela, you don't want to make Lady Datura any angrier. She already hates you." Fallanita begged.

"She's been waiting for the games to start since she made the team last year." Tara sighed as they walked out the door.

"I am so excited, Adela! You are going to love it. Did you finish the guidebook?" Fallanita asked her, ignoring her completely.

"You made her read the *Universal Natorbi of the Ages* guidebook?" Faye gasped, shocked.

"I haven't even read it all. It's, like, two thousand pages!" Tara replied.

Fallanita simply smiled. "We read it together, so she wouldn't be confused."

"Oh no, I'm still confused and tired." Adela laughed. She'd tried her best to pay attention, but after page eight hundred, she gave up.

"Hey, guys," Ryker said. He and Hector came toward them. They were also in their Natorbi body suits, which were only slightly different from theirs.

"Ready to come in third again, brother?" Tara smiled.

"I've gotten better." He glared at her.

"Only because I helped you," she teased. Hector looked too uncomfortable to speak. He was pulling on the collar and adjusting his sleeves.

"Are you all right?" Adela asked as they went down the stairs.

"I feel like a Power Ranger." Hector groaned, to which Adela broke out in a fit of laughter. She could always count on Hector to make her laugh.

"Which one? Mighty Morphin or Time Force?" She joked.

Hector smiled. "I can't believe you just said that. You're such a nerd."

"Do either of you want to share?" Ryker asked them.

"Never mind." They laughed, leaving the rest to stare oddly at them. They opened and entered the last door on the left.

"Sometimes I forget they didn't grow up in the same world we did. I'm glad you're here, Hector," Adela whispered to him.

"Me too, and congratulations, Golden Hive!" He smirked and held the door open for her.

"Thanks," she responded. She was shocked as she stared at the massive sea cave they walked into. Adela turned back to make sure the door was still behind them and, sure enough, it was. Now, however, they stood on the rock edge of a cave with no exit and an enormous body of water in the center. Adela couldn't see the bottom of it.

"So this is the Natorbi arena," Hector whispered beside her.

"Natorbi arena?" Adela asked, causing Fallanita to turn to her.

"Did you pay attention at all?" the tiny girl snapped at her.

"A little, yes," Adela replied quickly.

Fallanita sighed. "Hector, did you read?"

"Yes, Lady Foxglove." Hector joked. When she stepped up to him, the smile on his face disappeared.

"Well then, what are the rules?" She glared at him.

"I do believe that is my job, Miss Foxglove," Lady Datura stated as she emerged from the water.

Fallanita's tiny form jumped nervously and turned to face the frightening blonde. Lady Datura's wet hair did a poor job of masking the scar, which was easily visible now. Her red eyes narrowed at Adela before she turned to Hector.

"Well then, Mr. Pelleas, what are the rules?" she asked.

Hector stammered and seemed unable to speak under her glare.

"There are four rings, each moving faster than our eyes can see. Each light has five players. The first two lights to get all five players through their ring must play each other. The two sets of rings become goals. Red Diamond's ring is worth four, Golden Hives are worth two, Emerald Dens are worth one, and the Sapphire Falls are worth half a point. You may only use your feet, with the exception of the goalie, who may use any part of their body. Whoever scores the most points before the mermaids sing wins," Jeremy answered before Hector could find his voice. He didn't walk toward them, but rather followed a path up the cave.

There was Scarlet, standing as proud as ever, with at least seven Red Diamonds behind her. Two of them Adela knew from her Weeds and Needs class. She believed their names were Damien and Kol. She couldn't remember more than that because they never spoke to anyone. She didn't know any of the Sapphire Falls; they all seemed to be in their own happy little world.

"Now that we've settled that, get into your lines," Lady Datura instructed. She passed around a small blue pill. Everyone shifted quickly into formation except Scarlet, who walked past Adela, tripping her and sending her onto the cave floor.

"Oops, sorry." The blonde smiled.

Adela glared, her hand alive with light.

"No, save it for the game," Tara said, helping her stand.

"It's not a game." Fallanita smirked. "But she is right. Kick her butt. I will be rooting for you."

"Wait, where are you going?" Adela asked, turning to her.

Fallanita stopped on her way to the top of the caves. Adela noticed there were already students sitting there. They sat in packs, each one a group of five, except the Golden Hives. Fallanita was the missing person on that team. Adela noticed that Kalliden Caraway was there, along with three older Golden Hives who Adela didn't know. Sitting beside them was Lord Eli Figwort, who taught Light Sculpting. Behind them, next to the Sapphire Falls, was Lady Fern, and beside the Emerald Dens was Lord Myrtus. The only ones without a teacher were the Red Diamonds, where Jeremy sat proudly.

"These are tryouts, Adela. I am on the team. Every team member has to watch the tryouts and see who might get bumped off the team." Fallanita smiled before running to sit with the rest of the Golden Hives.

"Isn't she worried someone will bump her spot?" Adela whispered to Tara.

"No, she is the goalie. All the goalies have to be five feet or under. There is only one person here who meets that requirement, and that is Ian Nettle," she replied, pointing to the small boy at the end of their line. He looked like he didn't want to be there.

"I guess…"

"Miss Arthur, am I boring you?" Lady Datura hissed.

"No, ma'am," Adela replied quickly, taking the pill from her hand. She took a deep breath before she felt as though her chest expanded.

"This is the breathing pill," Adela said to herself as she took in air. This was one of the things she remembered from the book.

"Everyone get to the edge and dive in on my mark. Go all the way to the bottom and wait," Lady Datura told them all.

Adela moved toward the edge and stared down at the glowing water. Never before had she been gladder that her grandfather insisted she learn to swim in the deep end.

"Sapphire Falls."

Adela heard the splash, but she didn't look up from the water.

"Emerald Dens."

This time Adela's heart beat so fast she could hear it in her ears. Why did she have to be the first one on the Golden Hives?

"Golden Hives."

The moment she heard it, Adela dove right into the water. The suit she had on immediately expanded, spreading out to cover her fingertips as well as rising to cover her mouth and nose, as if it were a mask of some sort. Adela, however, didn't stop swimming and propelling herself forward.

The sea floor was lit perfectly, making everything easy to see. There on a large boulder were four mermaids with long golden tails and tentacle-strand hair. They all seemed calm and happy to have company. Adela also noticed the rings hovering in the water, each one the color of one of the four lights. She hadn't noticed until her foot hit the sand bed below that she reached the ground first. She somehow managed to outswim the other two even though they had jumped in first. When they reached the ground as well, each one of them stared at her as though she were some freak.

She hadn't really thought about it. She just swam the way her grandfather taught her. She also noticed the white lines that were on her suit had now changed to gold. Adela then met the red eyes of Scarlet, who glared at her.

"Adela," Hector called out, drawing her attention. Adela turned back to find Ryker and Hector now at the sea floor. Their suits now had green stripes.

"How can I hear you?" Adela smiled even though he couldn't see it.

Hector pointed to the mask on his face. "These are here to help us speak. You should've read the whole guide."

"Who needs a guide when you're an Arthur?" Faye said when she reached the ground. "You swim like a mermaid."

"Thanks," Adela said, glancing over at the mermaids who were contently eating a fish. Had this been any other time, Adela would have laughed. They reminded her of teenagers watching a movie, eating popcorn.

"Are you ready for this, Adela?" Tara asked, grabbing her arm.

"As ready as I'll ever be." She glanced around and noticed that each light had only five players, just like it would during the games.

Lady Datura was the last one down. However, she swam quickly. When her foot hit the sea floor, every last one of them stood taller. The rings began to spin so quickly that Adela had to blink to make sure she was seeing them correctly. *How in the world are we supposed to get through that?*

"On your mark. Get set. Go!"

Adela watched as everyone else ran headfirst toward the ring, only to be pushed back. It didn't seem to hurt. It was only like trying to get through a fence.

"Adela, go!" Faye yelled behind her.

But she couldn't. Adela watched for a moment before realizing what was going on. The ring moved faster than her eyes could see. Every time she blinked, the ring seemed to move even faster. It was as if intently focusing on the movements of the ring actually made it harder to see its position. When Adela calmed herself down, she felt each and every heartbeat, and she realized the ring moved slower. The ring moved in sync with her heart. The more panicked they were, the harder it was for them to make it through. By closing her eyes and calming herself, the ring was easier to see. She turned to her team, calling them all to huddle up around her.

"Swim toward it, close your eyes, and relax. That's the trick," she whispered to them before pushing off on her right foot and beginning to swim to the golden ring. The closer she got, the more she tried to keep calm. Taking a deep breath, she closed her eyes and swam forward as fast as she possibly could.

It was only when she heard cheering that she opened her eyes again. Sure enough, she'd made it through the golden ring before anyone else. Adela grinned widely before yelling for Tara to make it through. Adela waited on the other side for her. She watched as Tara closed her golden eyes and tried to swim through the ring. She missed it each and every time, her dark brown hair flowing all around her.

Adela yelled at her. After a while Tara went back and Faye tried to make it through. For a moment Adela thought Faye had it, but she never made it. None of them did. She thought even Hector had figured it out, but he was also pushed back each time he tried. Adela didn't know how long she waited on the other side, but before long she heard a loud whistle and saw the rings stop spinning.

"The mermaids have left and so the tryouts are over. Nice try, everyone. Heads up," Lady Datura told them all.

Adela looked down toward the now-vacant boulder. Sighing, she began to swim to the top of the water. She noticed Lady Datura swam beside her. She didn't know why, but Adela swam harder, pushing herself farther and farther to the top, only to have Lady Datura beat her by half a second. The moment she broke the water level, the mask over her mouth disappeared. When she pulled herself out of the water, Fallanita jumped her, which sent her back into the water.

"You are amazing!" Fallanita yelled when she surfaced again. "I couldn't believe you broke every single record. Where did you learn to swim like that? How did you get through the ring so quickly?"

"You just tackled me into the water." Adela laughed, surprised.

"Sorry, I'm just so happy. I can't believe it. You are so an Arthur! You broke your mother's time. You are now the Golden Hive record holder." Fallanita laughed as they swam to the cave's edge, pulling themselves out again.

The moment Adela stood, Fallanita grabbed her hand and dragged her over to the rest of the Golden Hive Natorbi team.

"Congratulations, my dear, this is where you belong. My oh my, I never thought I would ever see another young Volsin swim so fast." Lord Figwort chuckled as he rubbed his thick beard.

"She made it through the rings, but we still haven't seen how she is with her feet." Kalliden laughed as he, along with three other older teens, came forward.

"Very true, young Caraway, very true. We shall see you tomorrow for round two. Then we'll see where Miss Arthur fits in." The bearded man laughed again.

"You're just worried she'll steal your spot, Kall." The strongest looking one nudged Kalliden's shoulder.

"Adela, this Elthin Darkboom, our First Striker." Fallanita introduced them. The boy had golden eyes and blond hair. He pulled her into a hug that lifted her off her feet.

"I told you we were going to win this year. I get to graduate with a bang!" Elthin laughed, spinning her though the air as if she were a small doll.

"Elthin, put her down before you break her," said another strong-looking man. Adela was still shocked when Elthin put her on to the ground. She'd always thought she was somewhat tall for a girl. Next to the rest of the Natorbi team, she could have been mistaken for Fallanita.

"Theodore Doorsmen." The man introduced himself. "Second Defender at your service." He laughed.

Without the chance to reply, the third guy appeared beside

the other two. He didn't look as strong as Elthin or Theodore, but he was tall.

"I'm Kuper Endives, First Defender and team captain. You'll take Theodore's spot. My cousin needs a break," he joked, causing Theodore to chase him. They both kept running until they ended up back in the water.

"Are they always like this?" Adela asked Fallanita and Kalliden.

"Always. We're one big family." Fallanita grinned. "A family that you can be a part of... once you prove your underwater foot skills this evening."

"Yeah, now we need to eat." Kalliden laughed.

"Miss Arthur, Mr. Lamorak," Lady Datura called out, stopping Adela in her tracks. Adela turned back and came face to face with the scarred one. "I do believe you and Mr. Lamorak have detention. Change and head to Dragon's Landing. If you're quick maybe you two can catch the end of lunch."

"Yes, ma'am," Jeremy replied next to her. She jumped, not having noticed him before he spoke.

"Lord Myrtus will meet you there," Lady Datura replied before turning to leave.

Adela sighed as she watched the cave clear out. She waved to Hector and Ryker, then squeezed all the water from her hair.

"Are you going to move?" Jeremy asked her.

Adela scowled at him before turning to walk out the door. She would have kept walking had she an inkling of where she was supposed to go. She turned back to find the dark-haired Jeremy grinning at her.

"Are you going to just stand there or are you going to show me where Dragon's Landing is?" Adela asked him.

"I thought you were taking the lead on that," he replied, "Guess I was wrong."

When he turned around, Adela burned holes into his back but didn't reply. Their detention was going to be hard enough. She wasn't sure what it was, seeing as she'd never been to detention. Nonetheless, they wouldn't have called it that if it were going to be fun. As they walked, Adela noticed all the younger students smiled and waved at her as though she was somewhat of a celebrity. It wasn't the same look she'd received before. They were all gazing upon her uniform. They were all starry-eyed by Natorbi, reminding her of Fallanita.

"We're here," Jeremy replied, opening the door for her.

"Thank you," she said, staring at him oddly before stepping in. Instantly she was hit by a blast of cold weather.

The very first thing Adela noticed was the stable-like smell. Then she was blindsided by a flame that blew right into her face. She let out a scream before an emerald barrier of light came out to protect her from the fire. Once stopped, she observed that they were in a stable of some sort that led into the forest.

However, instead of horses, there were baby dragons. She only knew they were baby dragons because of how large her grandfather was. The dragons here looked to be the size of small horses.

"Hasn't anyone ever told you not to simply walk into Dragon's Landing?" Lord Myrtus yelled at her.

"Sorry, sir," Adela whispered glaring at Jeremy out of the corner of her eye. He was smug.

"Do not be sorry. Be smarter," Lord Myrtus replied, handing both of them dark coverall suits to wear over their Natorbi uniforms. Adela, taking it from him, sighed and stepped into it. She still wasn't sure why they needed it and she didn't know if she wanted to wear it. Adela was glad the material was thick because the room was so cold.

"You know the drill. Feed them from a distance." Lord Myrtus instructed them as he also handed them pitchforks. Adela stared at the steel in her hand, confused, and looked over at Lord Myrtus.

"Feed them what?" Adela asked, and as soon as she did, regretted it.

Lord Myrtus smirked at her and walked over to what appeared to be a massive treasure chest. The moment he opened it, Adela stepped back, covering her nose with her hand. It was the most horrid smell she'd ever experienced. Similar to a soup of rotten meat and… she didn't even want to know what else.

"They eat that?" Adela groaned as she tried to stop herself from gagging.

"Go up and down the rows. Never place your face directly behind the pitchfork. When each one of them is fed, you may leave," Lord Myrtus said before leaving them alone. Adela could hear the dragons as they roared in excitement.

Jeremy didn't speak. He simply walked up to the trunk, skewered the meat, and lifted it up to take to the dragons. Adela watched the slime-covered meat drip onto ground as he walked. Swallowing the bile rising in her throat, she walked over, copying his actions. Adela lifted the pitchfork into the stable of a small white dragon. It lifted its scale-covered head toward the meat before letting out a bolt of fire and swallowing it whole.

"You know, I could've died when you let me in," Adela told him as she walked back to the trunk again.

Jeremy rolled his eyes. "You wouldn't have died. Been burned maybe, but not dead."

"Thank you so much for clearing that up," Adela said to him before impaling more of the rancid meat.

"You're welcome, seeing as this is your fault," he replied. The dragon he was feeding unleashed a rain of fire onto his pitchfork.

"My fault!" Adela yelled before taking a deep breath that caused her to cough and gag at the smell. Jeremy smirked at her before getting more meat. He looked completely unfazed by the smell.

"How are you doing that?" Adela asked, walking up to him.

He simply glared. "Doing what?"

"You do smell that, don't you?" Adela replied, lifting the meat for the next dragon down the row.

"Do you always have to talk?" Jeremy replied.

Adela stared at him for a moment. He was hiding something and she knew it.

She walked in front of him, glaring at him. "If I don't speak, then I'll only think about the smell. If I do that, I might faint again. If that happens you'll have to sit with me again, so you see, I have to keep talking."

Jeremy sighed before zipping down his coverall slightly and pulling out what looked like earplugs.

"This will help with the smell. You're lucky they are brand new," he replied, handing them to her. Adela grinned before taking them from him. She looked them over before placing them in her nostrils. The moment she did, she no longer smelled anything.

"Thank you…"

"Only did it to get you to stop talking. So please, stop talking." Jeremy sighed as he walked back to get more meat.

Adela glowered at him. She turned back to the baby dragon and whispered, "We have a word for guys like that on the other side of the mirror. *Douches*."

"We have that word here too," Jeremy replied, feeding the dragon next to her.

"Look, okay, I'm sorry. I'm sorry for all of it. Everything I said and everything I did to you. But for the next two months, you and I are going to be spending time here. So we should at least try not to hate each other," Adela said to him as she turned to finish her work.

Neither of them spoke; neither of them even acknowledged the other. Instead, they fed the dragons as quickly as they could. Once they were done, Adela wanted to leave quickly. As she took off the coveralls, Jeremy stopped in front of her.

"I do not hate you. I was angry that my sister called out to you instead of me and I didn't understand why. I still don't understand why." With that, he simply walked out.

By the time Adela got back to the hive and changed into her uniform, she'd wasted at least fifteen minutes. She was so hungry she could eat anything without bothering to ask what it was.

"How was Dragon's Landing?" Fallanita asked, grinning as Adela took a seat at the round table. She glared at the tiny girl while grabbing an apple.

"That bad, huh? How can you even eat after smelling that?" Tara asked beside her.

"Jeremy gave me nose plugs. I didn't take them out until I ran out of the room," Adela replied as she ate.

All three girls turned to her in shock. "Jeremy gave you something?"

"Yeah, nose plugs, that's what I said. Why are you guys looking at me like that?" Adela asked, and they began to look away.

Faye simply shrugged. "He doesn't seem like the giving type."

"I don't know. He did give her a kiss." Tara joked, causing Adela to groan.

She could try to explain, but it wouldn't help anything. Instead, she focused her attention on the theme of the dining hall. The underwater hall was gone, now replaced with a cloudy sky where birds and baby dragons much smaller than the ones she just fed flew about without a care.

The four round tables and the single row for teachers seemed to be resting on clouds. Above them was an orange-and-blue sky. Upon some of the clouds were small dragons. She watched as two small white dragons wrestled with each other until they fell off the cloud, causing them to break away. They circled around the tables, rising higher in the sky to a slightly larger green dragon resting upon a cloud. Adela grinned at the small dragon that flew in front of her head. He or she was a light rose color. It spun around, flapping its wings and returning to the sky. They all made her think of her grandfather.

"They are infant air dragons. All dragons are born white. But as they get older, their true colors begin to take over. It's similar to our light. Whatever color they are resembles their personality." Kalliden drew her attention. The more she thought about it, the harder it was for Adela to think of a time when she had seen a white dragon… well, other than her grandfather.

"My… ugh, my grandfather is a white dragon. But he didn't look like an infant to me," Adela recalled. It was still odd calling her grandfather a dragon.

"That's because he is one of the four great dragons. The Dragon Elders, they are called. They live in the land of the seven Fire Mountains. When a dragon maintains its white scales, then it has stronger abilities than all others. They are the only ones that can mentally speak with us," Tara replied. Kalliden turn to her, impressed.

"Look who's been studying with the Emerald Dens now." He laughed at her.

Tara smiled. "I promised to teach Ryker Natorbi, and he shared his knowledge."

"Yeah, good luck with that." Fallanita joked.

"Why do we have that stupid ring anyway?" Tara frowned, grabbing a piece of food from the table in front of her.

"It proves dictation and skill. If you can't make it past the ring, you can't make it during the game," Fallanita replied.

"Yes, yes. *Natorbi today. Natorbi tomorrow. Natorbi for life.* We know." Tara pouted and took a drink of her Cielieu juice. Faye laughed beside her.

"And never forget it," Kuper Endives replied from behind. They all turned to face the older teen.

"Is it time already?" Fallanita and Kalliden replied as they both jumped out of their chairs.

"Yep, no other classes made it through the ring for the Golden Hives. But the Red Diamonds just got two new potentials." He turned back to point to the Red Diamond table where two teens were being cheered on.

"Seriously." Kalliden sighed.

"Are they any good?" Fallanita frowned. She looked as though she wanted to fall through the clouds.

"They are amazing. Nothing in comparison to *the* Adela Arthur of the Golden Hives, though." Kuper smiled. "We have to play them in order to find out who makes it onto their team. Lord Figwort thinks it would be the best time to see what Adela can do. So are you up to it?"

"Of course she is! That's why she tried out," Fallanita replied before Adela could even open her mouth.

"Oh, we have to see this," Tara said, standing up. But it wasn't just her; it was almost every single Golden Hive around the table.

An older teen on the other side of the table stood up and yelled, "Natorbi game. Golden Hives versus the Red Diamonds."

Every last student began to go crazy, cheering loudly. Fallanita, Kuper, and Kalliden all cheered beside her, making Adela want to go over and smack the daylights out of the one who started the new mess she was in. They were immediately silenced as some Red Diamonds walked toward them. Students parted to allow him to come forward.

"That's Rye Brier. He is the captain of the Red Diamonds," Fallanita whispered to her.

"Rye." Kuper greeted him.

"Kuper," he replied.

They stared each other down before shaking hands. At that, the whole dining hall broke out into cheers.

"I hope you both are aware that you must have permission to start an official game," Lord Elderberry replied, walking through the path the students made for him, Lady Datura, and Lord Figwort. Lord Figwort and Lady Datura stood at his sides. Both wore surprised expressions on their faces.

"My Golden Hives are prepared for anything," Lord Figwort replied, taking a step beside Kuper.

"I do believe that was a challenge, Mr. Brier, don't you?" Lady Datura smirked, taking a stand beside the Red Diamonds.

"Well, then why are we all standing here?" Lord Elderberry asked, causing everyone to jump and cheer. It was madness.

"I just changed," Adela cried to herself.

CHAPTER THIRTEEN

CHILDREN OF LEGACY

Adela stood in the cave, once again dressed in her Natorbi uniform. She watched as every last student and teacher entered. From what she understood, the cave worked somewhat like the dining hall. They would be able to see everything on the sea floor, and she could see them as well. However, she wasn't sure if she wanted them to see her. She didn't know what to do. She had broken her mother's record on swimming to the bottom and getting through the ring. But she wasn't sure if she could actually play.

"Nervous?" Hector asked, causing her to jump.

"Nope," Adela replied, pulling her hair up into a ponytail.

"Good, because I think you are amazing," he said, causing Adela to stare at him, bug-eyed. "I mean at Natorbi. You are amazing at Natorbi. That's because it's in your blood and you're a really good swimmer. Plus…"

"Thanks, Hector, I'm glad you'll still be my friend even if I make a total fool of myself." Adela laughed.

He simply nodded. "Yeah, but I might hide my face."

"Adela!" Fallanita called from the edge of the water.

"I should let you go. Don't worry, you'll be great." He smiled before walking over to sit with the rest of the Emerald Dens.

Ryker stood up, yelling her name, causing Tara to smile as she joined him in standing. Faye grinned at her, waving like crazy.

"Nice fan base you have, seeing as how you've never played before," Jeremy stated as he walked up beside her.

"I thought we were being nice." Adela sighed, turning back to walk toward her group.

He caught up with her easily. "That was nice, and how about we make this game more interesting?"

"The whole castle is watching. It doesn't need to be any more interesting," she told him.

"Really? Not even the chance to get out of feeding the dragons that horrible-smelling meat?" He smirked.

Adela's golden eyes narrowed at him. "Define interesting."

"It's simple. If we win, you feed the dragons alone after

Lord Myrtus leaves. If you win, and you won't, but if you do, I will do it."

Adela hated the smirk on his face. He really thought he was going to win.

"Deal," Adela said, reaching out to shake on it.

"So sad you're going to disappoint your boyfriend," he replied, and Adela knew he was just trying to get her worked up.

"Don't worry. Scarlet will still love you when you lose." Adela smiled before walking over to the rest of the Golden Hives.

Fallanita pulled her into the small huddle at the edge of the cave.

"What was that?" she whispered.

"Nothing," Adela whispered back. "So what's the game plan?"

Kuper's face became deadly serious. "We are all changing positions. I will become a striker and you, Adela, you will be taking Kalliden's position but as a defender. Which means your goal is to make sure no one gets closer to any of Fallanita's goals."

"You will jump in last. Wait five seconds before jumping in after me. This is different from tryouts. There is no stopping at the bottom. The moment we dive in, the rings will be moving. Get through it as fast as possible and then get in front of

Fallanita," Theodore added, handing her the same small pill Lady Datura had given her before.

"Don't be nervous. It's in your blood." Elthin smiled, giving her a pat on the back and adding himself to the long line of people who kept reminding her how great her mother was.

Adela took a deep breath as they began to line up at the edge of the cave. Fallanita looked back from the front of the line and smiled at her, causing her to smile back. Adela had never understood why people said they had butterflies in their stomach—until today. Her hands were shaking and she could barely hear anything. Once again she found herself staring at the crowd of people and, sure enough, her fans were just as crazy as before. She had never seen Hector look so… wild. He was screaming at the top of his lungs. Shaking her head, Adela turned to meet the red eyes of Jeremy. He looked just as smug as always. She also realized he was at the end of the line. This meant they would be swimming against each other.

"Great," Adela muttered to herself.

"Players, on your mark," Lord Elderberry called out to them. "Get Ready… Go."

Just like that, Adela watched as Fallanita jumped into the water. Five seconds after that Kuper dove into the water, followed by Elthin, leaving only Theodore and herself. Theodore jumped in, and she immediately took two deep breaths before diving in. The moment she hit the water, the suit spread to cover her mouth just like it had during tryouts. She saw the red of Jeremy's suit as he passed her. She began to panic but only for a moment. Seeing the golden ring at the far bottom, Adela closed her eyes and just kept swimming. Her grandfather always told her swimming was like flying. She never understood that until now.

She opened her eyes only for a second to make sure she was on the same path to the ring. Jeremy was right beside her. Closing her eyes once again, she swam through the ring. She only opened her eyes upon hearing the crowd cheering once again. It was like everything had changed. The rings now formed a circle around both goaltenders. Four rings, one goaltender. She was one of the two defenders to stop them. At the sea floor there were four mermaids holding a large white pearl. Surrounding them seemed to be every last student from the castle. They all looked like they were truly underwater.

"Adela, get into position!" Kuper yelled, swimming right in front of her. Nodding, she swam over to where Theodore stood a few feet in front of Fallanita.

"Remember, only use your feet," Theodore told her, and again Adela simply nodded.

"Here we go, guys," Fallanita yelled as the mermaid threw the pearl upward, making Adela realize it wasn't a pearl, but a ball.

Kuper swam straight toward the ball the same time Ryker did. Both of them collided against the ball, causing it to go wild. It was moving like it had a mind of its own. The four strikers were trying to kick it in the direction of the rings. However, every time they kicked the ball, it came around like a boomerang. Elthin and Kuper were all but flipping backward and sideways in order to get the ball into the ring. Kuper flipped backward, kicking the ball at an odd angle, causing it to fly toward Elthin. He swam forward and kicked it so hard he spun in the water. Adela realized the ball went in the opposite direction it was kicked. It also became faster each time. It was like Kuper knew where it was going and had already gotten there, kicking it into the Emerald ring.

Hearing what sounded like chimes, Adela turned back to see a golden one over their goal. However, there was no time to cheer. The ball was coming right at them with Jeremy kicking as hard as he possibly could. The ball flew above her head and everything seemed to just click into place. Adela swam up and kicked left, sending the ball spinning right. But Jeremy stopped it, kicking it straight past her head. It looked as though it was going to enter the golden ring until Fallanita threw her body in its path to block it. At the last moment, it bent left and went into the red ring. Just like that she watched as a red four appeared over his goal.

Jeremy swam right up into her face. "Good thing I gave you those plugs. You're going to need them."

Even though Adela couldn't see his mouth, she knew he was grinning.

"Sorry, guys," Fallanita yelled out to them.

"No, it was my fault," Adela called.

"I don't care whose fault it is. Just get into the game," Kuper yelled at them.

When the ball came back into play, Adela never let her eyes wander from it. That was difficult at first because of how fast it moved, but pretty soon she was starting to understand it and how the Red Diamonds were always in the right place at the right time. It was like poker. They all had poker faces, even Jeremy. When he was going right, his eyebrow twitched. When he was going left, he closed his eyes for a spilt second. By observing them, she knew where they and the ball were going before they got there.

When Jeremy squinted, she took off swimming into position faster than Rye could have gotten there and kicked it toward Elthin.

"Adela, switch with me," Kuper yelled at her.

"What?"

"Go!" he yelled again.

Not wanting to waste any more time, Adela swam to where Elthin was going as well. She had figured out his tell.

When he went left, he would clutch his fist; right, he would stretch out his fingers. He did this over and over again with each kick, making it easier for Adela to realize where he was going. However, Rye kicked the ball away from him, sending it downward. Jeremy and Adela locked eyes for a split moment before they both dove to the sea floor. She allowed him to reach it first and watched as his eyebrows twitched. The moment he kicked, Adela stole the momentum from the speed, flipping forward and kicking the ball straight into the golden ring. The moment it went through, Adela wanted to scream at the top of her lungs. It was such a great feeling.

"Adela!" her team yelled in celebration as a number three appeared over their goal. Smiling, she swam over to Jeremy before realizing she didn't have anything witty to say.

"Ha!" was all she could get out before she prepared for the next play.

"It's on," he replied.

"Like Donkey Kong," Adela told him, only to have him stare at her oddly. Once again she realized no one else understood her other-side-of-the-mirror humor.

When the ball came into play, it flew right by her head, and she didn't even move. It wasn't that the ball was going too fast. She knew Rye's kick would send the ball that way. However, she couldn't move. It was like she was frozen and suddenly someone was tearing her apart. She couldn't even speak.

"Adela," Jeremy yelled, appearing right in her line of view. That was the last thing she saw before everything changed.

One moment she was underwater playing Natorbi; the next she found herself in the middle of what looked to be a fog-covered maze. Backing up slowly, her back ran into a large hooded statue. It was almost like the ones she'd noticed in the castle. The one behind her, however, was at least a few hundred years older and was cracked everywhere.

"My prince," a soft snake-like voice hissed slowly.

Stepping away from the statue, Adela tried to hold back her scream. Instead, she stood completely still. There, no less than a foot away from her, were dark ghost skeletons draped in tattered cloaks. They weren't the only ones there. There was the woman. This woman with pure black eyes and pale skin reminded her of the woman who'd reached out for her in the school bathroom. They looked like they were speaking to her. Hearing a footstep beside her, Adela gasped.

Prince Delapeur was somewhat tiredly using his Chimera to stand upright. It was the beast that had taken Wilhelmina's life. His blond hair was now almost gray and his body looked tired and frail.

"I did not and I shall not stop until I have the power that is rightfully mine," he hissed, walking around her. It was like he smelled the air, and when he sniffed right next to her face, Adela bit her lips to keep from making a sound.

"My prince, the Lamorak girl's power takes time…"

"I do not have time!" he yelled. "Adela Arthur has returned. Do you not understand? I must have her light and then the world is mine."

One by one, Adela noticed what looked to be normal Volsin coming out of the maze and walking toward him. Each one had odd tattoo marks on their faces and each was dressed incredibly nice.

"My prince, we are close to figuring out the way to the castle," said a man with long silver hair beneath a top hat, bowing to him.

Adela watched in shock as Prince Delapeur all but flew toward the man and grabbed him by the neck. His hat fell to the ground, and he brought the man's face closer to his own. He hissed out what seemed to be smoke onto the man's face before dropping him. Adela bit down tighter to keep from crying out as the man screamed in agony, rolling around on the grass. Prince Delapeur walked over to another middle-aged man who bowed down low to him.

"I do not want close. I want now," he hissed out before pulling the light from the man's chest. Once again, Adela watched the light go out in the man's golden eyes. Prince Delapeur sniffed the air once more before turning back to her.

Adela thought for sure he could see her. However, he walked past her once again.

"You can hear me. I know you are able to. I feel the stench of your fear rolling off you in waves. It's just a matter of time, little Arthur. I am coming for you and there is no place for you to hide. Soon I will have your mind and then your light. Little Arthur. Little Arthur..."

His howls were the only sounds she heard before she gasped and leapt out of bed, screaming.

"Adela, you are safe," Jeremy called out to her. However, she couldn't stop shaking. She just wanted to stop shaking.

"You're safe," Jeremy told her again as he pulled her into a hug. Adela gripped him so tightly Jeremy had to shift so she wouldn't break his ribs.

"Miss Arthur, are you all right?" Lady Hellebore asked her. She realized she was no longer underwater, but in the infirmary with all the lords and ladies watching her.

"No, she is not all right," Jeremy snapped when they broke away. Adela did make sure to hold on to his hand. She wasn't sure why. She just felt that maybe, just maybe, if she were holding on to something or someone she would be safer.

"Mr. Lamorak, you have done a great job. But maybe you should go get some rest," Lady Fern said softly, causing Adela to squeeze his hand.

"I'm not going," Jeremy replied as he returned her squeeze.

Lord Elderberry came forward and glanced at her. He seemed like he was reading something on her face, not just staring. Adela couldn't bring herself to look into his red and blue eyes.

"What did he say, Adela?" Lord Elderberry asked her.

Lady Hellebore stepped beside him. "What did who say?"

"Miss Arthur, what did he say to you?" Lord Elderberry asked once again.

She tried to speak, but she couldn't find the words. It was like there was something stuck in her throat. Adela simply lay back and looked at the ceiling.

"You cannot possibly mean...," Lord Myrtus replied, stepping forward.

"Yes, Prince Delapeur. He called your mind. Is that not correct, Miss Arthur?" Lord Elderberry said to her.

Adela finally tore her eyes away from the ceiling to meet his gaze, but she still couldn't speak. Shifting her head to Jeremy, she stared into his red eyes before lifting their hands. Closing her eyes, she forced herself to replay everything she had seen, so he could see it too. But she could only last a few moments in those thoughts before she pulled her hand away. Sitting up quickly, Adela tried to control her breathing.

"Yes, she saw him," Jeremy muttered through clenched teeth. "He did not see her. He only knew she was there and stated he was coming for… that he was coming."

Lord Elderberry nodded. "Lady Fern, can you please take over Lord Aspen's classes next semester?"

Lady Fern stared wide-eyed before nodding. "Yes, I shall let him know."

"Get some rest, Miss Arthur. You and Mr. Lamorak may stay here, but do know that one of us shall come back to check on you periodically," Lord Elderberry told them before walking out.

Lady Hellebore was the only one who stayed back. The serious-faced woman took a seat on the bed, pulling Adela's hand into her own.

"I have seen your motivation, dedication, passion, and compassion, Adela Arthur. It is the reason you are so strong. He will try to steal it from you because he could never achieve that strength on his own," she said before turning to Jeremy.

"I am fine, Lady Hellebore," he said to her.

"I have no doubt of that," she replied. "I am, however, not a fan of you two alone. Especially considering the fact that both of you cannot go a moment without warfare."

"Apparently, we called a truce," he said seriously before turning back to Adela. Lady Hellebore did the same.

"Very well, then, but if there is so much as a shimmer of light, I'll make sure you both beg to be in Dragon's Landing again," she replied before taking her leave.

"Golden Hives…" Jeremy chuckled to himself when the door closed.

Adela turned to him but said nothing. She didn't want to talk. She didn't want to do anything but hide or maybe crawl into a ball. Just when things were starting to feel better, like she could be happy, he came back. She just wanted this to be over. She wanted to wake up in her old room with her old bed and eat her old cereal with the tiger on the front. If she could she would have dreamed about it. However, every time she tried to close her eyes, his words filled her mind.

"You do know you're going to have to speak soon," Jeremy replied. But Adela tried to pretend she couldn't hear him. She wasn't sure if she could speak right now even if she wanted to. Adela heard him sigh before she felt him rip the sheets from the bed.

"What are you doing?" Adela yelled, sitting up in order to grab the sheet back.

Jeremy smirked. "She speaks!"

"Seriously, Jeremy, what are you doing?"

He took her hand, pulling her off the bed before taking the sheet and wrapping it around her. Adela stared at him, confused.

"Jeremy—" she started to say he as dragged her to the door.

He glanced out to make sure the coast was clear. "Just trust me."

"We aren't allowed to just wander the castle," Adela whispered to him.

Jeremy stopped, turning back to stare her in the eyes. "Adela, trust me."

Sighing, Adela nodded. This was such a bad idea and she knew it. The last thing she wanted was to cause any more problems. But there she was, running through the dimly lit hall with Jeremy of all people. In her mind all she could think of was Lord Elderberry walking into the infirmary and finding them both missing. He was going to yell at them again and then Lady Hellebore would glare at them while Lady Datura would do something horrible. She could already feel her red eyes on her, wishing she were dead. The farther they ran up the stairs, the crazier Adela's thoughts became. She couldn't help it, though. Everywhere, in every shadow, and with every blink all she could see was Prince Delapeur. He was her new boogeyman, and she hated how it made her feel.

Jeremy stopped, turning back to her. "Ready?"

"No," Adela replied.

Rolling his eyes, he opened the door, and Adela took in the blast of cold air. It was shocking but comforting all the same.

Wrapping the sheets around herself even more, Adela walked out onto the tower. She could see the whole castle along with the forest. Reaching out, she couldn't help but smile at the snowflakes that fell onto her fingers.

"It looks like we are going to have a white Christmas," Jeremy whispered before sitting on the ledge.

"Christmas? When did it become Christmas?" *How has so much time already passed?*

"I am not sure how to answer that, but everyone has already started to go home," Jeremy replied, looking over at the treetops.

Adela stopped for a moment, looking at the school uniform she wore. The last thing she remembered was being underwater.

"How long was I…?"

"Three days. You woke up at times but only for a moment. It used to happen to the people my sister tried to get in the minds of. The better he gets, the less harm is done… or more if he chooses," Jeremy whispered.

Adela smirked. "Is that your way of making me feel better?"

"No. If I were going to make you feel better, I would tell you Lord Aspen is very good with mind defense. That's why Lord Elderberry wants Lady Fern to take over his classes next semester so he can teach you."

"Yep, that definitely made me feel better." Adela sighed before taking a seat on the ledge next to him.

"Fine, what will make you feel better?" he questioned.

Adela stared at the dark-haired teen in front of her. "Why do you care?"

"Never mind then, bossy," he replied, looking over at the trees again.

"Tell me what Christmas is like here?" Adela whispered as she watched the world beyond the castle become blanketed with snow. It was like being inside a snow globe.

"I don't know and I truthfully don't want to think about it. Christmas was Esthella's thing, not mine," he replied.

She could understand that. In fact, it was almost scary how much she understood that pain. Walking around watching families hug and sing carols with each other was one of the reasons she stayed home on Christmas. She even made sure they had enough movies and books to avoid the Hallmark moments.

"So what happens to everyone who doesn't leave for Christmas?" Adela asked him.

"We stay here and the lords and ladies give us gifts during breakfast." He sighed. Jeremy didn't seem to like it either.

"So are we friends now?" Adela asked him.

He smiled and it wasn't one of his half-smirk, half-grimace expressions. Jeremy was actually smiling like a normal teenager. Adela wasn't sure if she liked it or was worried about it.

"What?" she asked.

"We will after you finish the rest of Dragon's Landing."

"But…"

"No buts. We won the Natorbi game and you were supposed to take my spot. But since you conveniently fainted again…"

"I did not faint!" Adela yelled. "My mind was hijacked."

Jeremy rolled his eyes. "Yell any louder and you will not only wake up the whole castle but also the Stygian forest."

"I didn't faint again." Adela frowned.

"If you say so. I still can't believe we destroyed Avalon's Field, though." He laughed, forming a small orb of light in his hands.

"Won't it grow back?" She hadn't been back to that room since their fight.

"Avalon's Field is where the castle was first built by our families, the Arthurs and Lamoraks. Lord Ethelwolf goes into more details of it in his class. When the first Volsin came through the mirror, they settled in Avalon and as more of us were born, the need for a school became greater. The first Elderberry asked the Arthurs and Lamoraks to help form a school that would be strong enough for protection. When they did, they kept part of the field so we could always remember where we started. No one else can use light there except for us."

"And we destroyed it...," Adela groaned. "On a scale of one to ten, how badly do you think we are screwing up our families' legacies?"

Jeremy actually looked shocked for a moment before smiling again. "They shouldn't have left such big legacies. I would have been proud to just be another—"

"Face in the crowd." Adela finished for him, reaching over to take the light from his hand and changing it to gold.

"Yeah, another face in the crowd," he replied as the light shifted colors.

"Has he tried to get into your mind?" Adela whispered, but she couldn't bring herself to look into his eyes.

"Yes, I feel it sometimes. But I spent most of my life protecting myself from a nosey sister. He won't be able to, and now that you're here I am second on his list. Thank you, Arthurs, for being just *slightly* more powerful." Jeremy joked, even though it wasn't as funny as he hoped it would be.

Adela sighed. "Someone has to stop him. I just don't think it can be me. When I was in that maze..."

"Adela, I know. I saw. You don't have to say it and no one is asking you to stop him. I plan on doing that by myself." Jeremy interrupted her with a smile on his smug face, but Adela knew he was serious. In her mind all she could see was him on top of a snow-covered mountain, watching his sister die. If Jeremy was given a chance, she knew he would do anything to avenge Esthella and his family. The problem was she wasn't sure, from what she saw of Prince Delapeur, if anyone was capable.

Chapter Fourteen

Unexpected Presents Are The Best Kind

The moment Adela stepped into the room, she felt an uncanny wave of déjà vu shower over her. She knew she wasn't late. Her uniform was fine, she was sure there wasn't anything on her face or hair, yet everyone was staring at her. It wasn't the same stares she'd gotten when she first came to the castle. No, it was the same stare that she got on her birthday after she freaked out in the bathroom. The type of stare that made her feel like the word *freak* was tattooed on her forehead. Keeping her head low, she walked as quickly as she could to the back of Lord Figwort's classroom.

"Morning—"

"How bad?" Adela cut him off.

Hector frowned. "It doesn't matter what anyone says. They're just a little bit spooked, but once everyone comes back from Christmas break, it will be old news."

Adela just stared blankly at him for a moment before groaning. "Is it really that bad?"

Usually, he just told her honestly and that's how she knew everything would be okay. But if he couldn't even do that, then it meant she really didn't want to hear what people were saying about her encounter with Prince Delapeur. She knew they knew. Fallanita had asked her bluntly about it and so had Tara.

"No, it isn't." He was lying and she knew it, but she wouldn't bring it up anymore. She opened her book and a shrill scream erupted, causing her to squeal in return. She snapped it shut. *Don't look up, don't look up,* she told herself, but she did anyway. Adela found everyone staring at her, again.

"You grabbed the wrong book." Hector smirked beside her.

"Yeah, I realize that." She glared at him. He was looking at her oddly. "What?" He shook his head, sliding his book to the middle to share with her.

"Hector, what?" she whispered, pretending to look for the right page.

"I've just missed you," he finally whispered.

"We see each other every day." How could he miss her

when she was in every class with him and ninety percent of the time they always sat together?

He shrugged before finally meeting her eyes. "It's different now from back home… if it can be called home, I guess. It was kind of just you and me facing the big bad world of high school. Now there's all of this stuff and you're an Arthur…"

"Oh, not you too, Hector. I've always been Adela Arthur. You know, the girl who can't do physics to save her life and who hates spiders, frogs, and insects—"

"And snakes," he added.

"Yes, and snakes. Just because my family name is big here doesn't mean I'm any different from who I've always been. When everyone leaves for Christmas, I'll remind you of that by beating you in a snowball fight," she replied as he rolled his eyes at her.

"Don't you think we're too old for a snowball fight?"

Adela pretended to be hurt. "Hector Pelleas, you bite your tongue. One is never too old to indulge in the sport of throwing snow."

"Just because you say it with an accent doesn't make it true." He laughed at her.

"Just because you're afraid of losing doesn't mean we're too old to play," she reminded him, trying hard not to laugh.

"That's because you cheat," he whispered loudly.

"You have gone too far, sir. Have you no sense of decency?" Adela gasped out.

Hector straightened his back. "I have not gone far enough, my lady." They stared at each other for a moment before breaking out into a fit of laughter.

"And she is supposed to be an Arthur. She looks more like a Dingle Bird. A very annoying Dingle Bird." Scarlet smirked and a few other Red Diamonds laughed along with her.

"Hector, are the Daneworts known for anything?" Adela turned back, making sure her voice was loud enough.

"No, I don't think so," he replied, unsure why she asked.

Turning her head back to Scarlet, Adela just smiled. "I guess it's easier for you to wonder about my family when yours isn't known for anything and you need to be the center of attention."

There were a few gasps and a lot of wide eyes in the room when Scarlet stood up in rage.

"First, both my parents own almost half of Cielieu City, and second, what family? Last time I checked, Prin—*he* had wiped out your whole family, and everyone knows he is coming for you next. You were stupid for coming back here. No one in their right mind would want to be an Arthur. Especially since we all know he will get into your head again and steal your light the moment he gets a chance," she yelled, causing every last person to turn toward Adela once again.

Luckily for her, Lord Figwort had, at that exact moment, chosen to walk in. The older man was completely oblivious to what had transpired only a second earlier, and no one wanted to be the one to inform him. Scarlet simply sat down and everyone pretended to pay attention to what Lord Figwort was saying.

"Are you all right?" Hector whispered to her.

"Yes. What's a Dingle Bird?" she whispered back to him.

Hector gave her an odd look before replying. "Imagine a baby hyena with wings."

She nodded and smiled, even though she didn't want to. Opening the book—the correct book—Adela began sculpting the images in the book as Lord Figwort instructed.

Light Sculpting really wasn't that difficult. It just took a lot of concentration, which Adela was thankful for. If everyone was concentrating on forming objects with their light, they couldn't pay attention to her. She only wished she could concentrate more on her light and not Scarlet's words. They took her back to that maze. She'd just learned how to close her eyes again without panicking.

The moment class was over, Adela grabbed her things and left so quickly it almost looked like she flew. She stopped for no one and had no idea where she was going. She could have sworn she saw Fallanita out of the corner of her eye, trying to get her attention. Yet her feet seemed to have a mind of their own. For hours she wandered the castle, not even bothering to stop. Every time she did, she watched parents coming for their kids, kissing and hugging. It was nice at first. She stood in the tower overlooking the castle and smiled as the gates opened for them. Seeing people care for each other, love each other—it was refreshing after everything she'd seen in the last few months.

But after a while, watching became painful. It almost burned her eyes. She was jealous, so very jealous of all of them. She was jealous of the little girl who was so excited to see her parents she tripped in the snow and her father had to pick her up. She was jealous of the teen who tried to pretend he was too cool to hug his mom but smiled when she pulled him into one. Then there was Scarlet. Even from the tower Adela could see she got her looks from her father. He was a tall, broad-shouldered man who seemed to walk with a limp. But that wasn't what Adela noticed. It was his eyes, his very bright blue eyes. He seemed to hold all the love in the world for his daughter in his eyes. That's how Adela knew Scarlet was right. Why in the world would she want to be an Arthur when Scarlet could be a Danewort and have a father like that?

Adela stayed in the tower until the wind was so cold her eyelashes and lips began to frost over. The halls were eerily quiet as she began her trip back to the hive. The whole place was empty, but she knew she wasn't completely alone. She still had Hector, Fallanita, and Jeremy… Well, she kind of had Jeremy. If she knew him the way she thought she did, then he would probably try to hide out from everything.

The moment she got into the hive, she crawled into her bed and pulled out her parents' yearbook. It was all she had, but it was better than nothing, and she was grateful for it. The tears that dripped onto the pages were happy tears because she was finally able to watch her parents.

She had her eyes closed only for what felt like few moments when she heard someone screaming her name.

"Adela?"

Maybe she'll go away if I don't move, Adela thought to herself as she held her pillow just a little bit tighter.

"Adela?"

She's not here at the moment. Can I take a message? she replied in her mind.

"Adela, help me please!"

Jumping out of bed, Adela turned to the small girl inches from her bed. Fallanita was smiling so hard it looked like her face was going to crack. "What! What's going on?" she asked, panicking.

"Merry Christmas!" Fallanita replied.

Adela groaned before lying back down. "I don't celebrate that holiday."

"How could you not? Never mind. Can you? Please, you have presents and I don't want to open them alone. It reminds me that I am not home like everyone else, drinking warm Jumble cider in front of a fire. But since you're basically my sister now…"

"Okay. Okay, you've convinced me." Adela laughed, getting out of bed slowly.

"Hurry!"

"I am coming. I'm coming," Adela replied, this time sliding out of bed.

The entire time Adela was getting ready, she could feel Fallanita's stare burning a hole in her back. It was funny how excited she was. She even wore a golden Christmas hat. Adela was expecting her to break into carols next. As she moved around, she noticed their whole dorm room was covered in golden Christmas decorations. It was breathtaking to see. Her grandfather had always decorated, but nothing like this.

"Are you ready yet?" Fallanita sighed.

Adela rolled her eyes before walking to the balcony. "Yes, Fallanita. I'm ready."

"Finally!" She blurted out.

On the way down Adela noticed that not only had her room been decorated, but so had the hive. It was like a Christmas shop had exploded and things were just flung everywhere. But what made it so shocking was the massive Christmas tree that extended all the way to the top. Adela would have questioned how they'd gotten the tree in there, but she remembered that she was currently flying on a disc of light and about to go to a magical dining hall where the scenery changed daily. It had taken a lot of effort to stop questioning the things she once thought were impossible.

When Adela and Fallanita walked out of the hive, Hector was already waiting for them both. He seemed nervous for some odd reason.

"M-morning," he stuttered.

"What's wrong with you?" Adela asked him carefully.

"Nothing," he said a little too quickly. She stared at him for a moment and glanced at Fallanita, who just shrugged, pretending she didn't know anything.

"Okay, if you say so," she muttered as they walked in silence.

Once again it was eerie walking through the castle with so many people gone. She could even hear their feet echo as they moved. It was about to drive Adela crazy when finally she heard laughter and feet as they ran past them and toward the dining hall.

"Fallanita, come on!" a few of the younger kids in white cloaks yelled.

"Finally, the Christmas spirit!" She joked before running after them.

Adela couldn't help but smile at her. Fallanita was so tiny

that if weren't for her cloak, you would have thought she was the same age as they were.

"Is it just me or does she look like them?" Hector joked.

"I was just thinking that." Adela laughed before entering the dining hall.

The moment Adela stepped inside, she let out a gasp, blinking repeatedly as her eyes adjusted to all the colors. If she thought the hive was an explosion of a Christmas store, then the dining hall had to be the explosion of the North Pole. Gone were the four round tables, and in their places were four Christmas trees, all representing each light. They seemed to be in some sort of ballroom with chandeliers of different-colored flames. In the center of the room was now only one large round table where everyone sat together, whether they were Golden Hive, Red Diamond, Sapphire Fall, or Emerald Den. Underneath each tree seemed to be enough presents for everyone on the naughty and nice lists—plus elves.

"Geez...," Hector whispered.

"I know." Adela laughed while walking over to her seat. Hector sat by her side. Just then Fallanita ran up to Adela with a mug of steaming gold liquid. After staring at it for a moment, Adela took it from her small hands.

"Nothing's going to happen to my voice, will it?" Adela asked. She turned to face Hector, who just grinned at her.

"Nope," they said at the same time, which didn't help at all.

"Can I know what it is?" Adela asked them.

They looked at each other before Fallanita spoke. "Jumble cider."

"Is it…?"

"Just drink it." Hector laughed.

Sighing, she took a small sip before looking back up to their grinning faces.

"It's the best thing you've ever tasted, right?" Hector said. She didn't want to give them the satisfaction of admitting it was really amazing.

"It's okay," Adela muttered behind the mug.

"She loves it. I see it in her eyes," Fallanita replied, plopping on the seat.

"My eyes say nothing," she replied, taking another sip.

Before any of them could speak, the presents that were once under the tree suddenly began parachuting from the sky, causing everyone to break out into cheers. Adela waited patiently for the gift to land in her hand. When it did, she wasn't sure if she wanted to open it. She wasn't a gift person, especially when she couldn't thank the person who gave it to her. Adela looked forward, trying to meet the eyes of the lords and ladies who still sat at a separate table. Lord Elderberry was the only one who met her gaze. He winked his red eye at her before returning his gaze to the other students.

She wasn't sure what she expected to see when she opened the tiny golden package. She thought nothing could really surprise her anymore. It could be a talking frog for all she knew. However, when she pulled out the small vial, she was completely confused. It looked like ground white powder, and it glistened whenever the light hit it. The moment she lifted the lid, a puff of smoke came out as though it were a chimney.

"It's a dragon's tooth," Hector told her as he stared at it.

Adela stared at the vial. "This is a dragon's tooth?"

"When baby dragons lose their teeth, you can make them into powder and use it to heal any type of injury," Fallanita replied, taking the vial from her to look at it more closely before handing it back to her.

"I'm not that much of a klutz." Adela joked.

Hector grinned. "You're going to jinx yourself. I can feel it."

"Adela, you have another one." Fallanita interrupted, handing her another small gift, this time with a letter attached to it. Taking the letter off the gift, she started at it oddly before reading.

"Your father found comfort in this. Maybe you shall as well."

She stared at the letter until the ink began to fade from the parachute. Knowing it had something to do with her father,

Adela ripped through the wrapping quickly. It gave way, revealing a small pocket watch that was no longer ticking. Lifting it by its gold chain, she gazed at it, confused.

"A pocket watch?" Hector asked. "What does it do?"

"I'm not sure, but the note said it was my dad's," she whispered.

"There is an inscription on the back." Fallanita pointed to it. Flipping it over, Adela ran her thumb over the engravings.

"Time brings all that is…," Adela read.

"Time brings all that is what?" Hector asked.

Adela lifted it for him to see "That's it. It just says *Time brings all that is*. Does that mean anything, Fallanita?"

"Not that I can think of," she replied, lifting the necklace she'd gotten before placing it on her neck.

Adela shrugged before glancing back at Hector. "What did you get?"

"Some new books about the history of Cielieu. These are the ones Ryker and I have been trying to find forever. We checked the library, but all of them were gone. These actually have live pictures and voices," he said, unsurprisingly excited.

Adela glanced over to Fallanita who was trying not to laugh. Hector tore his gaze from the books to stare at them before shifting uncomfortably.

"I also got an emerald ring. It is very cool and definitely not nerdy," he added, showing off the new ring in front him.

Adela grinned. "Yeah, sure, that's cool, but I liked the book too."

"Liar." Fallanita coughed, causing Adela to kick her.

Hector rolled his eyes. "Fine. I like books for Christmas, so sue me."

"I didn't say anything." Adela smiled before standing up.

"Where are you going?" Hector asked her.

"Bathroom. I'll be right back," she replied, grabbing her watch and dragon powder and stuffing it in her pocket before she forgot it.

"Hurry back or I am drinking your Jumble cider," Fallanita yelled.

Adela almost wanted to go back and take her mug but thought better of it as she walked out the door. She couldn't help but smile when she noticed some of the younger kids flying airplanes down the hall. They all looked so happy… until one of the lords demanded they clear the halls. She was just about to enter the bathroom when she noticed Jeremy sneaking into Dragon's Landing. He checked backward twice before finally going. It took only a second for Adela to decide to follow. She walked as quickly and softly as possible until she reached the door at the end of the hall. Her hand hovered over the door handle, unsure of what she was going to walk in on.

"Hello?" Adela called when she tiptoed in. The stables

were as cold as ever, but she couldn't see anyone. Instead, she heard a painfully loud whine before an ear-scathing cry.

"Jeremy!" Adela now yelled as she ran toward the noise.

He jumped out of one of the stables. "Adela, what are you doing here?"

"I could ask you the same thing," Adela retorted as she tried to calm her panicking heart. She thought he was hurt or something.

Before he could reply, another loud cry rang through the air. He rushed back into the stable and fell to his knees next to a large dragon. Jeremy petted its side, slowly running his hand over each of its black scales. It looked like it was dying. It struggled with each breath it took and its eyes began to close.

"What's going on?" Adela panicked and kneeled next to him.

Jeremy shifted his red eyes to her. "Do you know how to help a dragon give birth?"

"You're joking," Adela replied, but Jeremy just shook his head. "How is this possible? I thought they weren't full-grown dragons! We have to call somebody. Jeremy, do you even—"

"Adela, please stop panicking," he demanded.

"I'm way beyond panicking! We're in a stall with a pregnant dragon," she snapped before taking a deep breath.

Jeremy sighed. "Are you done? Because I need help."

"What do I need to do?" This was crazy, but she couldn't just leave.

He looked around the stable for a moment before pointing to a large padded blanket hanging on the side of the stall.

"Hand me that and then lay her head on your lap," he told her.

Adela stared at him, wide-eyed. *Did he just say what I thought he said?* she thought.

"Hurry!" he yelled, forcing her to move again. Tossing him the blanket, she rushed to the head of the dragon, unsure of how she was supposed to support that much weight on her lap. But as the female dragon let out another cry, she lifted as much of the mother dragon's head as she could onto her lap.

"I thought dragons laid eggs," Adela said, trying to calm herself down again.

"Only fire dragons lay eggs. Air and water dragons don't." That made as much sense as anything else.

"Jeremy, do you even know what you're doing?" Adela asked him as he placed the towel on the dragon's stomach, right under its wing.

"Not really. All I know is that we are just supposed to make them as comfortable as possible," he replied, petting her again. There was no escaping it now.

"We're going to be in so much trouble," Adela whispered as she petted her scales.

"You can leave," he told her seriously, but before she could speak, the dragon below them began to screech loudly, flapping its wings so wildly it could have caused a small tornado.

Dust along with tiny rocks on the stable floor pelted her as the cries increased. Adela wanted to scream along with her before finally everything just stilled—the wind, the screeches, and the dust all stopped at once. But just like that there was a small cry that broke the silence.

"What is going on here?" Both teens turned to find Lord Myrtus, whose eyes widened at the sight of the small white dragon in Jeremy's arms.

"Oh my!" Lady Fern gasped, running in only seconds after Lord Myrtus. "Lord Myrtus, you take the dragon into the snow before it burns Jeremy's poor arms," she directed.

Lord Myrtus's green eyes narrowed as he took the baby dragon from Jeremy's arms. "You should have called. This could have been very dangerous. But good job to the both of you."

"Thank you, sir," Jeremy replied while Adela nodded.

She didn't do anything. It was all Jeremy.

"You two, please go get cleaned up," Lady Fern stated as she helped them from the ground. "Oh, and Mr. Lamorak?" she called before they could make their escape.

"Yes, Lady Fern."

She simply smiled. "A dragon birth on your birthday is a sign of luck."

He nodded before leaving quickly. They weren't that dirty, but if there was any chance to get out of trouble, they were going to take it. By the time they made it outside, there was already a group of nosey students. Among them was Hector, who seemed to be glaring at Jeremy.

"What happened to being right back?" Hector tried to joke when Adela reached him.

"Somehow I ended up helping a dragon give birth." She laughed before turning back to Jeremy, who was wiping dirt off his uniform.

"You were amazing—a little crazy, but amazing." Adela laughed at him.

"More crazy," Hector muttered under his breath.

Adela and Jeremy turned to him before he spoke again. "Thanks, I think."

"So were you going to tell anyone it was your birthday?" Adela asked him, not forgetting Lady Fern's words.

"It's Christmas. I didn't want to spend my seventeenth birthday surrounded by decorated trees and overzealous kids who are also getting presents." He sighed.

Adela thought about it for a moment before frowning. "Yeah, I see your point."

"It's not bad. It's just your outlook," Hector muttered again.

Jeremy glared at him, and Adela wondered where all the hostility came from. They were ready to kill each other and as far as she knew, they'd only spoken to each other this once. If it weren't for the fact that they were all going to the same place, she knew they would separate. As she turned the corner beside the stairs, Jeremy pulled her back.

"What…?"

"Shh." He hushed her.

"What…?"

"Stop talking, look," Jeremy hissed, glaring at Hector before pointing around the corner.

Adela glanced back, as well as Hector, only to see Faye staring into the flame of one of the statues.

"It's just Faye…," Hector whispered.

"Thank you, genius. Only problem is Faye left for the holidays. Listen to what she is saying," Jeremy hissed.

At first Adela couldn't hear anything, but she could see the tiny girl speaking quickly as though she were in a trance. It was haunting, and if it weren't for Jeremy's hold on her arm, she would have run to her.

"Adela has the clock… You said… You promised," Faye whispered into the green flame before letting out a small whimper of pain, holding her head.

"Let go of me," Adela hissed at him.

"Adela, wait!" Hector said quickly. She broke away from him, running toward the statue, only to find Faye missing.

"Where did she go?" Adela yelled, glancing around the hall.

"Better question is why was she talking to Prince Delapeur?" Jeremy asked her.

Adela froze before glaring at him. "You don't know that. She could have been… Look, we don't know what she was doing."

"Adela, she talked about the clock. How would she know about if she wasn't even at the dining hall?" Hector questioned.

"So what, Hector? It's just a pocket watch and she could have been talking about anything. Before jumping to conclusions, can we talk about whom you're assuming she spoke with—the prince of darkness? It's sweet little Faye, and until we know what we heard, we don't talk about it, okay?" she yelled at both of them. Jeremy and Hector glanced at each other but didn't speak. Taking a step forward, she glared at them both. "I am serious, guys. Do not bring it up ever again."

"Fine," Hector muttered.

"I don't trust her," Jeremy hissed.

It only made Adela's blood begin to boil. "You don't even know her!"

"Do you?" he asked before walking away.

Do I? Did I really know Faye? The moment the thought

entered her mind, she tried to push it out. But even she couldn't deny the goose bumps on the back of her neck.

Chapter Fifteen

Nothing But A Bunch Of Time Skippers

"Anything?" Hector asked, causing Adela to jump out of her chair.

It took her a second to stop yawning before she could speak again. "Sorry, what?"

"Have you learned anything new on the object?" he whispered, dropping even more books on the table before taking a seat across from her.

"Not even a little bit," she muttered. Sighing, she shook her head, flipping through pages upon pages of useless information before her. Christmas was a little over ten weeks ago and with each passing day, Faye was acting more and more oddly. The only problem was that the only ones who could tell were Hector, Jeremy, and Adela. Small things, which under any other circumstances wouldn't have been seen as so odd, tipped them off. It made sense that Faye was always tired and had headaches. All the tenth years were stressed about the upcoming finals. That would be the logical conclusion, except for the fact that they'd seen her talking to the castle flames that one time. Truthfully, if it weren't for the fact that Hector and Jeremy were there as well, Adela would have thought her mind had played tricks on her.

Then there was the object, which was the worst code name anyone could come up with for a clock. It was the only way they could bring it up when they were in public. For the last ten weeks, Adela had felt as though she were sleeping with one eye open, and she didn't like that at all. To her, there could still be some logical explanation, and maybe finding out more about the clock would help. However, there was no information about it anywhere. She wanted to clue in Fallanita and Tara, but she wasn't sure how they would take the news. They'd been the best of friends ever since their first day. She didn't want to accuse Faye of anything without knowing anything solid. Sadly, between classes, lessons on defending her mind with Lord Aspen, and Natorbi, she was already feeling drained. When she wasn't in any of those three places, she was studying in the library. She was there so often even some of the Cartus Worms were mistaking her for an Emerald Den. Nothing makes you judge your sanity more than having worms laugh at you.

"Any luck?" Jeremy asked as he pulled up a seat.

"If I read any more, my eyes are going to burn." Adela joked, leaning back on her chair and rubbing her eyes.

"Maybe we should go to Lord Elderberry," Hector finally suggested.

Adela sat up immediately, leaning over the stacks of books to whisper to him, "We are not going to Lord Elderberry. We could be very wrong and just paranoid. We can all agree that we have caused enough drama for one school year."

"But, Adela..."

"Hector."

"Can we at least put it to a vote?" Hector sighed. Honestly, he looked as though he was just as tired as she was.

"Fine, all in favor of telling Lord Elderberry, raise your hand," Adela stated, glancing between Hector and Jeremy, who kept his arms folded.

Hector called, "All in favor of not going to Lord Elderberry?"

Only Adela raised her hand.

"Jeremy, the only way this works is if you raise your hand for an option," she told him.

"I know that. I just agree with both of you. Does Lord

Elderberry even know about the clock?" he replied, shifting in his chair.

Hector sighed as he began flipping through his book again. "Only way to find out is to ask him, which means we need to go to his office."

Adela pulled out the pocket watch again, running her finger over the engraved words. It still hadn't changed time, forever stuck at five minutes before midnight or noon, depending on the time of the day.

"I think he knows. He was the only person that could write the note… I mean, my grandfather could have, but he's a dragon so I'm unsure," she whispered. No matter how often she said it, she couldn't believe it.

"It doesn't look that old either," Jeremy replied. "Maybe we are just a little bit paranoid and it's nothing but a normal clock. But why was she still in the castle after she left for the holidays?"

Adela shrugged. "Maybe she forgot something and came back. She might not have even said *clock*. It could have been *rock* and she could have been talking to herself."

"But that glazed look in her eyes. I saw it in your eyes too when—" Jeremy stopped, looking around the library before leaning closer. "I saw that same look in your eyes during the Natorbi game right before you completely blacked out."

Frowning, Adela tried to think of a way to debunk that theory. If they could explain that small detail, then everything else didn't really matter. If she wasn't talking to him, then it didn't matter what she was doing. It wasn't their business then.

"Guys, I think I found it!" Hector stated, sounding more shocked than anything else.

"What?" Adela asked, rising to her feet.

Placing the book in the center of them, he pointed to the same text above the very small picture of her pocket watch.

"The Creator's Clock," Adela whispered, gripping the object in her hand tighter.

Hector read aloud, "When Cielieu was created, in order to separate the Mortalis from the Volsin, time was fractured evermore for the safety of all. Should that safety ever be threatened, rumors of a clock arose, with not only the ability to foretell the future, but also reveal the secrets of the past. With it any true Volsin from the house of Arthur may discover the truth they seek and…"

"And?" Adela asked him, panicked.

Hector flipped the page before turning back. "That's it?"

"What do you mean that's it?" Jeremy snapped, taking the book from him.

"I mean it just stops," Hector replied, taking back the book. "The next page is missing. What is with this place and completing sentences?"

Adela wasn't sure what to say. In truth, she was starting to consider a name change. With each passing second, the clock in her hand seemed to be on fire. She knew it was only in her mind, but it felt odd holding something so simple yet so dangerous at the same. She had half a mind to throw it into the forest and walk away.

"Adela?"

Hearing her name she finally broke eye contact with the object in her hand to meet the green and red eyes of Hector and Jeremy.

"Yes?"

"Are you all right?" Jeremy asked her.

Nodding, she placed the watch in her skirt pocket before standing back up.

"What do you think we should do?" Adela asked them.

"Go to Lord Elderberry," Jeremy said.

"Or not," Hector replied. "We know the watch belongs to the Arthurs, so therefore it's hers. I just want to know how something rumored to exist ended up in your possession."

"Aren't you the one who wanted to go to Lord Elderberry?" Jeremy sighed, more than a little annoyed.

"I know, but we should talk about what this means. There are so many questions now."

Adela pressed her temples as she tried to calm her

pounding head. She couldn't think, not with them bickering away.

"Look, I have to meet Lord Aspen for my mental defense training. Can we all talk about this tonight at the tower?" she asked them as she collected her books.

"Yeah."

"Okay."

"Remember, we don't talk to anyone about this yet," she whispered.

"Is that wise? I mean, he could find out what you know," Jeremy questioned, and he had a point.

"I know, but whenever I'm there, I just try to think of things back home." The more she thought, the bigger the risk seemed to grow her mind. She'd hid it from Lord Aspen for the last ten weeks because it was never in the forefront of her mind. But this was big now, and she couldn't just forget the ticking time bomb that was her clock.

"I'll figure it out," she replied, only leaving when they nodded.

Leaning against the wall after she exited, Adela took a deep breath before she could find the will to move again. As she roamed the halls, Adela wished she could trade places with anyone else at the moment. But she couldn't think about that. She didn't want to think about that before going to Lord Aspen. Everything he tried to teach her, she forgot within a day. Her head felt as though it were on fire, and pretty soon she would get nosebleeds. He couldn't get into her mind like Jeremy and, she suspected, Lord Elderberry could. Instead, he was training her to put up walls in her mind. He had an uncanny ability to read her facial expressions. He knew what she was thinking without even having to try. He said something about the eyes and how she always spoke a lot with them.

"Miss Arthur, you're late." Lord Aspen sighed from behind the very thick book he was reading. Lord Aspen was a very short man with an oddly crooked nose and a large mole right under his ear.

"I am sorry. I was studying in the library."

Lord Aspen tilted his book only slightly to get a better look at her, twirling the hairs that sprouted from his mole. Adela tried her best not to cringe under his gaze. He did that often, and it creeped her out.

"Are you telling the whole truth?" He didn't blink at all as his blue eyes stared her down.

"Yes, sir," she replied.

"Huh, you are not telling me all of the truth," he said before dropping the book on the table. "All the training we have done and your mind is nowhere near where I thought it would be. At least you can keep a secret. The only problem is I can *tell* you are keeping a secret."

"I will get the hang of it, I promise. I've been practicing with Jeremy, but it's like I wake up every morning and I have to start over." Adela frowned.

Lord Aspen just sighed. "You have the potential. You just seem to be losing it after a day of work. Strange. Very well, then, we will work on it next class. I must be going."

"Wait, what?" Adela asked as the hobbit-sized man wobbled past her and out the door. Following him quickly, she forced herself to walk slowly to match his pace.

"You must learn, Miss Arthur, that everything in life is nothing more than a managing act in which time creates a sequence of events. You spent too much time in the library, thus losing time with me, costing you the very few moments I had to spare today. Which is why I must be going. See you tomorrow. Do not be late. Some of us have important dates!" Lord Aspen waved as he wobbled down the hall without her.

Standing in the middle of the hallway, Adela tried to wrap her mind around what just happened. Lord Aspen had to be the weirdest Sapphire Fall she'd ever met. He was always on the move and yet every time she saw him, he wasn't doing anything but reading.

"What are you looking at?" Fallanita asked, making her jump.

Tara stared at her oddly. "Are you okay?"

"Yeah. I'm fine. It's just finals." Adela smiled, hoping it didn't look as fake as it felt. She didn't like hiding things from them. They were the closest things she'd ever had to sisters.

"Don't worry. You have been doing amazing and I know the teachers will give you some slack." Faye smiled, making her feel worse. How could anyone like Faye ever be anything but a good person? It didn't make sense. Faye was a good person and Adela believed that. Whatever was going on was just some big misunderstanding.

"Are you sure you are okay, Adela?" Fallanita asked her again.

Once again she lied through her teeth. "Yes, I'm going to be fine. I'll see you all later."

"Don't forget we have Natorbi practice tomorrow." Fallanita grinned.

Nodding, Adela hoped with all her might it didn't look like she was running away. She was just confused, and it was all because of that stupid pocket watch. She just wanted it to go away. She didn't want to lie to her friends or even think her friends weren't who they said they were. She'd never had friends like she had here. She always had her grandfather and Hector. Now that her grandfather was gone, there was nothing but this big hole she was just starting to fill. Running to open the window, Adela all but ripped the watch from her pocket. Once again she read the engraving, and with each word she felt herself becoming enraged.

"Time brings all that is… bothersome," she snapped, winding her arm back to launch the blasted watch into the forest. Before she could send it soaring through the air and be rid of all the problems that came along with it, she was blinded by a flash of light. The flash happened quickly, like someone had taken a picture right in her eyes. Still holding the watch by its chain, she blinked a few times before taking a step back.

"Kaila!" Hearing her mother's name, Adela's head whipped around quickly. Maybe too quickly, because what she saw wasn't possible. She must have snapped her neck, because there was no way her mother or father could be running toward her.

Taking a step back, she watched as the dark-haired woman she knew to be her mother stopped only an inch away from her. Her beautiful young face was stained with dry tears. Reaching out, Adela tried to wipe them, but her hand simply went through her as if Adela were a ghost. She watched her father run forward as her mother wiped her face as best she could.

"What?" her mother snapped. Adela turned to her father, wondering what he could have done to make her so upset.

"Kaila, I know you are…"

"No, you don't know. Everyone bows down to you because you're an Arthur. I deserved to win and you know it.

Lady Melbourne chose you, so you want to know what I think? I think you, being an Arthur, is bothersome, Lliam. I hate it," she yelled at him before turning back and continuing down the hall.

Adela glanced at her father, wide-eyed. "Dad, go after her." He didn't. Instead, he walked back to the window and pulled out the same watch she still held in her hands. Standing beside him, she watched as he sighed angrily, glaring at the object in his hand.

"Being an Arthur is bothersome…" He chuckled sadly to himself.

"Dad…"

"She is right. I don't want this," he snapped angrily. Pulling his arm back, he prepared to throw the watch out the same window. Again, there was a flash of light and when Adela blinked again, they were gone. Adela was left dumbfounded as Lord Elderberry walked alongside Lady Hellebore. She immediately hid the clock behind her back.

"Miss Arthur, do you not have class?" Lord Elderberry asked her.

"I had training with Lord Aspen, but I was late, which made him late for something," Adela said quickly.

Lady Hellebore stared at her for a moment. "Then shouldn't you be studying? Finals are around the corner."

"You're right. I should go the library. Thank you, Lady

Hellebore. Good-bye, Lord Elderberry," Adela replied, running down the hall.

She was doing that a lot today, running from place to place. She hoped maybe she could outrun her problems if she just kept running. She didn't want to see or talk to anyone; all she wanted to do was sit down and put the pieces of her life in order. Somehow all her running led her to the tower, and there she barely even took a breath as she went up what felt like never-ending winding stairs. It was only when she was at the very top, overlooking the woods, that she formally placed herself on the ground and allowed air to fill her lungs.

As the wind howled and the world stopped spinning, Adela finally took another look at the clock in her hand. It looked exactly the same as before. It still looked brand new and was frozen at five minutes to noon. She couldn't believe she was about to send the tiny golden object through the skies. It had just given her the best present an orphan could hope for—a moment with her parents, her younger parents, but that didn't matter.

Now she had a new memory. Adela wondered what would've happened if her parents were still alive. Would her father have told her that story? What happened in those few minutes before he tried to send his watch through the skies?

"Time brings all that is bothersome," Adela whispered, waiting to be blinded. Nothing.

"Time brings all that is bothersome," she said again, just a tad bit louder, and again nothing happened.

Rising to her feet, she turned back toward the opening and prepared to throw the watch just as she had earlier, repeating the words again. Instead of a blinding light, Adela's eyes widened as the clock slipped from her hands, plummeting to the earth hundreds of feet away. Before it could make it any farther, it was encased in an emerald light and began to rise toward her.

"What are you doing?" Hector yelled at her once the clock was back in her hands. Adela, for a moment, didn't understand why she hadn't thought to do that instead of just watching it.

"Earth to Adela?"

"I'm sorry, Hector, my brain… You'll never believe what happened to me," Adela began, but she wasn't even sure how to say what she needed to say.

Somehow Hector understood her speed-talking as she went over every little detail, from missing time with Lord Aspen to meeting up with Faye and the others to the final the incident with the clock.

"So that's how it works," Hector whispered, taking the watch from her hands and lifting it to his green eyes.

Adela just stared at it along with him. "What do you mean?"

"It's kind of like my mind. I have a photographic memory, but when I'm in current places, I can actually remember the way things felt and even smelled. It's almost like a movie I can stop and watch at any time, not just a picture. Like the first day we met and the day Wilhelmina died," he explained before handing back the watch and taking a seat on the ground. Adela stared at him for a moment before taking a seat next to him. She wasn't sure what to say to him, but she was glad she didn't have to lie.

"I think about her sometimes," she told him. "Whenever I'm feeling low, I always wonder what she would say to me."

"She'd probably make you feel lower. I know she wasn't nice. But she didn't deserve what happened to her. She should be here with us. She should be taking How to Defend Yourself from Terrifying Creatures 101," he muttered.

She hadn't even remembered that was the class he'd joked about only a few months earlier. He was right; she should have been there and she wasn't.

"Can you imagine Wilhelmina with light here?" Adela asked with a smile. She could see it now, Wilhelmina taking charge of the whole castle.

"She would have people eating out of her hands in no time." Hector joked.

Adela simply nodded before realizing something. "You skipped class."

"I'm already ahead. It's fine."

Before she could reply, the door opened and they both

jumped to their feet just in time to see it was Jeremy. He looked just as surprised to see them.

"You skipped class too?" Adela yelled.

"Do you want the whole castle to hear you?" Jeremy replied. "Yes, I skipped class. But so did you. Why is that?"

Hector rolled his eyes. "She figured out how the clock works."

"I have to be in a certain place, doing the same action as my parents, or any Arthur, I guess. That could be anything and anywhere." Adela sighed. This wasn't helping their cause at all. The only reason they cared about the watch was because of Faye. Now they only had more questions.

"Let's figure it out, then," Jeremy stated, reaching for the clock.

"We did figure it out." Hector glared at him.

"No, we figured out how it worked. Now we need to figure why Faye brought it up and who she was talking to," Jeremy added, his red eyes never leaving the inscription engraved into the gold.

"We know who she was talking to. She's on the other side, which is why I say we go to Lord Elderberry."

"Has anyone ever told you you're abnormally indecisive? We aren't voting," Jeremy said as Adela took the clock from him and turned her back.

They were worse than cats and dogs. They couldn't just get along even though they were all on the same side.

"Adela, we have to go to Lord Elderberry," Hector told her. "It's his job to figure out what Faye is up to, not ours."

"Or we can figure this out now. We can figure out the truth." Jeremy's eyes narrowed.

Adela looked between them both, the green and red of their eyes reminding her of Christmas lights, before glancing back at the clock that was burning a hole in her hand. If she went to Lord Elderberry, he may want to take it away, and she wasn't ready to part with it. She just wanted to see more of her parents. She wanted to know the truth behind Faye and the reason she had spoken to Prince Delapeur.

"We should…," Adela started to say when the door opened again, causing both Hector and Jeremy to stand in front of her like she was in need of protection from someone.

"Hey, guys, what are you doing up here?" Fallanita asked with a skeptical golden glaze, allowing everyone to relax only slightly.

"Just talking." Adela smiled, breaking out from behind her protectors. "What are you doing here?"

Fallanita frowned. "I really hated my Light Mediation class."

"You skipped too?" Adela sighed. They were going to get

in trouble; she could feel it. She didn't want to have to sit in front of Lord Elderberry.

"Is that the Creator's Clock?" Fallanita asked, causing everyone in the tower to freeze. Adela stared at her with her jaw dropped before Jeremy took a step up again.

"How do you know about the Creator's Clock?" he demanded.

"Adela talks in her sleep... a lot," Fallanita replied, taken aback by Jeremy's demeanor. "Do you mind getting out of my face, please? Why are you all acting so odd?"

"Give me your hand," Jeremy stated to her.

"What?"

"Jeremy, what are you doing?" Adela demanded.

"I am going to make sure by reading her mind." He turned back to her. "We have to be sure."

"It's Fallanita," Hector told him.

"And we are unsure about Faye," Jeremy reminded him, causing Hector to just stare at Adela.

"Whatever. Fine. Here," Fallanita said before handing her arm over to Jeremy, who held on to it while staring into her golden eyes. It was like he was reading line by line, then as quickly as he could, he let go.

Turning back to Adela, he nodded before taking a stand at the farthest edge of the tower.

"Now that I've passed the secret handshake, can someone tell me what's going on?" asked the small girl, who simply crossed her arms and waited.

"It's a long story. I'm sorry. I think this clock is making us paranoid. We're just trying to figure out the truth about what's going on," Adela told her.

Fallanita took only a single step forward, leaning in to look at the device but not touch it.

"Have you asked it?"

"What?" Hector said skeptically.

Standing straight again, Fallanita glanced at him "Have you asked the clock for the truth or does it not work that way?"

"No, we have to be in a certain place," Adela said. "But then, it wouldn't hurt to try."

"Time brings all that is true." The moment the words slipped from her lips, she was blinded by a flash once more.

When the light of the flash dissolved, they were no longer in the tower of the castle, but now among the leaves and twigs of the forest floor.

"Where are we?" Fallanita uttered as she held on to her head, rising from the dirt.

Hector rose next to her, glancing around wildly at the massive trees that surrounded him. "This is—"

"We are in the Stygian Forest." Jeremy interrupted him. He

was the farthest away from the group. His red eyes scanned the tree line and the roots at their feet.

"Stygian Forest?" Hector hissed through his teeth. "How in the world did we get in the one place we're never supposed to go in?"

"That doesn't matter. We have to get back before it's dark and the moon is full. The Stygian Forest will come alive then," Fallanita replied quickly. She didn't seem as afraid as Adela thought she would be.

Adela couldn't help but remember a time when there were no such things as forbidden forests. Times when her biggest problems were passing physics and trying to avoid breakdowns. This wasn't normal, and right now she'd give anything to be out of the heart of the almost lightless and eerily quiet Stygian Forest. She remembered reading about it in her Archery and Defensive Intelligence class with Lord Silverweed.

The Stygian Forest was the house of darkness. Everything that could ever be brought to life in a nightmare dwelled there and came out when the moon was full, destroying everything in its path. The very creatures that had taken Wilhelmina, Chimeras, hunted at night there along with Reaptors. If Volsin stayed within in it for too long, their ability to use light would fade. The darkness fed off their light so much, weak Volsin wouldn't be able to handle it.

"Adela," Jeremy called, snapping her back to reality. "We need to go now. We are burning moonlight."

She nodded but didn't follow him. She made the mistake of looking at the clock in her hands. No longer was the clock fixed at five until noon. Instead, it was now pointing in the opposite direction of where the rest of them were going. Frozen amongst the roots of the massive trees around them, Adela looked north and south. There were few times in anyone's life where they could actually realize when they were at a crossroads, and Adela knew she was at hers.

"Adela, what are you doing? We need to go!" Hector yelled.

Adela knew, from the way his hands fidgeted, he was more scared than he wanted to admit. But then again, they all should've been. Yet she wasn't afraid of the Stygian Forest. She was afraid of what would happen if she never found out about her family. About why she now had this clock, which no one else knew existed.

"You guys go. I'm going to follow this through," Adela said before turning her back to them.

Before she could take a step, Hector was already in her face. "You don't have to follow anything through. We're not on a quest. This was a bad idea and we need to go."

"Hector, you need to go forward and I need to go back. I have to understand and maybe this is the only way. So can you people move out of my way?" Adela sighed. She didn't want to fight him on this, especially when the light flowing between the tree lines decreased with each passing moment.

Jeremy took a stand beside Hector, glaring down at her just as angrily as the boy with the emerald eyes.

"Turn around or I drag you kicking and screaming," he hissed at her, allowing the axe he'd formed to rest on his shoulders.

"What if it was your clock and you were able to see your parents and find out more about them? Would you turn around?" Adela asked him, and when he couldn't respond, she knew she had him.

"Which way?" Fallanita asked, taking a step up with a large grin on her face.

"No. You guys need to head back," she replied.

"We will if you will, and since you aren't, lead the way. If it were me and there was anything I could do to see my family even for a split second, I would do it." Fallanita smiled. "Are you in or out?"

"I have a bad feeling about this," Jeremy whispered, and Hector simply agreed.

Chapter Sixteen

Two Truths And One Big Lie

"We are so going to die," Hector mumbled under his breath as they climbed over the dying tree trunk that now rested on the forest floor.

They all walked so closely together that if anyone took a wrong step, they would all fall to the dirt alongside them. All the light that once streamed through the lines of the trees was now only a faint glow, making Adela more and more scared for her friends' lives. As though their fear was not heightened enough, what sounded like a muffled growl broke though the air, causing each one of them to freeze in place.

"We're definitely going to die," Hector whispered.

Jeremy glared over at him. "You keep saying that, I will kill you myself."

"And I will help," Fallanita hissed as her golden eyes skimmed the tree line but couldn't see anything.

"We need to keep moving," Adela replied, giving all her attention to the watch in her hands.

"Why can't we just make discs and travel that way? It will be so much faster." Hector sighed. He glanced around at the massive trees, which all seemed black at this time of night.

"Faster, yes, safer, no," Fallanita answered. "If we use all our energy forming discs, we will be too tired to fend off anything."

Jeremy stopped, staring back at the sea of trees behind him. "It isn't safe for us to stay still. We need to keep moving."

"Jeremy, what's wrong?" Adela asked, stepping forward. But before they could take another step, the ground beneath their feet began to shake with so much force Adela fell to her knees.

"What's going on?" she yelled over the rumbling. None of them could speak over the loud growls that were headed their way, making the ground shake even worse.

"They are black unicorns!" Fallanita yelled.

"I thought black unicorns were friendly!" Hector howled, unable to rise to his feet.

"Not when they are being chased by a silverback ogre!" Jeremy answered, his red eyes widening as the stampede made a mad dash toward them. The force of their hooves shook the group, along with the giant, three-eyed silverback ogre. It made standing all but impossible. As they came closer, the group had already become frozen in fear.

Adela didn't have time to think. She broke through the fear and formed a golden lasso, swinging it high over her head and letting it catch on one of the branches.

"Guys, go up," she yelled, holding on for dear life.

They watched for a moment before copying her actions. They each made their own ropes and pulled themselves up into the dark tree branches. One by one, seven black unicorns running for their lives passed right under Adela and her friends, but she knew the unicorns wouldn't make it. She could see the sliverback ogre catching up to his meal.

She had no idea where she got the strength or why she did it at all, but Adela took action. She pulled herself up just a little bit higher before making another golden rope that she tossed toward the tree opposite her and into Jeremy's arms. He stared at her for a moment, and she nodded toward the approaching ogre. And he nodded back. They waited just long enough until the ogre ran right between them, not even slowing down. Just slightly before he passed, they pulled as tight as they possibly could.

That was all it took for the giant sliverback ogre's feet to fly toward the sky just before his body slammed down hard on the forest floor. As it flew, the ogre let out a scream of pain loud enough to wake anything that was once sleeping. The force of the impact also caused the rope of golden light to snap, sending a sharp pain throughout Adela's arms, forcing her to let go of her lasso on the tree and fall to the earth almost as hard as the ogre did.

"That was such a bad idea," Adela muttered as she rolled to her side, trying to ease her pain.

"Are you all right?" Hector yelled, dropping down beside her.

"No," she muttered before rising from the ground and cradling her arm to her chest. Hector and Fallanita helped her stand as Jeremy tiptoed around the unconscious ogre.

"Is he dead?" Adela called out to him. She didn't want to kill him, just stop him before he hurt the black unicorns. From what she learned in class, they were endangered anyway.

"No. Just unconscious. Must have hit his head too hard," Jeremy replied. "We should head back to the castle. There has to be a safer way to figure this out."

"He's right, Adela," Hector said, still helping hold her up. She must have hurt her ankle as well because every time she tried standing, her knees buckled.

"Umm, guys," Fallanita whispered, her eyes wide. "I think he's awake."

Sure enough, the massive silverback ogre shook his head before spitting out a tooth. He balanced himself against one of the giant trees. After gaining composure, the ogre grabbed the tree, severing the roots from the trunk.

"How angry do you think he is?" Adela whispered as they all backed up slowly.

They didn't need to answer, because the moment the silverback ogre saw them, he let out a thunderous growl, shaking the air.

"Very, very angry," Hector whispered back. "I don't understand! Silverback ogres don't attack Volsin! We aren't big enough to eat."

"We are better than nothing, seeing as we stole his dinner," Jeremy yelled. Just then the ogre's hands decimated the trees right beside Jeremy, forcing him to duck for cover.

"I take it back," Fallanita yelled. "Form your disc now!"

"Wait, you still have the dragon's tooth," Hector yelled.

Adela, remembering, pulled it out of her pocket.

"We have to go!" Fallanita yelled once again.

"Distract it so I can heal her," Hector screamed back.

"Easier said than done," Jeremy replied, forming an arrow of shimmering red light, aiming it away from them. Fallanita sighed loudly, turning to help Jeremy. Each of them tried to confuse a creature five times their own size.

"I wish this thing came with directions," Hector replied as he took the vial from Adela, uncorking it as fast as possible.

"I'm just happy you remembered it," Adela replied.

"We can't do this forever, Hector. Hurry up!" Fallanita yelled as a tree crashed down beside them. The ogre stumbled back and Hector jumped. He spilled half the bottle, and the wind blew it across Adela's face.

She coughed so hard she forced herself out of Hector's arms. She tried to clear her eyes and realized she was now walking just fine and the pain in her wrist was gone.

"I'm okay. We need to go!" she yelled, focusing on the ogre that kept trying to crush her friends to death.

Shooting another arrow into the monster's face, Jeremy took a few steps back. "He is just going to follow us."

"I have an idea," Fallanita screamed over to them as the ogre slammed his fists into the ground, forcing both Hector and Adela to jump out of the way. They rolled over to where Jeremy now stood.

"Anytime you want to share would be nice!" Jeremy yelled back.

"Everyone at once shoot an arrow over his head. The light will blind his third eye," Fallanita replied, taking another shot at its ear. The ogre screamed in pain.

"On my count," Hector yelled, forming an emerald bow. Adela focused on the space right above the ogre's bald head.

"Now!" Jeremy yelled, and at once four arrows—two gold, one green, and the last red—collided over the ogre's head, creating a flash so bright even they had to turn away for a moment. When they looked back, the ogre was on his knees, shaking his head over and over again in hopes of clearing his blurry eyes.

"Now's our chance," Adela replied, backing away slowly before they all turned and ran as far as possible from the monster whining in pain behind them.

None of them stopped. They jumped over fallen logs, dried leaves, and dirt, not wasting time to talk. They kept running in the direction they thought was the castle. All that pushed them forward was fear, fear of what else in the Stygian Forest was hungry and looking for Volsin to eat. When they saw the trees thinning and the moonlight streaming in, they thought they had finally made it home. But instead of seeing large statues, they were met with a run-down cottage. Even that appeared to be taken over by the forest.

"Where are we?" Adela whispered, walking on the path of broken tiles leading to the house.

"I'm not sure, but who was crazy enough to build a house in the Stygian forest?" Hector replied.

"Maybe they learned that the hard way," Jeremy whispered, using his foot to kick away the broken pieces of glass.

"Or maybe they just couldn't make it back," Fallanita whispered, brushing her hand over the broken-down mailbox. The faded letters spelled out the word ARTHUR.

Adela reached out to touch it, but Hector stepped forward, pulling her hand back. "It's a common last name."

"No it isn't," she replied with a sad smile, forcing him to let her go.

Once again she found herself at a crossroads. She wasn't sure if going into the rundown cottage, her parents' rundown cottage—her rundown cottage—was a good idea. Not now, anyway, not after they'd just encountered an ogre hell-bent on having them for dinner. She just stared at it for a moment longer before turning back.

"Are you really going to walk away?" Fallanita asked her. "I mean, this is why we came here, for the truth. We'll never have this moment again."

"She's right, Adela. We can spare a moment. We all know Lord Elderberry will kill us when we get back," Hector whispered, even though he didn't truly believe it.

"This forest will kill us if we don't get back. I've caused enough trouble and you guys almost got hurt because of it. There's nothing here, and maybe I can come back someday, but we need to get going," she replied sadly, golden eyes still fixed on the cottage in front of her.

Jeremy took a step beside her. "It is your choice. We will back you up either way."

"So we have voted." Fallanita smiled, reaching out her hand to pull Adela toward the home.

Adela felt fear and worry creep up her spine as they moved closer and closer to the door. What if it wasn't like she imagined it to be? It already wasn't, but she didn't want to see the inside and have all her dreams shattered at once. And that's exactly what happened when they opened the front door. Adela's heart fell to her stomach and shattered. There on the opposite side of the door was a large picture of her father, her mother, and her infant self. It had a slash through it, inflicted by whatever creature came before them.

Holding her breath, Adela reached out to touch the image. It came alive, projecting out into the weather-torn, hole-infested, tattered house. The image was fuzzy and shook every three seconds due to the tear in the picture, but Adela could still see her father clearly, spinning her around in the air before her mother stopped them for a photo. That was it. Nothing but a picture on a wall remained. She would have reached out to replay it but was distracted by the sound of glass connecting with the floor. Hector.

He lifted what was left of a small teacup.

"Sorry," he said, but she couldn't reply.

She was too overwhelmed to speak. For years she wondered what her home looked like, what it would have been like to grow up in a house with her parents.

Moving through the broken remains of the home, Adela took a deep breath and created a disc of light to take her up the stairs since there were just too many holes in them to climb safely. She floated into an open room before the disc disappeared under her feet. Spinning around, she realized the room was meant for her. Adela could feel the sob building at the back of her throat. They hadn't even finished painting her room. It was a golden room with the start of emerald flowers, most of which were unfinished.

"Adela, are you okay?" Jeremy whispered behind her. Beside him were both Hector and Fallanita with worried expressions glued to their faces.

"I'm not sure," she whispered.

"It must be hard to take in," Fallanita replied. "Do you think this is the truth the clock wanted to show you?"

Adela's eyes widened as she searched all over her uniform. "It's gone."

"What do you mean it's gone?" Fallanita panicked.

"I mean I don't have it anymore. I must have dropped it when I fell," she replied.

"We can't go back for it," Hector said to her. "Not now, at least."

"Fallanita, what's wrong?" Jeremy asked the small girl, who stopped her fidgeting and gave them all a sad smile.

"I really just wanted this to be over," she whispered, pulling Adela into a hug before kissing her cheek. "I am so sorry."

Once again Adela felt herself taken over by fear.

"Fallanita, why are you sorry?" Adela asked the girl when she broke away, taking a few steps back from the three of them.

"What would you do to get your father back, Adela?" Fallanita asked her seriously. All the kindness, the light, Adela had once seen in her friend's eyes were gone. All that was left was emptiness.

"You didn't," Jeremy hissed, rushing to the window to find a group of pale-skinned reaptors along with one Chimera closing in on the cottage.

"This whole time you were working for him!" Hector yelled. Adela just stared, frozen in shock. "You knew what word to use in order to bring us here. I bet you probably sent the ogre as well. They hunt in packs, never alone. This whole time you've been playing us like fools.

"And you let me. I will do whatever I need to do to get my father back—including deceiving Adela Arthur and giving her the Creator's Clock. Then Prince Delapeur will set my father free," she replied emotionlessly.

Adela took a step forward, trying to control the rage she felt in her soul. "This whole time we thought Faye had betrayed us, and it was you!"

"She was a puppet. Next time Faye will know to keep her mind out of the sky and in reality. With the light Prince Delapeur gave me, it was easy to get into her head." Fallanita smirked, making Adela wonder who was this girl she'd shared a room with all semester.

Shaking her head, Adela took a step backward. "He's going to betray you. He isn't going to let you or your father be free."

Sliding up her sleeves, Fallanita exposed all the dark tattoos taking up her arms. "Volsin lie all the time. Prince Delapeur gives his word."

"And what happens now that you've lost the Creator's Clock?" Jeremy snapped at them. "Your deal was for Adela and the Clock. He owes you nothing. You are nothing but a—"

Before Jeremy could even finish, a bolt of dark golden light came in contact with his chest, sending him flying out the back window.

"JEREMY!" Adela yelled, rushing to the new hole in what was once her nursery. Jeremy rolled onto his side, the dirt on his red cloak making it look as though blood poured out of his chest. Adela panicked, thinking that it just might be.

"He will be here soon. You better run." Fallanita smiled. With a flick of her finger, the whole house began to go up in dark golden flames.

"Adela, we need to go now!" Hector yelled, pulling her out of the burning house and falling toward the ground beside Jeremy.

The two-story fall was easy to recover from. Hector wrapped his arm around the bloodied Jeremy, helping him to his feet as he held onto his chest. Hector formed a disc of light underneath them and took to the sky with hopes of getting far away as fast as possible. Adela stood on her own plate of golden light, watching her house go up in flames as Fallanita's darkened eyes watched from the hole she'd created.

"Adela!" Hector yelled, pulling her out of her trance. She kicked off, starting after him.

Both of them put as much energy as they could into getting away, but the farther they went, the harder it was to maintain the light. Adela was so clouded by the recent events, she wasn't even sure she could see straight. It all made sense, yet it didn't. She didn't want it to. She remembered the mornings she'd forget some of the basic mind tricks that she'd learned only a day before, how she always felt fear and the need to do better, be stronger. She just thought she was being hard on herself. But it was Fallanita breaking the walls of her mind. Just over Christmas, Adela felt so happy to have Fallanita say they were as close as sisters and now… and now she was serving her up to the one Volsin who made it his life's mission to destroy lives.

Before Adela could think even a moment longer, her light, along with Hector's, went out and they were sent crashing into the clearing below. Rolling and tumbling onto the weeds and dead grass, they let out coughs and groans of pain. Pushing herself off the ground, Adela noticed both Hector and Jeremy, no longer moving, near a familiar-looking hooded statue. At that moment her worst fears came to life. She realized they'd fallen into the heart of the same maze Prince Delapeur had taken her mind to before. She turned back to find not one, but dozens of black-eyed reaptors. Each one had overgrown fingernails and scars all across their faces. They looked human and yet not so.

Adela stood in front of Hector and Jeremy, taking comfort in the fact that they were still breathing, but unsure how much longer that would last. She tried over and over again to form a shield over them, but nothing was working.

"My precious little Arthur. How long I have waited for you to return home," a voice, softer than a whisper and colder than the night's air, rang out.

She knew whom it belonged to, but she couldn't see him anywhere. Then the sea of reaptors parted, allowing the frail man in all black to glide right through. She felt a chill go up her spine and the hairs all over her body stick up. For the first time, she stood face to face with Prince Delapeur. He grinned wickedly and circled her slowly, his feet never once touching the ground. Adela didn't move. She dared not even breathe as she tried to fight back her fear and tears. She tried to remember what Lord Elderberry said to her about how he feeds off fear, how it made him stronger. His white-blond hair looked to be about the same blond she had seen on the mountaintop after he killed Jeremy's sister.

"Tell me, my precious little Arthur, are you afraid?" he asked, stopping right in her face and taking a deep breath.

"I am not your precious anything," she hissed back.

He let out a wild, icy laugh before backing out of her face. "You remind me of your mother. So stubborn. Such is the nature of a Golden Hive, I suppose."

"You don't get to speak of my mother—or my father for that matter," she yelled. "Not after what you did!"

Prince Delapeur looked surprised. "What did I do, young Arthur?"

"Don't pretend like you didn't kill them. You were too weak to do it without stealing the lights of other people because you are a coward." The moment the words spilled out from her lips, he sent a blast of dark light right past her head. It sailed into the thorn bushes behind her, burning right through them.

"Careful, little Arthur, or the next one will hit your pretty face. I can take your light whether you are damaged or not." He grinned before his eyes became cold. "Your parents would have been alive today if they had only given me what I wanted and joined sides with me. We could have ruled both realms, gods among Volsin and humans alike!"

"You wanted to control both realms," Adela whispered, thinking of how no one in the lesser realm would ever be able to stop him. No amount of modern technology would defeat him.

"I *will* rule both realms. It is only a matter of time. I have seen it through your mind. It is in desperate need of a ruler, a king, one I am more than prepared to offer. A kingdom that would have been ruled together, but instead, they stood against me!" he yelled out into the silence of the night.

Adela wanted to run but couldn't—one, because she no longer knew how to walk and, two, because of Jeremy and Hector.

"Why would they stand with you? Why would anyone stand with you?" Adela whispered, unsure what had happened to her own voice.

Prince Delapeur simply stared at her before asking, "How could a sister not stand beside her own brother?"

Adela's eyes widened. "You're lying."

"You will soon learn, my dear niece, that I never lie," he

hissed, hovering closer and closer to her as Adela took a step back from him.

"My sister decided to stand by her Arthur and plot against me. It cost her life. Do not make the same mistake. Follow me and I will you show the ways of true power. We are all that is left of our family," he replied, stretching out a hand toward her.

Adela only stared at it for a moment before glancing back up at him. "Go to hell." She mustered enough light within herself to throw a bolt at him. He simply stopped it with his palm and looked back at her.

"What? Was I supposed to be hurt by that?" he asked her. "My turn."

Adela had no time to even move before the bolts of light connected with her chest. They sent her flying backward into the statue, which broke against her back. She fell upon the ruins. Holding back a scream, Adela looked through her scattered hair to find Fallanita. She was behind Prince Delapeur, just watching, not a speck of emotion on her face.

Pushing herself back up, Adela was met with another bolt of light that sent her sliding farther on the dead grass. Tired, bloodied, and broken, Adela just wanted to shut off the pain. There was so much flooding her mind at once, she wasn't even sure if she could move. Lying on the grass, she watched as he and his dark army came closer and closer, but it was only when she saw Fallanita walk toward Jeremy and Hector that something in her woke. A soft voice echoed in her mind.

You are much stronger than you believe. Fear has no power over you, sweetheart. You have power over fear. Do not lie to yourself.

She didn't know where the strength came from, but it flooded her system faster than the pain could. In her mind she called out for help from whomever could hear her, but nothing happened. She rose to her feet and Prince Delapeur stared, somewhat shocked, before a grin broke out over his flawless face.

"So much light." He grinned.

"Yes, and it's mine, not yours," Adela replied before sending out waves of light. It was like she had stolen the light of the sun. One by one she released bolts of every type of light, from gold and red to blue and green. It was a never-ending assault of lights at anything and everything that dared to come in front of her before she collapsed to her knees.

This is not over, my little niece, a cold voice said in her mind, but she just pushed it away and gave in to all the lights.

Chapter Seventeen

We Rise And We Fall Together

"Did her eyelid move?"

"It's just relaxed."

"There, it did it again. That is not relaxed." The voice argued as Adela tried to awaken from her slumber.

"Told you. It's just reflexes."

That sounds like Hector, Adela thought to herself.

"She is waking up, you dimwit."

That was definitely Jeremy.

Sighing, Adela opened her eyes quickly before shutting them again due to brightness of the room.

"Do you guys ever stop fighting?" Adela muttered, rubbing her eyes as she tried to sit up. Both of them quickly reached over to help her. Adela just stared at them, but seeing their scars—one right at Hector's sandy-brown hairline and the other on Jeremy's wrist—made all the memories of the maze rush back to her. Before either of them had time to adjust, she hugged them both tightly, ignoring the pain in her arms.

"You're all right," she whispered to both of them.

"Thanks to you," Hector replied when they broke away. "You kicked some serious—"

"Serious what, Mr. Pelleas?" Lord Elderberry inquired as he walked in.

Both boys stood up quickly. "Nothing, sir."

"Why don't you two go spread the news about Adela's awakening?" he told them, causing them to both look back at the dark-haired girl in the bed.

"She will be fine. Now go." He reassured them. They sighed and left quickly, most likely so they could return quickly as well.

Between Adela and Lord Elderberry there was nothing but silence. Adela just hung her head low. "Lord Elderberry, I am so sorry. They wanted me to tell you about the—"

"The Creator's Clock." He interrupted her, walking to the front of her bed. "Had you done so, I would have told you the real Creator's Clock was destroyed when your mother used it to open the door to the lesser realm, and the one you had was a replica, most likely made by Prince Delapeur to draw you out. A plan that seemed to work flawlessly."

Adela opened her mouth to speak, but no words could convey how stupid she felt at that exact moment. She had caused so much trouble, searching out clues like she was some kind of supernatural Nancy Drew, but she and her friends almost lost their lives.

"That being said, none of this would have happened had it not been for Fallanita," he added, causing Adela's back to straighten and her face to harden, but they both knew that was only her reaction to her feelings of betrayal.

"I should have known," Adela whispered. She didn't know how she should have known, but she felt like she just should have.

"If you had, then you deserve to be headmaster and not me. I do not know when or where we failed her, but we did, and this happened as a result. For that I am truly sorry," he told her.

Adela wiped her unfallen tears, refusing to cry for a Fallanita she never really knew anyway.

"He told her if she brought me and the Creator's Clock, he would set her father free. He lied to her," Adela replied, unsure why she was even bothering to make excuses for Fallanita now.

"He told her half of the truth. Since the clock was nothing more than a replica that he controlled, he could have hidden it at any moment while you were in the maze. There was no way for her to ever win. Neither she nor her father will have an easy path ahead of them now."

"How did you find us?" Adela asked him, not wanting to think about Fallanita. All she could remember was her father's voice before everything became a sequence of lights.

"You led us to you." Lord Elderberry smiled. "Somehow you were able to connect with the minds of every last Volsin in all of Cielieu. Each one of us felt your pain and your desperate call for help, for light. Each and every person allowed you, for a spilt moment in time, to tap into it."

"I tapped into all of the Volsin light?" Adela whispered in shock.

"And by doing so you were able to not only push back the darkness around you, weakening Prince Delapeur badly, but also to heal part of the Stygian forest. A pocket of light in a sea of death—that is what you, Adela Arthur, were able to do," he replied. He was neither amazed nor stunned, as if he knew she could do it all along.

"But he isn't gone."

Lord Elderberry just frowned. "No, he is not gone. He is still out there, waiting for his chance again. But because of you, he, for the first time in sixteen years, has had to stare death in the face and remember that, even with all the light he has stolen, he is just a Volsin capable of dying. That is a very powerful lesson to learn for anyone."

"Did you know?" She didn't want to ask, but she had to. "Did you know who he was to me?"

"Your mother's brother was named Leo Harding. The man who put you in this bed for a month and the man who once carried that name are two very different Volsin. I wish you could have met Leo Harding. He was a good man," Lord Elderberry replied, not giving her a straight answer, but it was enough for Adela to understand what he meant.

Nodding, she stared at her hands. "So what happens now?"

"Your friends will come in. And afterward, you will need to be ready before the moon is full and daylight fades," he stated just as the doors to the infirmary opened, allowing in Faye, Tara, and Ryker, along with Hector and Jeremy.

Adela glanced back at Lord Elderberry, who winked while making space for her friends to come jump onto her bed. Lord Elderberry had powers no one could even imagine.

"Adela, we were so worried when we heard your call." Faye spoke louder than Adela had ever heard her speak before.

"The whole castle woke up. I still can't even believe it. I got goose bumps on my toes!" Ryker added, feeding off Faye's energy.

"I still can't believe she faced him and won. Do you know how cool that is, Adela? Everyone all over Cielieu has been cheering for weeks." Tara grinned, seated right beside her.

"Guys, we don't want to overwhelm her. She just woke up." Hector sighed, even though Adela was fine. She enjoyed their rambling. She wasn't really paying attention, but it was nice to hear people with joy in their voices.

"You have become such the mother hen, Hector." Tara groaned, rolling her eyes at him.

"I have not."

"Maybe he thinks we're like Fallanita," Faye whispered, now back to her normal voice. They all went silent, forcing Adela to address the pink elephant in the room.

"I'm sorry we suspected you, Faye." She wasn't sure if she knew, but it was better to let her know either way.

Faye frowned. "Yeah, I am too. I don't even remember some of the stuff Hector told me I did. But hey, now you and I get to take Lord Aspen's mind defense class together. At least this way we can make sure neither of us is ever late. He always says he's late for some important date when we're late too."

Adela smiled, remembering her Alice in Wonderland moment with Lord Aspen.

"How did the rest of the castle take the news?" she asked, glancing over everyone.

"Not well, as you can expect. I think the angriest was Lady Hellebore. She had every photo and plaque of Fallanita's wiped out of the castle. Others didn't believe it at first. They don't understand how someone who seemed to be as kind and fun-loving as Fallanita could go so off- course," Ryker replied.

Jeremy nodded. "The lords and ladies didn't want to tell the students because it would cause people to lose the hope you had given them by calling out to them. However, Lord Elderberry said no one else was going to fall through the cracks, and in order to do that we needed to start telling the truth, even the bad truth."

"I think everyone just feels betrayed, but we will all help each other rise. I am guessing that is the motto for next year. We fall together. We rise together," Faye replied.

"What if you're tired of falling?" Adela laughed. She'd taken enough falls for one year.

"You get over it, because it is going to happen and we are all going to be here." Jeremy sighed. "This time, hopefully conscious."

They all laughed before the topic changed once again. This time Adela didn't speak; she simply leaned back and allowed her friends to talk amongst themselves. She threw in a few smiles and nods every once in a while. She didn't expect Jeremy to socialize. He just sat in a chair and listened as well. While she was watching them laugh and smile, it was almost easy to forget how messed up her life had become. In a way it made her very happy, and in a strange way, it also depressed her. Why couldn't she be this happy without trying sometimes? It seemed simple enough, but when you thought about it, it really made sense. How could she ever be happy knowing that the only family she had left was trying to destroy her and everything she cared about?

She found herself wanting to know more about Leo Harding before he became Prince Delapeur. But that would have to wait for another time, because all too soon, the flames in the infirmary began to transition from green to yellow. As she rose to her feet and grabbed the golden cloak left for her, Lord Elderberry returned.

"What happens when the daylight fades?" Adela finally had the chance to ask him. Her friends must have been in on it because they all simply grinned.

Lord Elderberry walked to the back of the infirmary, tapping once on the stone wall, morphing it into a large door.

"You have a visitor." He smiled.

Before Adela could see who it was, Jeremy grabbed her hand. She turned to him and he kissed her again.

Breaking away quickly, he never broke eye contact with her. "You almost died. Promise me we will talk once you get back."

Dazed, Adela simply nodded. "I promise."

Hearing Lord Elderberry cough, they let go of each other. Turning back to the newly formed door, she prayed with all her might it was who she thought it would be. Adela pulled it open and there, hovering over the castle, was a massive white dragon with wings large enough to cover the tower and with a tail as long as a football field.

"Hello, little bumble bee." His ancient-sounding voice rang out in her mind.

"Hi, Grandpapa," Adela said excitedly with a large smile. Turning back to Lord Elderberry, she said, "I thought you said dragons weren't allowed here?"

"I said dragons are only allowed in case of emergencies. I do believe, after everything you have been through, this would count as an emergency." He smiled before nodding toward the golden-eyed dragon. "Go on. But you have missed a lot of school, which means you will be making up classes in the summer."

"That seems fair." Adela grinned as the white dragon before her wrapped his tail around her waist and placed her on his back.

She waved at her friends before they took to the sky in a single swift motion.

"Tell me about your year," he said to her. Adela sighed, not wanting to ruin the moment.

"On the downside, I met my uncle. On the upside, I got my first real kiss." Adela laughed as they flew into the fading light of day, knowing full well he wasn't going to be happy. She was just glad he was there with her, dragon or not.

ACKNOWLEDGEMENTS

I want to thank God, for so many reasons of course. My parents who have given me so much love and support! Thanks so much mom and dad! I love you both.

To my best friends Bethany, Tara, Toni, and Sahara, along with my high school teachers Ms. McAllen and Mrs. Skica-Cole. Without any of them I know that *Adela Arthur* would have never been written or published.

Thank You All So Very Much!

ABOUT THE AUTHOR

JUDYANN MCCOLE, aslo known as Judy Onyegbado, was a senior in high school when she started working on Adela Arthur and the Creator's Clock during her history class. It started as a short story for a group of young kids she babysat for and grew into an adventure she herself wanted to go on. She is currently attending college in Virginia, where she hopes to finish the next adventure in Adela Arthur's life.

COMING SOON...

ADELA ARTHUR

AND THE

ETERNAL EVERGREEN

Made in the USA
San Bernardino, CA
31 July 2013